T0333603

Breaststrokes

Breaststrokes

Margaux Vialleron

**SIMON &
SCHUSTER**

London · New York · Sydney · Toronto · New Delhi

First published in Great Britain by Simon & Schuster UK Ltd, 2024

1 3 5 7 9 10 8 6 4 2

Simon & Schuster UK Ltd
1st Floor
222 Gray's Inn Road
London WC1X 8HB

Simon & Schuster Australia, Sydney
Simon & Schuster India, New Delhi

Simon & Schuster: Celebrating 100 Years of Publishing in 2024

www.simonandschuster.co.uk
www.simonandschuster.com.au
www.simonandschuster.co.in

A CIP catalogue record for this book
is available from the British Library

Hardback ISBN: 978-1-3985-2577-1
eBook ISBN: 978-1-3985-2578-8
Audio ISBN: 978-1-3985-2975-5

Typeset in Bembo by M Rules
Printed and Bound in the UK using 100% Renewable
Electricity at CPI Group (UK) Ltd

For Valentina,
to us, à nous,

A feather is trimmed, it is trimmed by the light and the bug and the post, it is trimmed by little leaning and by all sorts of mounted reserves and loud volumes. It is surely cohesive.
– Gertrude Stein, 'A Feather', *Tender Buttons* (1914)

I am made and remade continually. Different people draw different words from me.
– Virginia Woolf, *The Waves* (1931)

Chronology

Prologue

Someone, One Day

'Liars always get caught.'

The girl stays silent.

'Do you understand?' the woman adds.

The girl nods seriously.

The woman massages her forehead with the tips of her fingers, and the girl can't take her eyes away from the skin tag that hangs on the woman's right cheek. Hyper-pigmented, it flows like an off-beat pacemaker – it shows compassion but her words speak disbelief.

'Have you thought about the implications of your accusation? We'll have to question your friends and suspend him.' She picks at her thumbnail, spittle. 'And he could lose his job.'

The girl evaluates her self-esteem: her grades, varnished shoes and brushed hair; asexual but sexy, pleasing but not pleased; polite and quiet – a good girl.

'Liars get caught when their stories are confronted with the recollections of others. They don't align. So, you must tell me: is this revenge?'

The girl shakes her head.

'You're not upset with him?'

Behind the woman's chair is a cramped office where walls are covered with files, the objectification of monotonous administrative assignments or the nets of her dreamcatcher. Children come in here either to raise concerns or to be raised as a concern. The room smells of sweat – puberty trapped between four walls. The green colour of the tissue box on the desk clashes against the yellowing sheets of paper. Ring marks from coffee cups testify to the woman's work.

'I'm scared,' the girl mutters.

'I should call your mother.' She unclasps the phone from the monitor loudly, the promise of a slap.

The girl thinks about her mother: warmth and lactose, hours in the kitchen standing before the stovetop; chocolate melts and spreads on crêpes, wax melts and spreads on legs; she speaks about dignity often, a weapon that will smooth the angular characteristic of stubbornness.

The girl lifts one hand shyly. The woman puts the phone back down.

'Is there anything else you'd like to add?'

The girl thinks about him: a mild smell of urine, chlorine; sticky, like the tubes of glue she squeezes for scrapbooking.

'I don't have a choice but to see him every day.'

The woman blinks, speechless: both pet their hands,

clammy. The girl has a red eye with a stye; a chemical aura exudes from her – tiny, blurry, unformed, or that is how the woman sees her. The presage of a sexualised body. The adult trembles; she calls him a friend.

This isn't a story about what you know or believe to be true, nor what I know or believe, but about permission – *granting* – and agreement – *obtained* – or the performance of consent. This isn't just about consent. This is about pleasure, too.

PART 1

Sunday Morning

1

Cloe and Sarah

Cloe has two options. Either she takes the longer but direct route home or the faster way, with a connection between means of transport. Decisions always come in pairs – to take the Tube or the bus, to cook a red or a white pasta sauce, to turn left or right. She failed at making one, an ambidextrous child and an indecisive adult. *Unpolitical*, people call her. There are days when such a characteristic comes across as a compliment, a quality that highlights her empathy, although guilt overcasts most of her choices. She should be more political, *a woman like her*. It hits at night and during the day equally, from the stabbing pain in her pinkie finger to cravings and a cricked neck. The hair loss she isn't as certain how it started; perhaps she should change her comb for something gentler, or take zinc as recommended on the posters that are displayed inside buses. She could chew one of the sweets aimed at 'those who don't take vitamins'. That is the conclusion she reaches when she decides to wait for the bus. On the Tube, however, she would have been compelled to invest a disproportionate amount of money in comparison to her earnings on iron supplements. 'Tired of being tired?', a woman yawns holding a hand up in front of her mouth, posters framed alongside the escalators, a descent among ads. Online software, a grey background against a vivid colour to highlight the figures she could wire into her bank account if she had signed up. The dream, another promise, the confidence; the lure of making money. Can she say no to any of this? Hope can be dangerous.

Last night, Cloe took a decision. She chose to stay out longer, to dance instead of going home. She twisted the knot inside her stomach tighter with a round of shots – white alcohol, the kind that makes her drunk. Cloe didn't think of her bank balance before making the payment: it would be one bill to settle next month; she was merry enough to forget her aversion to risks. Who did she buy the extra shots for? She has exhausted the trial period on her credit card – the interest rate has jumped to 3 per cent. Unread messages from her banking app ping, unnoticed.

Her phone buzzes inside her jeans pocket, a missed call notification from earlier this morning, followed by a text message received *now*:

Hey C, can you call me back? Last night was fun.

The phone number isn't in her contacts list. This message about a fun time she can't remember reads like a threat: her instincts howl an alarm bell. *Who are you?* Cloe stands at the bus stop, the monitor showing disco lights instead of line numbers. Her headache has passed, now her eyes burn before the light and a migraine kicks in.

Cloe waits for the bus.

Sunday morning, still. Sarah stands on the other side of the road, with each of her fists clenched inside her coat pockets, self-conscious that the back of her white trousers are stained with slush. The April showers cast a spell on clothing, the shop windows are luminous when the sky falls low, and clouds thicken with a grey texture. She is self-conscious of how much she complains about the weather, how boring she sounds, how insensitive she is when parts of the world are experiencing record-breaking temperatures, well over fifty degrees Celsius. *Hyper-emotional* is what her family calls her, often shortening the expression to the singular and hurtful adjective, *hyper.*

It began the evening she threw up in the car after a gallery opening. She had held back her tears for the entire night and the overload of salt and gasps had soaked oxygen away from her lungs like a sponge does with water. Sarah had witnessed the woman in front of her being refused entrance at the door after she failed to show an invitation, a stranger, as it seemed her parents nor her sister took notice of what had happened. Sarah grew up in a family of liberals where art was part of the children's education, yet this anecdote introduced her to empathy as an unjust cognitive response. Her breath skips a count in memory of the unknown woman. She recognises the weight of her head bending downward, when she had first walked in with her perfectly brushed ash hair; she was turned away in a flash. She can still picture the woman's large and glittering pearl earrings, her burgundy nail polish; Sarah has a photographic memory. Years later, both her parents and her sister still have asthma inhalers strategically positioned across the house and inside their jackets' pockets, though paper bags will do the trick, Sarah reassures them when she senses an episode mounting.

Her eyes water; she inhales, exhales.

Sarah crosses the road towards the bus stop. The pedestrian light is red, a driver honks their horn, and she runs even though she will arrive before Mathilde. Sarah will be early, admittedly, and her sister will be late, undoubtedly. It has become a ritual – not the order in which they both enter the Oldfield Tavern, but Sunday lunch – at least since Mathilde announced her engagement two years ago. But Mathilde's postponed wedding is a story for later. What matters for now is that Sarah meets her sister at this gastropub on Oldfield Road once a month, where they catch up about wedding preparations. The significance of flower varieties and the meaning of the petal colours, the social strategies behind making a guest list bid for a gambit of compromising and pleasing, Sarah learns, earnest and scared of disappointing her mother and sister. No hesitation on the subject: their mother asked Mathilde to involve her. To *choose* her sister, *hyper* Sarah, as the maid of honour, because Mathilde wouldn't dare contradict their mother (Sarah wouldn't either; nobody in the family would).

The bus arrives and Sarah heads upstairs – *Why can I not breathe properly?* She has a long journey ahead, there will be traffic, the people who stand still make her pernickety. A little envious too. *My chest feels tight.*

2

Gertrude

First thing in the morning, the room shines, a bright hour for happiness in Gertrude's east-facing kitchen; time to discard some of her sourdough starter. Two spoons at least. This is her method to keep it balanced, its perfume malty and its flavour nutty, the composition purely made of wholemeal flour. She pours in two generous spoons of fresh flour, then lukewarm water, slowly, to avoid drowning the mixture, and then combines both ingredients with a wooden spoon. Her pace is energetic. The addition of water is key; the lactic acid awakens, her starter feeds. She has cultivated it from scratch, initiating the process months ago, at home on her own, accounting for longer hours than the sunlight does, feeding it a bubbly mixture of flour and water at regular intervals, discerning its fragrance, which has varied widely between both sour and sweet. She toyed with the idea of adding grapes and yoghurt to boost its growth when the mixture would not rise, nor go down, the defeated mother she had created. But she worried that she would betray its organic equilibrium, she who believes nature selects its disciples before archetypes cancel them. She started growing a starter before researching the chemistry behind its composition – she holds a deep aversion to rules – so she learnt about the demands of having a wholemeal-based starter later in the process. The enzyme and microbe levels are higher in wholemeal preparations than in its rye counterpart, which makes it more sensitive to any change of habits or new seasons. Good thing that Gertrude finds repetitive patterns soothing. All the articles she found, either written by bakers or scientists, by amateurs and professionals alike, included at least one line about the *feel* of a starter – its odour and texture – and that a good breadmaker should get to know their mother starter. Other than the commitment involved in feeding these molecules for breadmaking daily, it is the beast's individuality that scares Gertrude. She has always responded to facts better than to feelings.

> *it's not that i don't feel at home in my body,*
> *i'm not at home in my body*

Gertrude's brother, Liam, with whom she lives and shares a choreography of battling for shelving space and incompatible timetables, criticises her breadmaking when it causes the sink to block. The bags of flour Gertrude spreads over the kitchen counter before kneading, the discarded starter

13

residues that stick to the wooden spoons and then peel away when warm water and washing-up liquid enter the stage, the whole operation of making the bread Liam eats, and then puts on trial.

Soft-boiled eggs with miso mustard spread for breakfast; sandwiches of leftovers for lunch, watercress braided between slices, Cheddar cheese but no tomatoes since Gertrude is allergic to them, the red fruit banned from their kitchen; his obsession with air pockets, unsolicited advice about how his sister could make her next loaf sweeter, softer, better.

Gertrude rejoices as she feeds her sourdough starter, messing with the kitchen and leaving for work without Liam noticing. Transgressive independence, Sunday morning. She anticipates Liam will sleep until the late hours of the afternoon, when the sun will have rolled onto his side of the building and will pierce through his bedroom's thick curtains.

Signs of his early presence include a leftover glass of water and breadcrumbs scattered above the small fridge. Gertrude smiled when she first walked into the kitchen this morning, finding Liam's stamina for the London nightlife endearing, his first year at university, his passionate heart and influenceable mindset.

it's my skin that i want to discard

Gertrude returns the fed starter to its usual corner of the kitchen, placing a round cork coaster underneath the jar to secure it a warm place, and heads to the bathroom.

*

When she makes her way to work, the streets are quiet: a few runners, fewer dogs and their owners who are walking absently, the occasional car passing by her side. Gertrude has kept her outfit minimal, her hair tied in a high bun (countless pins to hold it), the curse of overly thick and curly hair for someone who dislikes being at the centre of attention. She walks. Her pace is fast and sustained, her fingers brush over the brick walls and their blanket of wisteria flowers. She looks at the flats with the balconies she wishes she could afford to rent with their colourful outdoor tables, pots for herbs and a view over the city that connects one's life with the mirage of others. She enters the local park, spotting a sleepy swan and walking through the football pitch, the sour odour of wet grass after a morning shower, cherry blossoms and, finally, the main road. Coffee-shop owners have lifted the blinds up, independent stores are getting ready to do so, but the lights inside the Oldfield Tavern are off when she arrives.

She unlocks the front door and curses at the stains from last night's dinners and spilt beer trapped inside, the smell of rotting chestnuts. The refrigerators work loudly at the back when the place has been disarmed of its primary function; that is, to host guests. Gertrude walks straight into the kitchen, where the ceiling settles high and creates an echo chamber, chopping boards are organised by colour (red for raw meat, blue for raw fish, yellow for cooked meat, brown for vegetables and green for salad and fruits), three fridges, metres of cling film and arguments about how to cut it properly so it doesn't break into unsuitable pieces, so there is no waste at the end of the shift. Phil, the head chef, has a tender heart but no patience for those who 'blow goods', edible or not. His brusque cockney accent guides his team through the rush of delivering meals. He is the one who hired Gertrude and they have worked together ever since. They reached a balance between Phil's lack of patience and Gertrude's wittiness eventually. He taught her about the organisational rules of a kitchen – assigned stations, cleaning up after yourself, acknowledging before fulfilling an order – and she followed the pathway from polishing steamy glasses and emptying dishwashers on to peeling, chopping and frying potatoes. In the kitchen at work, Gertrude abides by the rules. Her skin has developed an oily complexion, her vision often blurs with fatigue, quiet tears flow when she finds herself alone in the pantry room, the blisters on her ankles crack open, but she hasn't missed a single working day. She dreads orders of aïoli sauce, the method precise and the chemical equation complex, and she loves making risotto the most, one spoonful of broth at a time, the squelching sound of Parmesan cheese melting against the Arborio rice. The happy memories triggered by spotting peas in a dish.

Sundays have their own pace.

'Is there anyone here?'

'Sorry, coming!' Gertrude ties an apron around her waist hastily, the thick cotton kind, dark blue with white, thin stripes, gloves tucked inside the front pocket. She signs the delivery receipt, time and date are registered carefully, and steps aside so the man she now calls by his first name can carry the squeaking, polystyrene boxes into the kitchen.

The Sunday menu is special, a selection of meat to roast, the range depending on the morning delivery. Gertrude switches the radio on, catching the breakfast show, and makes herself a bacon roll.

This is prime time in the kitchen at work.

Only the one chopping board is out, a rule is broken, and the music mingles with the chatter of the broadcasters. A toasted bun, the crunch and the light smell of bonfire, the fat from the flesh melting in her mouth.

The preparation of the meat will be down to Phil, his sous-chef and their trainee, while Gertrude is assigned to the Yorkshire puddings and cooking the vegetables. *A woman's job*, her colleague added once, unsolicited. And she won't forget. She pours flour and salt into a bowl and adds the milk slowly, stirring continuously until there are no lumps. Gertrude breaks the eggs and whisks. Her wrists work hard while her mind begins mapping out the work that needs to be done with the vegetables, the silent and unifying components of a roast. The stocklists don't lie; since Gertrude has taken charge of the veggies, there are fewer returns. The roots make the animal whole; her cutting and baking tray spreads bring balance to the meal. Crispy but not dried, so the sprigs of thyme she has convinced Phil to buy come through with a second wave of flavours, woody and rounding out the dish.

Its Sunday roast is what makes the pub a success with families and locals. Gertrude stows the Yorkshire pudding batter away in the fridge, a clean cut of cling film to seal the bowl on top, and then begins preparing the vegetables.

> *a pretty girl like you,*
> *single and working in a pub,*
> *a waste they say, but*
> *i sing a praise for*
> *a pretty girl like me*
> *to do as she pleases*

The chairs slide against the wooden floor; tables creak. Casks are being checked and replaced. Pans and pots fill up with water, oil sizzles, the meat is sliced on the steel counters – the rest of the staff have joined the show and their first booking is due to arrive at noon.

3

Mathilde and Sarah

'Since when do you smoke?' Mathilde asks as a means of hugging her sister hello.

Sarah waited outside the pub on Oldfield Road. She feels ugly every time she declines a waiter's invitation to order a drink – *I'm waiting for someone*, their body language and her interpretation. The irrational fear that they don't believe her. Sarah could have said *yes* and ordered a drink, a simple agreement between a customer and waiting staff, but she wouldn't want to choose what Mathilde will be drinking today.

'I vape. It's not the same.'

'Smoking isn't good for your condition.'

'It's listed as one of the risk factors. I already have the thing, so I may as well kill myself faster.' A year ago, Sarah was diagnosed with a long-term autoimmune disease that causes chronic pains and swelling in the joints. While her life isn't directly threatened, flare-ups are difficult to predict, and her lifestyle has needed adapting. She is learning to manage her symptoms.

Mathilde gives her sister a dead look.

'I vape when I'm on a deadline,' Sarah clarifies before she draws in a last breath of nicotine. She files the electronic cigarette as she would a silver pen inside her jacket pocket and drops a soft kiss on her sister's cheek.

Challenged, Mathilde responds with a corner smile: 'Mum has developed a hoarse voice; be careful with that stuff. Shall we?'

The thing to know about Mathilde is that she would have voiced her opinion with Agnes the same way if she was present today.

They step inside while Sarah mutters, 'I don't smoke. Tobacco gives me eczema.'

'Most vape juices contain nicotine, which comes from tobacco.'

Sarah cracks her knuckles, and Mathilde rolls her eyes as she unbuttons her coat. A long olive-green parka, her fingers thread down her stomach agilely.

At the pub's entrance, a 'Please wait here to be seated' sign stands, a marker pen that imitates chalk letters polices them; they stop. A quick scan through the room gives the sisters insights about the demography of lunchtime: push-chairs, greying haircuts, a low hum of background noise, the scent of bleach conceals the night before. The front of house arrives – curly hair, round glasses, average size and matching navy t-shirt and trousers – and asks if they have a reservation.

'For two people, under the name of Mathilde Jenkins-Bell.' She pauses, fleetingly, until she must add: 'With an "h". Mathilde, but spelt with an "h".' She enunciates each syllable slowly, but she doesn't go into the detail of specifying each letter.

A polite smile, the soft flutter of paper menus sliding from the folder into his hands, and then he asks them to follow him. The noise changes as they walk past the kitchen, banging pots and pans and heated air, plates lined up in a row for the staff to collect and take to the tables. The smell is strong, velvety, a note of damp moss: Sunday roast is on today's menu.

The gift of being two siblings around the table is that Sarah and Mathilde don't need time to adjust to one another's presence and habits. One grabs the jug and serves water to them both; the other spreads the paper napkin over her skirt (chiffon material, long, emerald colour); each takes a sip of water, and so the conversation begins.

Mathilde digs for more specifics, but only briefly. She queries the deadline her sister mentioned when they stood outside the pub, and Sarah avoids the question, saying something about submitting a chapter from her thesis to her supervisor by next Wednesday. They comment on their cousin's divorce and note their father has been texting more regularly on the family chat recently, admitting Agnes must have had a tantrum after he failed to respond about some dinner party's menu (particularly rude since their mother insisted it was *his* friend who was the one guest that followed a strict vegetarian diet). Mathilde brings up a case of sexual harassment from the local MP's office where her partner works that has broken in the news, only to reassure Sarah that Chris has nothing to do with it and that his reputation is safe (Sarah had not asked). And they debate a few TV shows they have been watching recently, but without much enthusiasm.

They stop talking as they read through the menu. Pork belly, Bramley apple sauce for Sarah and chicken for Mathilde, bread and butter for the table. They keep their choice of roast to themselves, but Sarah unveils her appetite: 'Can we order a side of cauliflower cheese?'

'If you eat it, then yes,' Mathilde replies.

Silence.

When they place the order, Mathilde asks for the cauliflower cheese. She announces the wine colour, also, when she demands two glasses of the Sauvignon Blanc, medium size. A top of ice cubes for Sarah.

The polite dance ends here, and so the anticipated monologue begins. Mathilde starts layering fabric samples over the table so Sarah can visualise her ideas for a colour scheme. 'They are samples only,' she repeats to fill the silence left by Sarah, who glances at the spread. Mathilde's pupils bounce between the table, her sister and the room, worried the food might arrive any minute. 'We still need to take the samples

to the venue so we can choose a scheme that fits the location,'
she says with confidence this time.

'The earth tone would be lovely with the barn.'

Mathilde gives her sister a brilliant, agreeing twinkle,
and she continues with conjugating each verb as *we*. They
want to modernise the decor, something 'bohemian chic',
but also the ceremony itself. *I'm cold.* They don't want something patriarchal during which only men do the talking and
Mathilde is handed over like a silent prize. *Please don't make
me do a speech. I wouldn't know how to be funny.* They went
sampling cakes last Friday and they were all 'to die for!'; it
will be 'literally' impossible to choose. They will open the
ceremony with a Spritz and burrata bar – smooth, explosive
balls of mozzarella cheese served with beef tomatoes, wheels
of sourdough bread, tumblers to serve the cocktails. *Are my
desires unimportant if they are different from those of my sister?* The
most fun part is still to come with auditioning bands, and
Sarah should join them when they do. *We were raised under
the thunder of the same nursery rhymes.*

The food arrives – an end to this linguistic feast for a happy
couple and Mathilde returns to the use of the first person. 'It
hasn't been straightforward this past year with my incident
and everything, but I know that I want to marry Chris.'

'Cheers to that,' Sarah says cheerfully, looking Mathilde
in the eyes to keep her gaze from lowering to her sister's
scarred hand.

Compared to the year before, Mathilde's face has length-
ened. The physical manifestation of a depression she works

hard to hide behind the fence of a confident voice. Sarah is approaching the portion of meat carefully, putting her cutlery back on the table between each bite, slowing down her eating so she can match the tempo of her sister, whose speech is taking her attention away from her plate. The only dish Mathilde has tasted so far is the side of cauliflower; as always, a vocal approbation had followed the first forkful, which was rapidly washed away with more talking. The recipe is creamy and rich. Sarah itches to comment, to remind Mathilde that she didn't want to order the dish in the first instance, but she is too afraid of picking an argument with her sister. On the other hand, she could remind her of how much they both love cauliflower cheese, the only thing their father can cook, except that in the Jenkins-Bell household they use Comté cheese only. 'The result is more generous,' their father had explained. She stops herself from interrupting Mathilde, who is still debating whether to dress the tables with flowers or plants, while swirling one of her carrots into the gravy sauce. It has thickened, an unpleasant foam appearing, the result of her snail-like speed; the dish is getting cold, and this bothers Sarah more than she would like to admit.

'I'll send you notes, so don't worry too much. And, of course, a list of who you should be inviting to my hen do.' Mathilde stops and stuffs a chunk of chicken inside her mouth – then she exhales loudly through her nostrils.

Sarah says she will go get them a glass of wine so they can have another toast. The repetition makes the intention convoluted – an echo settles between the sisters, and Mathilde eats fast while her sister heads to the bar. Her masticating is rushed and distasteful. When Sarah sits back at the table, they clink their glasses, and Mathilde switches topic.

'I went out for a bottomless brunch near Paddington with the girls yesterday.'

Sarah swallows a large sip of wine, excluded by the tidings *the girls* evoke, a magpie lands on the windowsill, and Mathilde talks more. 'The couple at the table next to us were on a first date. How wild is that?' She pauses, then repeats: 'Going for bottomless brunch for a first date.'

'How do you know they were on a first date?'

'It was obvious.' Mathilde's tone is sharp.

Sarah fails to find something to add quickly enough, so Mathilde continues. 'She arrived before him. Pretty girl, long legs and beautiful red curly hair. She was wearing red lipstick and she kept taking her phone out of her pocket to check if her make-up looked good. When he arrived, she stood up, he moved forward, and they hugged awkwardly like people who have texted a lot but never met do.' She is talking fast, smiling and moving her hands. 'Then, when they sat back at the table,' Mathilde lowers her voice as if she was holding a secret, 'he asked her about her journey to the restaurant.'

They both take a sip of wine. Sarah ponders over the level of detail Mathilde absorbs from her surroundings.

'You don't ask your mate that,' Mathilde sherlocks. 'This is a typical icebreaker for when you meet a stranger.'

Sarah disagrees and they debate this briefly.

At this point, the conversation could have moved on organically, except that Sarah's anxious instinct forbids her. She presumes her sister would seize the opportunity to ask for an update about her dating life – *the* worst topic – analytical in her approach, Mathilde would make Sarah feel nude and vulnerable. Instead, Sarah keeps the ball rolling: 'Did they stay longer than you and the girls? If so, that was probably one of the longest first dates recorded on one of those applications.'

The joke falls flat. Sarah makes a mental note to remove the 'if so' next time. Or was the sentence too long to be funny? *Mathilde is razor-sharp; our mother would sing her praises.*

Mathilde responds as if her sister had shown a genuine interest; the pair always play games of chess. '*App*, Sarah. Nobody says *application* anymore. But they did anyway. It felt like they were having three dates in one. You know the deranged pace of meeting someone you might never see again.' (Sarah doesn't know, yet she is nodding like a bluffer would.) 'They had some quick exchanges, a heated conversation, she laughed loudly, and he put his hand over hers a couple of times. It was quite sweet to watch, weirdly enough.' She rolls her eyes, pleased with her summary, her cheeks coloured from the food and wine.

Sarah finds it gratifying that a brunch with *the girls* means that Mathilde spends more time people-watching than chatting with her friends. Then she worries: *Does Mathilde do the same when we are together? What is going on at the table next to*

26

us? Has Mathilde noticed? Sarah doesn't ask because Mathilde would respond.

Mathilde picks at her nails now that they have pushed their empty plates aside, waiting for them to be cleared. No dessert.

'Anyhow, we left but they stayed on. I can't help but wonder if they woke up in the same bed today.' Mathilde ends her sentence with a testing tight smile, as if she had said something controversial.

The rest of the conversation follows the lives of others, with comments and opinions about friends and family members, and the afternoon moves on. The crowd at the pub renews. In the room next door, a football match has kicked off, supporters with red t-shirts wait and shout at the bar, the signal that the sisters should leave.

4

Cloe

Cloe steps on board the bus but stays downstairs. She is standing up, with one arm circling the pole, a turquoise pouch bag weighing down her left shoulder. Unkempt hair, her lipstick is fading. She rests her forehead against the cold metal. Her eyes close. She read an article about this bus route in the local newspaper once, in which a study had proven that if a chicken were to walk the same path that this bus follows, then the animal would arrive at its destination before the double-decker. Cloe devours the papers, a preference for the local gazettes and their peculiar life testimonies, itching with envy because of a bittersweet dream of a career as a staff writer for a renowned magazine. She earns a salary writing copy for various websites and marketing newsletters instead. She is a talented copywriter and can sell a wide range of products, a useful skill rooted in regrets. Today, she is travelling between her favourite part of London and the one in which she lives, a journey during which she has spent more time than she would dare say wondering how the chicken piece came to be written and published. Cloe wouldn't confess this, but it must baffle her that she can't secure a commission when there is a budget for editing and publishing articles about chickens racing with London buses. Did they time an actual chicken as they herded the animal along the roads? Presumably not. Drivers honk, cyclists give the finger to black cabs, cars overtake bikes. They must have agreed an average pace for the chicken and applied the figure to the distance involved instead. How does one determine an average? How much data makes a sample a reliable representative for the whole? Unanswered questions keep her alert. Cloe's toes flex inside her shoes, anchoring, stabilising her feet as the bus makes its way through engineering works and traffic lights. She would not want to trip over.

The rain cleared the sky earlier this morning, brilliant blue and full of undisturbed sightseeing opportunities. Her thoughts would have unleashed if she had sat comfortably upstairs. Here they come in waves, acid reflux and suspicions – *What did I do last night?*

As a young athlete, Cloe trained six days a week. A mixture of Pilates classes and runs before school, raw eggs and protein powder shakes for breakfast; supervised sessions at the swimming pool afterwards; and Héloïse drove her to competitions at the weekend. Cloe's mother fulfilled the role of being both her cheerleader and harshest critic, until everything ended.

The 400 metres freestyle race is where Cloe took risks, her favourite distance to pair crawls and breaststrokes, the latter movement being her strongest. She found her thrill up and down the pool lanes. The butterfly stroke highlighted the weakness in the right arm she had broken on a swing when she was little, as well as her indecision (in her mother's words) as Cloe failed over and over to find a rhythm between raising her head at the second or third stroke, and backstrokes bored her. Braided hair, purple swimsuit with a white star featured above her right hip, hair clips to keep her vision unobstructed, and waterproof glitters spread over her eyelids to remind the judges they were girls when they pulled their bodies out of the water. Only girls, despite the goggles that sucked their blood. They wore colourful caps that matched the elastics of their braces, the intention to pop, until they were thundered by the spotlight they had shone over their insecurities.

Cloe won her first medal in a 100-metre breaststroke race, 'Rebellion (Lies)' by Arcade Fire blasting inside the local swimming pool, chlorine flaking skins and children screaming between their hands. She dislocated her left shoulder, stubborn with the butterfly strokes she hated doing, fears she would never be *this* good again, until the injury healed. The speed of a teenager's life. Voltarol gel, homeopathic pills, water bottles advertising the highest rates of magnesium and calcium minerals, food supplements, a strict diet and a meticulous sleeping timetable. Cloe's calves have thinned since she walked out of the pool for the last time – the end of a systematic practice, breathing every two strokes, her body the conductor for achievement before her team's ambitions, and a denied puberty. These girls whom she used to shadow every day – changing-room chats. She has close to no contact with them these days, the meaningless likes on their social media posts aside, the occasional comment or message around their respective birthdays, each one of them spread across the country and abroad. Only one of them kept up with the practice of competitive swimming, and this saddens Cloe.

Silence leaves room for interpretation, not for forgiving.

Cloe exits the bus at an early stop and inhales the sweet fragrance of melons, followed by a row of colourful crates – aubergines (white and purple), asparagus, radishes, apples (Gala, Golden Delicious, Granny Smith), juicing oranges, tangerines and red plums. Her ability to focus is a skill she owes to athletic training. The chicken and the route ahead were useful distractions against the flashbacks from last night that have started running through her mind. Dancing shoes. Disco lights and beaming smiles between blinding flashes, faces close up. Too close. A drench of guilt, shame. Cloe heads to the coffee shop, where she meanders around the counter of baked goods before stopping longingly in front of the Danish pastries – crispy, golden, square, with a bleeding sticky heart of cherries, an unusual craving for her savoury inclination. The coffee machine works loudly and repeatedly behind the counter, yet she turns away empty-handed. Her stomach flips, bitten nails with the skin around them dry. She enters the corner shop next door and snatches a can of Coke from the large refrigerator.

'And two Millionaire scratch cards, please.' Cloe pays and waits for the cards.

The woman lowers her spectacles and heads to the other end of the counter. Her lips mutter with small movements, her aquiline nose performing a slow dance behind each breath.

The wait draws the ghost of Héloïse, who bought packets of Marlboro Red cigarettes every few days. And two Millionaire scratch cards; one for herself and one for Cloe, except that she always handed over the lighter to her daughter so Cloe could scratch both cards on their behalf. *Spare change for a house by the sea*, Héloïse would say with confidence, the cigarette ash long like an eel. She never looked back at Cloe when they stepped inside the fire-proof hallway of the council building where they lived. *I cannot have you stink of chlorine for the rest of your life. Children should swim wild*, she added as she washed her hands with the posh orange and geranium soap she had bought with the spare change. Three rounds of foam against the persistence of yellow fingers, tobacco tattooing Héloïse despite her imagination.

The pond on the other side of the road is a sought-after location in the neighbourhood, the ducks well-fed and the benches consistently warm from the first school bells to dusk. Cloe passes the grey heron's nest where the path narrows down, elevating herself on tiptoe, jumping from one rock to another between puddles until she arrives at her chosen, hidden corner of the common. She drops under the Holm oak tree. Evergreen, this is her favourite place to think. She scratches the cards first, a prize of £6 is attached to one but the other is void; she has paid back the expense of buying them at least, she smiles briefly. She has cracked the code – the cash she thought they had won as a family before, the money they would splash inside TK Maxx, was in fact the reimbursement of a loan they had taken at the corner shop beforehand. Vicious lifestyle, circles, continuity.

Cloe goes through her stuff: a leather wallet, all her cards present and filed away; a pack of tissues and one bottle of hand sanitiser; pink lipstick and the keys to her flat are in her bag. She palms her phone inside the pocket of her jacket, then she reaches for a receipt in the other, eager for a clue, if the date wasn't from two weeks ago. The ink stamp on her wrist has washed off, a distinguishable circle, but the letters aren't legible enough to reassure her. The postcode on her card statement is from south of the river, SE15, or where she woke up and took the bus this morning. The ground is wet, tears run down her cheeks.

Time to go home.

The way back is brightened by the sight of bluebells. Bees return to London and the local elections are due next week.

I mean to care. I meant to read the leaflets so I could pick my candidate, one that would listen, so I would feel involved enough to be heard. Héloïse says that to make a lie disappear one should tell it plenty of times, so it becomes real. But I didn't come home last night.

Cloe returns to the coffee shop where she had stopped earlier and heads straight to the till. The chocolate bars are stored underneath: 75% dark, orange and geranium flavour. She taps her card and pays with the loan from the scratch cards she keeps safe in her pocket. Cloe has worked out the maths in favour of her gain, a fable to cast away consequences.

When she finally arrives home, Massimo, an overnight-hungry pet, greets her. She serves half a tin of cat food inside his bowl, her stomach lifts and she grabs her phone. She presses the contact name, stands still as the ringing tone triggers a shiver down her spine, a ghost taps her shoulder and the voicemail drums in.

'Hey, Mum, can you please call me back?' She hangs up and goes to hide under the duvet, a childish cover with sailing boats and a single pillow. Cloe bites into the chocolate bar as the clocks approach their peak: noon.

5

Gertrude, Mathilde and Sarah

A member of the kitchen staff called in sick. Colleagues distrust the story, a form of reckoning the morning after Saturday night. Phil burnt himself within the first hour of cooking, the line derails, and Gertrude's shift lengthens by the second. Paper scraps with food orders scribbled on them pile up on the counter, the small bell rings as soon as a new plate is ready and placed under a heating lamp, until one of the waitstaff collects it. Tea towels are layered over their shirtsleeves to protect the skin on their forearms. *Watch your back*. The tone is friendly before one o'clock, and increasingly hastened as the afternoon meets hands with the evening. The smell of melting butter. They run out of pork belly, the information filters through slowly and a customer complains before a colleague could strike-through the dish on the chalkboard. Beef falls next, and the team serves chicken and vegetarian roasts as long as stocks last; after that, it will be chips for everyone or nothing.

Gertrude wonders what she would hear if the brouhaha at the pub were to be broken down into comprehensible conversations. She imagines that she would pick up the newly famous word 'partygate', replacing what was called a government once, or the square c-words that paralyse with fear, 'climate change', or 'cost-of-living crisis', or the more individual causes such as health and stories of doctors' waiting lists, dating apps or nursery school fees and enrolment paperwork. Out of desire, the frustration caused by her shifts and the scorching air inside the kitchen, she imagines the lives of the people she serves food to. She knows someone is celebrating their birthday from the two cardboard boxes that are stored in the kitchen's fridge – one with three different layers of chocolate and the other with a Victoria sponge cake (with blackcurrant jam) inside – a reminder for the pub owners that the dessert menu needs rethinking, Gertrude tells Phil. *Sticky toffee pudding*, caramelised sugar for the toffs, tough under the teeth, sweet and sticky; the sound of it repulses, a pudding more than a dessert. 'They have come to eat out. They want dessert, Chef,' Gertrude argues with Phil. His response focuses on the rising cost of goods, utilities and taxes: 'Gas and the use of the ovens must be regulated and kept to a minimum,' he adds authoritatively. Gertrude's solution is a panna cotta; she emphasises the words, insisting on the doubled letters. *Panna cotta*, she repeats softly, the glutenous texture that will remind customers of their childhood; poached rhubarb to make them see pink, a leaf of basil on top to win them over. 'Easy,' she concludes. Phil says there is no budget, adamant and losing patience, and clicks his tongue: it must be sticky toffee pudding, served with a scoop of vanilla ice-cream, or the ice-cream on its own, or nothing.

Gertrude returns to the fridge, curls her lips after catching sight of the chocolate cake whose ganache had melted, then solidified again into ugly bits that stain the packaging.

Mathilde stops at the bathroom door, nodding ahead, a permission for Sarah to leave. They hug rapidly, an innate movement between the two sisters, and say goodbye.

Sarah exits the venue into a harsh light – grey and bright, intense and disorientating. The bus comes less frequently than the listed times at the stop suggest. She squints at the pavement across the road, dense with pedestrians dressed in suits and smart long skirts; choirs and preachers' songs echo through the stained-glass windows of the church around the corner. The charity shop boils with people digging for records and vintage wine glasses, wearing fleeces and hiking boots, while the old man behind the till jokes that he had only come in to greet his colleagues. But there is so much stock to tidy at the back: bin bags are dropped outside the door overnight despite the polite note that advises against it. Even though it is getting late in the day, the queue in front of the one popular bakery remains, whereas the other baristas along the road are cleaning coffee machines.

When her bus finally emerges from the roundabout, high and imposing, Sarah's neck stiffens and her mind startles; a light headache kicks in.

> Have you told Mathilde to go for the earth tones colour scheme?

The message has interrupted the flow of her podcast, an episode from the *Desert Island Discs* archive. Sarah relaxes with the knowledge of having listened to this interview before, while Maya Angelou selects the first of her eight tracks: Mahalia Jackson's 'How Great Thou Art'. She pushes back the switch at the top of her mobile phone, silent mode activated, and places the phone on her knees, with the screen facing up. Push notifications with Agnes's name pop up and Sarah delays her response. Maya Angelou's voice grows distant.

> The citrus palette is vulgar and the ocean one doesn't go with her skin complexion. Did you tell your sister?

> It's better if these comments come from you. She'll listen to you.

> What did you have for lunch? Did you ask about Chris and those awful rumours in his office?

> Do you think she is concerned about this? Your father
> says that she should be. I don't like this, she has had
> enough stress recently.

There is a longer pause than before between the previous
and next message.

> How are you, dear?

The sixth message is the one. Sarah types a brief, summary
response to all the above as part of a new message – earth tone
has been chosen; these aren't 'rumours', but there is no need
to be concerned about Chris or about his job or about his
reputation (/Mathilde's); they each had a roast and they shared
a side of cauliflower cheese for Dad; she looked well today –
and then she follows up with a second message, attached to
its original question, *How are you, dear?* The thought of typos
troubles Sarah as she types hastily, her fingertips winning the
race with her mind before she censors herself:

> I'm heading back to the library. I have this deadline
> coming up and am behind with my word count. And
> now I need to start organising M's hen do. She wants
> to go to Mallorca with the girls. I don't think I have
> the energy or the money mum.

She regrets her words as soon as she sends the message. The
aftermath of wine spoke on her behalf; an ache, a call for

her mother's attention. Everything Agnes dislikes. Maya Angelou has played another three tunes before the phone lightens again, a photo of her and Mathilde in Cornwall from before, sun-kissed and dripping hair after a surfing class shows up as her screen background, as well as another text from her mother.

I can help you, love. You only have to ask.

You must start looking after yourself and stop making yourself sick with these word count goals. Remember what the doctors said about stress being bad for you.

Stress is bad for anyone. They call it an invisible illness, yet its diagnosis has granted everyone around me the right to decide what is best for me and my body. Suddenly anyone can guess my pains and cure my ills. Anyone but me, that is.

Mathilde says you've been quieter than usual.

To ask her parents for money will handcuff Sarah with the knowledge she will need to be *nicer* to her mother as a trade-off, the acknowledgement that she depends on them, however vocal she may be about her independence. Michael Parkinson is still casting Maya Angelou away, the music is playing, but Sarah missed the context around the song. Still, she discerns words: someone has called to say how much they care – the misplaced lyrics make her smile nonetheless. Sarah will ask her mother to contribute to the cost of Mathilde's hen do – her taking care of the logistics and going is more of a favour to them anyway, *isn't it?* She too knows how to lie to herself to protect her privileges.

I thought she wanted to go to Tenerife? Agnes can't help but text.

For the hen do, I meant.

Sarah puts her phone away and jumps off the bus. A dual carriageway, the road must be crossed in two sections; the frustration of pedestrians is palpable. Sarah's vision blurs, her legs like jelly, and she focuses her mind on the woman who is pushing a buggy in front of her. She can't see the child inside, but there is a trail of regurgitated milk on the mother's sleeve, her hair is rough and long, toys and a baby coat are crammed under the buggy – *'Don't you see me, Sarah?' I can hear Mathilde calling me* – the light turns green, and they go their separate ways. She steps inside the building, opens her bag with a polite expression to the security officer she recognises – *even if he doesn't recognise me* – he nods, and she heads to the locker room. Laptop and phone in one hand, she pushes her bag inside, closes the door, 2704 once, 2704 twice, and heads upstairs.

I'm back, third floor. Usual spot. Sarah presses send before considering the implications of sharing this information. Like a pyromaniac, she wants to light a spark for herself; a quiet force, *hyper* Sarah.

Then comes Gertrude's favourite moment in the working day, when orders wind down and she has a chance to reach for a cocktail tumbler, the thick, short and heavy type. She drops four ice cubes and pours in a small bottle of alcohol-free ginger beer; she scratches her thumb with the cap. The fizz stings her tongue, the spice numbs her gums, a reward at the end of the lunch rush. Gertrude sits on the small stair outside of the kitchen. She can hear her colleagues in the background, a melting pot of chatter about a new council regulation for parking authorisations and fees, a brief mention of the Eurovision show. She stops listening, the cold liquid has reached her forehead.

A crackling sound before the smell of burnt toast, the ash-tail lengthens at the end of the cigarette. 'Mad busy today,' Stefano exhales, half a pint of beer in his spare hand. He sits next to Gertrude, and she drops her head on his shoulder softly.

'I'm doing a double shift, covering for our sick colleague.' *Sick.* The tone of her voice implies disbelief.

'I really can't do it today. Sorry, mate,' Stefano replies.

Two puffs of the cigarette; a colleague strides over them with a bin bag.

'I wasn't asking, just complaining. I'd rather be here than at home.'

'How is Liam?'

Their colleague returns, climbing up and walking back

into the kitchen. Gertrude wheezes and rubs the palms of her hands against the scratch of her petrol-blue-dyed jeans. Tobacco, like any other nightshade plant, releases alkaloids and, in the case of Gertrude's immune system, histamines. She wouldn't give herself a swollen face or eczema for the sake of a mouthful of tomatoes, but smoking is a different temptation. The spectre of devotion, a dependence.

'He hasn't washed his bedsheets for about three months, but he has befriended the hot new neighbour. I'm not sure if he's attending classes.' Gertrude shakes her head tenderly. 'Little brother is doing just fine.'

Stefano laughs and Gertrude smiles. 'That brat. I'd have killed to be able to go to university in London.'

'And not having to work extra shifts to pay for it,' she glares. Gertrude pictures her parents with their frozen gestures and plain clothes. Her memory comes in fragments, talks about actions and people being 'good' or 'bad', her screaming and them declining to respond, conditioned by a strict duality that influences their decisions. Gertrude hasn't seen her parents in years. Still, she often wonders what they would think of her if they met their daughter today, anew, like a stranger who walks into someone's life and brings revelations. They wouldn't like the smell of cigarettes attached to her shirts, nor the sound of Stefano being her closest friend, or that she works in a pub. When she was growing up, prescribed books were stored by Gertrude and Liam's bedside tables, caffeine and branded products were banned from the house. The front door stood for the division between those who believed like them and the others – their household's rebellion against the separation of Church and State. Religious studies on Saturday morning instead of sports practice, a sharp dichotomy between what Liam could do and the things Gertrude wasn't allowed to try. The word luck was removed from their family lexicon for fear of tempting sins, and Liam was better at playing the good child game than Gertrude. She grew up wishing she was someone else, until she left home. She headed to London and checked herself into a hostel, where all the principles that had been drilled into her rusted upon contact with bodies and minds that had been shaped outside of her life-long community. This is when Gertrude met Stefano; there, in a dormitory where each bed came with a small locker. Gertrude had to fend for herself and to hunt for ideas of her own – the course of emancipation. She worked hard, doing double shifts until she saved enough money to share a flat with her brother. Their parents pay for Liam's rent, and she hasn't asked her brother if they know that he lives with her; she doesn't want to know.

Stefano scrapes the ciggy against the cement stair, then runs his hand through Gertrude's hair. 'Red like fire,' he whispers as he gets up. 'Inferno,' he mutters as he stretches his arms high, a tall and thin man. He throws the cigarette butt into the rubbish bin and they both stare at the dustbin for a few seconds. They share an ambiguous relationship with guilt, an instinctive emotion that has chaperoned their education – fire and light, two magnetic poles – and the consequent need to rebuff it.

Stefano was raised just outside of Naples and he often blames prayers for taking away his parents' agency. Bitterness doesn't come to Stefano's mind when he hears Gertrude; their families don't share a Church, but their respective educations have resigned them to lie low so they can live as they please. Gertrude hands him her glass so he can wash his mouth out with the last sip of ginger beer.

Time inside the British Library works differently than anywhere else in London. The hall fills with tourists who have come to visit the exhibition of its 'treasures, books, maps and manuscripts', going on a journey of learning from the Magna Carta on to Florence Nightingale and Shakespeare. The inside walls are covered with journals and reviews that knit centuries together. A crowd of doctorates meander through the library, spanning from students who went directly from undergraduate on to postgraduate studies to retired workers who have decided to occupy their spare years with academia. A group of out-casts too, headphones plugged in, carrying niche reference books alongside those who come to access a computer and an internet connection. More than past events are stored inside the British Library: a present timeline develops in the shadow of its archived pages and artefacts; the institution praises its collection with items that date as far back as two thousand years before Christ, and history is rewritten every day.

A visitor coughs and the cry from their throat resonates through the building, spiralling white staircase, red bricks outside. The Wi-Fi signal is unreliable and the workings of the website puzzle Sarah, who comes to the library for research.

She joined the Institute for Environmental Design and Engineering as a PhD candidate last September. One of few women attending the school, Sarah studies 'access to water', and its subsequent issues. She obtained a studentship, three years of funding to research water management in the City of London, with a focus on community engagement. *And a special award from the Mayor of London's office for my proposal too.* Sarah was born and educated in the city.

Format, page number, insert. View, show ruler. Tools, word count – *Nothing promising to show you.* Format, headers and footers, she arrived almost one hour ago and all she has done is play with the formatting of her document. *Where is she?* Silence reigns. Paper sheets with a dated infographic of a man bringing his finger to his mouth are stuck on the columns with Blu-Tack. The stains of oil from the tack's chemical decomposition repulse Sarah. *Quiet please.*

But I cannot write anything worth breaking the silence for.

Quiet, please. I won't tell you what I'd rather be doing instead of studying.

Sarah can hear the familiar and assured footsteps before she pivots her head. When she does turn around, a wide smile escapes; *my feelings always run away before me.* Kristina wears the plastic carrier bag from the library like a fashion accessory, descending along her arm but not swiping the floor. She hugs Sarah hello from behind, slides her hands from the top of Sarah's shoulders onto her hands, gives them a squeeze and sits next to Sarah.

'That's a well-presented document,' Kristina whispers.

Sarah scrolls through the file, up and down, the rhythm fast enough that the lines merge, a black hole of aborted intentions instead of red shoes tiptoeing over a dance floor. 'I had lunch with Mathilde today.'

Kristina looks at Sarah with close attention, her pupils abnormally large and chalky, the colour of a winter sea. 'You smell of wine,' she adds, provocatively loud.

Sarah moves a hand in contestation, but Kristina doesn't allow enough time for Sarah to say no: 'Sweet. Lemony.' She pauses. Her hand reaches for Sarah's leg, closing firmly at the top of her knee. 'Peachy. Sauvignon Blanc?' Her accent shows in the word *blanc*.

'Mixed with Picpoul,' Sarah says.

'Picpoul,' Kristina repeats slowly.

Sarah shakes her head. 'I'm not teaching you French today.' Kristina doesn't loosen her grip. 'Seriously, Tina, I'm so behind.'

'Don't be silly. I'm your supervisor. You can't be in trouble unless I say that you are.' She blows inside Sarah's ear.

Margaux Vialleron

Warmth.
Goosebumps, Sarah gets up.
'Usual location. Ten minutes,' she says.
Sarah walks out first.

6

Cloe

Ten months ago, Cloe moved from a flat share to a studio in north London. The place was advertised on someone's Instagram story; she sent a direct message to a stranger, which turned into a sublet lease agreement, or a useful exception to justify the amount of time she spends online. Massimo, the ginger cat, came with the flat and the proprietor included a clause about the specific brand of canned food she must feed him in the contract. The owner self-identifies as a 'digital nomad', but such a lifestyle doesn't suit a cat.

The lease was one of those agreements that are available to buy, the paper thin and the vocabulary punitive. The room is soulless, but it is her own and there are large windows. The neighbours added her to the street's WhatsApp group as soon as she collected the keys, yet they still haven't eaten a meal together. The intimacy of a converted Victorian house means that they know each other's habits – poor wall insulation.

Things Cloe has learnt since she has lived on her own: pets have a far more balanced and scrutinised diet than humans; the börek with feta and spinach from the deli next door has become her breakfast of choice; where her glutes are (after a round of body strength classes she found on YouTube); butter spreads best when stored in an appropriate dish and left out on the counter, rather than being hidden in the fridge; she prefers books that are reviewed as *entertaining* rather than *thought-provoking*; she has a habit of leaving pasta in the pot, and overnight gluten sticks like leeches at the bottom of a terracotta pot. It was not her flatmates she was avoiding, but herself.

She brushes her teeth, spits. Blood. Cloe returns to the changing rooms that populated her girlhood. *The benches were made of dark oak wood, a row of thin horizontal bars, a small space in between each, wide enough to catch a pinch of skin while we sat and pumped ourselves up. I bruised easily but healed faster back then. The changing room was compact, no windows, and a shower room next door. A wall was left free, centimetres and metres data was engraved on it – 'the Tuesday wall', as we, my teammates and I, called it. Tuesdays, or when our coach was officially allowed to ignore the female symbol on the door, walking in with the notebook in which he recorded our growth after a close inspection. Our bodies replaced our life experience. We were pressured to meet the*

requirements for the practice of our sports – height, weight, BMI.
The blue mosaic tiles, six shower heads in a row, deep and wide
toilets on the other side, a long mirror at the top. Three soap bars,
bright yellow like Sicilian lemons, hanging at the end of thinning
ropes. The one door only we opened, the cleaners aside – the
toilets – also located in the shower area. We taped a calendar on
the back of the door with the other girls, the glossy paper and the
division competitions spread across months: it featured iconic photos
of Britney Spears. I can clearly picture how she was crawling on the
front page, pearls of diamonds covering her toned and naked body,
Toxic and unapologetic. The strident music, the groaning noise
of the door lock, we made crosses with our initials on the days we
wanted to mark, since some of us had started menstruating; bleed-
ing days when we weren't allowed in the water, but we were still
expected to attend training; the things we don't talk about. The
relief of spotting when we knew what our bodies could produce –
another life that would end ours prematurely. We were a team and
we lived to execute our training schedule. Loyalty and the menace
of a betrayal sealed our relationship with one another: we weren't
friends, you must understand; we were teammates. Everything we
did was for the team to win.

We started collecting our pocket money into a communal pot, an
old custard creams box, which we hid behind the toilet's cistern. We
waited patiently until we finally had enough coins to ask Vivienne's
mother to shop at the Superdrug for us. The girls insisted she was
the cool mum with her deep throat laugh, single and smoking in
the car park while we trained inside the leisure centre. I think they
didn't trust Héloïse and the French words she threw in mid-sentence.

51

Emily had stolen a paper catalogue from her older sister, and I wrote our shopping list carefully. I can recollect each detail about it with my eyes closed – the attention, the calculations we made, the wrong but appealingly gluey texture of the paper. I remember it with the dexterity my teacher had hoped I would apply to my learning of the mathematical tables. I do because the logic was ours, softening our skin before polishing it with gloss, an alliance between girlhood and beauty, the strength we bought for ourselves:

Veet Hair Removal Cream Body & Legs 200ml × 2 – £7.49 × 2 = £14.98

Veet BodyCurv Hair Removal Cream Bikini & Underarm 100ml × 2 – £5.88 × 2 = £11.76

Superdrug Vitamin E All Over Body Cream 475ml × 2 – £4.99 × 2 = £9.98

Barry M Instant Blur Body Foundation (Waterproof) – Medium/Dark (Buy 1 get 2nd ½ price) XL × 2 – £9.99 × 2 = £19.98 – £4.99 = £14.99

Vo5 Ultimate Hold Hairspray 400ml × 2 – £3.59 × 2 = £7.18

Superdrug 24 Pack XL Bobby Pins – Black (Buy 1 get 2nd ½ price) × 1 – £2.99 = £2.99

Superdrug Bobby Pins 40 – Blonde (Buy 1 get 2nd ½ price) × 1 – £1.99 £0.99 = £0.99

Girls4Girls Kids Unicorn Goo – Glitter Goo
× 1 = £1.49

Revolution Precise Brow Pencil Dark Brown (Waterproof
Edition) × 1 – £4.00 = £4.00

Superdrug Micellar Face Cleansing Wipes 25's × 2 –
£1.00 × 2 = £2.00

Grand total = £70.36

We twittered until the last line, one for the necessary cleanser to wipe away our little lies before going home to our parents. We thrived and we didn't bother dividing the total amount due between us. Our money had become one sum in the box – we were a team, of girls, but we were a team nonetheless. Our bodies were vessels.

The toaster hums, the bread pops up; Cloe spreads a generous layer of peanut butter on top of toast, a childish snack for the heart. The fog inside her brain draws a curtain over the past twenty-four hours. She reads the message again. Flashing lights, cigarettes before the dance floor, and her head spinning.

Hey C, can you call me back? Last night was fun.

The choice of the initial instead of her forename makes her want to vomit. She finds it rude to shorten names – it steals someone's musicality – and the spelling of her name is short.

Cloe. She likes its shortness, the phonetics of a valley, and the story behind it. Her parents had thought about their decision carefully – and perhaps they had fought as well, as this was their favourite language, a feisty and passionate couple – their fear for their daughter to be misnamed her entire life. Neither of Cloe's parents are native English speakers, but she was born in London.

They wanted all sides of the family to be able to pronounce her name equally: her paternal, Catalan family back in Barcelona; Grandmother Colette and her French spiritual ancestors, when they have no family left on the other side of the Channel; the present, English context of their European roots. *Cloe* – four letters because her father argued against adding a syllable English speakers would try hard to pronounce, a forced dictation that confuses. His daughter would have to spell her name on repeat to all types of administrative services. F for foxtrot, R for royal, A for appetite, N for November, C for cat, E for email, S for Saturday and C for care. Francesc was adamant; they couldn't be good parents and write their daughter's name *Chloe*. H for history. The last letter jarred the correct pronunciation too, the intention for it to be a hard 'e', except that English speakers would soften it, naturally. But Héloïse put a veto on the addition of an accent, the skin on her face wrinkling with the frustration of receiving an error message each time she submitted an online form, her home address impossible to prove, the accents relentlessly abandoning the letters that puzzle her name. Héloïse. Chloé became Cloe and Colette still disagrees.

Cloe prevaricates when she is hung-over.

She climbs and sits on the kitchen counter and starts to Google. The cupboard where she stores snacks is located behind her right shoulder, within reach; a breath of fresh air comes through the window. A pack of popcorn. She types in the number. A page featuring websites that start with variations of the same question appears – *who called me?* No reported scam, but no concrete answer either. More popcorn, a crunch; she reaches for the box of granola next, a recipe made of nuts, dried pineapple and sunflower seeds, more nuts and the dreadful sultanas. Cloe hates their composition, sticky, sweet and sour, an ambiguous topping that reminds her of her indecision. She adds 'reported scam' next to the phone number – *Your search did not match any documents*, then a list of suggestions. *Make sure that all words are spelled correctly*: she deletes the mention and reads over the number slowly. Her fingers skim underneath the typography lines on her screen, the oil from her fingertips underlining her state, confused. *Try different keywords*: she specifies the UK international code 0044, then she removes the 'who called me?'; no luck, so she tries similar iterations such as 'who is it', 'number finder'. Nothing. She snatches another mouthful of granola or popcorn, whichever box sits at the front; the flavours have merged into one craving for blinding sugar.

Héloïse had warned Cloe before – liars get caught. *But what about the lies we tell ourselves?*

She opens a new browser tab, in incognito mode this time, and types: *What should I do if I don't remember if I consented to have sex with a stranger last night?* The sentence reads long and clunky, the ↵ key symbolises what her future could hold – disquieting possibilities. Cloe locks her phone away before the temptation to click 'enter' overwhelms the cautious side of her personality. Right and left, left and right, the ambidextrous child who became an indecisive woman, prey. She chooses not to know; *what I don't know doesn't exist, correct? I need to know in order to be telling lies.*

PART 2

Saturday Morning

7

Cloe and Gertrude

As is her custom on Saturday mornings, Cloe catches the 9:24 a.m. train departing from London Euston. The information display announces a terminus at Milton Keynes. The sight of high-rise buildings is replaced with detached houses and the horizon line clears behind patches of grass and tansies – Cloe falls asleep. At the destination, habits set in motion: she heads to the local supermarket inside the station and pours herself a black Americano coffee at the self-service machine, grabs a cheese and onion twist at the in-store bakery, and she buys both a bouquet of violet tulips and malted milk biscuits, the packaging distinctively pink. She goes to the self-checkout tills and exits the shop. Cloe doesn't pay attention to the people around her – joggers, tote bags advertising bookshops and exhibitions that happen in London, flare jeans – nor to the diversity of coats and

layering, in between seasons, and a self-indulgent disappointment about springtime. She walks purposefully.

In this market town, the density of lives means that schools,
pubs and various shops gravitate within a close perimeter,
which unsettles Cloe when she walks along the high street.
Bright yellow reduction signs at the mountain and sports' gear
store flash, a tailored window for the independent clothing
shop, a candied smell outside the bakery dedicated to special
occasions, a hairdresser, one letting agency and the funeral
service branch of the same supermarket where she goes food
shopping, each located in a row. Until Cloe turns left into
the residential area of town. Now the gates stretch higher,
painted in black, interrupting the lower brick walls that spread
on each side – owners claim a right to privacy to justify the
construction of fences, but they fear trespassers. Cloe peeks
at the houses. The gardens are tidied, textured green with a
few light spots of petals, trees in some instances; the facades
are freshly painted, the homes spacious. The road goes uphill,
and she walks to the top, where a Georgian house stands its
ground with white walls blending into a shade of cream,
stains as the witness of the years that have passed and a lack
of funds for repairs. The garden is at the back. She steps into
the entrance hall, a room dissonantly modern in comparison
with the rest of the building, a ramp and sliding doors large
enough to accommodate wheelchairs.

'She is waiting for you in her room,' the usual nurse welcomes Cloe warmly. 'She is in a good mood today,' she adds
with an encouraging voice.

Cloe doubts the nurse from experience. 'Wait until she sees my breakfast,' she responds as she goes upstairs.

First floor, further down the corridor, she knocks softly on the door, which has been left ajar.

'Who is this?' Colette pretends to be surprised her grand-daughter has come to visit her (she puts on the same act each week). It works; Cloe's stomach liquifies, the guilt for not visiting her grandmother enough mutes her.

'Come on in.' Colette initiates a truce agreement. This too happens each week.

'Morning, Mamie. Let's open the window, shall we? I bought you flowers.' Cloe begins her routine in showing how much she cares – she slides the curtain to one side, then she unlatches the window and takes the temperature of the wind with her finger, pours water into the kettle and pushes the switch down, the sound of boiling water mounts and she infuses a teabag. Colette hasn't moved. Her gaze follows her granddaughter as she sweeps through the room with purpose. The tea brews, Cloe approaches the bed, drops a peck on her grandmother's forehead and asks, her tone apprehensive: 'Would you like to sit on the chair today?'

'Maybe later. Did you bring biscuits?'

'Of course.' Cloe fetches them from her bag. She takes a small tray out of the kitchenette cupboard (flaking Liberty pattern), lays out a few milky but crispy treats on a small plate, throws the teabag in the bin, a drop of milk, and she unveils the brown bag from her shopping carrier. She gives Colette a look out of the corner of her eye. Closed lips, she waits.

'How can you eat this cheesy pastry for breakfast? It stinks. Your cholesterol, darling.'

'Mêle-toi de tes oignons,' Cloe interrupts Colette playfully. Her French is poor, the idioms she has grasped a sense of from her grandmother's repartee aside. The school she attended didn't offer French classes and she is convinced that she can't perform the brain gymnastics learning a language requires. Her grandmother smiles with her teeth at the sound of her 'petite fille', an instant joy that delights Cloe, until she notices the lipstick stains on Colette's incisors – crushed raspberries that show her mamie has lost her independence. The end, a red line every human recognises; death doesn't differentiate. Cloe turns her eyes away from the lipstick splatter. She remembers Colette so vividly, with her skinny calves the shape of walking sticks, orchestrating lunches for the family and dinners for both family and friends all summer long, every year. Melons, prosciutto, pissaladière and grilled sardines, the velvety garnish of olive oil and the sound of the cicadas. Cannes, the part of the French Riviera where Colette was born, the heat enhancing glamorous scenes and the Mediterranean azure. The apartment was located on the eighth floor of a building called Le Marly, its architecture typical of a delicate compromise between tourism and inhabitants of the booming French city, with a swimming pool at the back. Cloe would wake up before anyone else to lane swim as, after nine-thirty, the pool edges overflowed with glossy magazines, teenagers smoking and children jumping with their knees up and arms circled around their bodies.

The more water they splashed out of the pool, the louder they were, whereas Cloe liked to slide efficiently underwater. A methodical swimmer, her arms and legs propelled her harmoniously. She nibbled croissants by picking each layer of pastry with her fingers, patiently, an attentive girl who was unnerved by the cheerful joy of the other children dancing before the burning sun. She would spend her days sitting under a parasol, filling exercise books in preparation for September, in denial of the holiday period. Balconies featured thick, bright shades and there was an old and compact lift whose squeaking noise threatened Cloe's survival instinct enough for her to climb the stairs up. Colette's balcony was covered with white tiles to halt the heat, but grandmother still had to remind granddaughter not to walk barefoot, the sea at the bottom and the île Sainte-Marguerite pocking the horizon with its rocks. 'Avenue du Moure-Rouge', where Colette lived, the home she inherited and refurbished after her mother died, and the flat where she spent every summer since she had moved to England. Cannes is where Cloe got to meet the Colette she admires the most – when she stood with class in her linen dress, the colour of a ripe pear, vocal and holding a broom in her hand to battle dust against the persistent mistral wind, popping to the pharmacy for the neighbour and speaking bad words about those who bought the terrasse houses on the roof.

Colette's husband, Cloe's grandfather, had been asked to drive all the way to London to investigate the *thing* about pubs. It was the '60s; the Beatles and the Rolling Stones had launched the so-called 'British Invasion' and the owners of French bistrots worried that the pub culture might come knocking on their doors next. Alain came back, in Colette's words and a strong French accent, 'a very French man dressed up in an English outfit'. She could not get him to re-acclimate and to forget what he had discovered in London – the business opportunities – the quick turnover of chips and beers, the wine he could import from France and capitalise upon. They moved to London permanently in the wake of this, whereupon he launched a wholesale business to channel crates straight from the vineyards of France on to the British islands. Colette never worked, not *officially*, not enough to earn a pension despite the hours of administrative work she did for Alain's business during their marriage, because the labour of a supportive wife is not recognised by the government, while the contribution she earns for the hours she dedicated to raising their three children doesn't cover the meals of an adult in a hospital-ised infrastructure. Alain died young. 'He was a cheater,' Colette responded to the news of his heart failure. The 'ch' became a soft 'sh' between her lips, *cheater* like a snake threatening to spread venom. The business was sold for *breadcrumbs*, Colette deplores, misled by the French idiom 'pour des miettes de pain', after a run of making ends meet with the leftover money from Alain's schemes. She rented a small one-bedroom flat in a north-west suburb of London, the rooms pungent with potpourri and a collection of old *Gala* magazine editions on the coffee table that gathered dust. Colette is unbeatable on the ins and outs of the royal family – don't test her.

Until the day she fell and the week when she tripped twice and dislocated her hip. The family sold the apartment in Cannes so they could afford the cost of a bedroom in a facility for pensioners; still, London is too expensive, and Colette was cast away. Héloïse terminated the lease agreement for the flat with the NW postcode and moved Colette into the present care home. *She couldn't travel to the shops on her own, never mind cross the border, change train stations in Paris and head down to the south of France,* Héloïse repeated to Cloe, each word stuffing the gaps between inhales of nicotine. One hangs on to the pragmatism the final years impose over the execution of life to justify breaking the heart of one's own mother.

Cloe sits at the end of the bed, her legs crossed to fit in between the security barriers. She drinks her coffee while Colette sips tea and dips half a biscuit between each intake.

'Why are you grimacing like that?' Colette asks.

Cloe responds fast: 'My coffee is cold. It tastes like mud.'

'How often have you tried mud?'

'You can't help yourself, can you, Mamie?'

'Will you help me cut my toenails today?'

They look at each other. The power dynamic rebalances, two women who share a name, silence.

'Only if you let me win our game of Othello.'

Colette nods in the direction of the dark green cardboard box and Cloe jumps off the bed before returning with the game set. The board is perched between them,

Cloe levelling her knees up to her chin, hands crossing underneath, the ring piercing on her nose jiggling as she thinks. She plays with her thumbnail, the scratching noise getting under her grandmother's skin, an itch on her scalp, a marked pause; she takes her time before making the next move. The only chance for Cloe to win is to play unfairly and to distract her grandmother – a family of *cheaters*. One piece eats the other, Colette wins anyway and Cloe escorts her to the bathroom. Her guard has lowered, Cloe fits the shower cap on her grandmother's head gently (only the hairdresser is allowed to brush and wash her hair; once every two weeks as per the silver care plan or what they can afford) and she begins washing Colette with a glove and a soap bar – argan oil. Cloe would never miss a Saturday, a promise she made with her mamie, an unspoken rule to strengthen their relationship. She ends with cutting her grandmother's toenails and Colette agrees to stay in the chair for a short while.

Everyone who works in the kitchen at the Oldfield Tavern, apart from the head chef, gets a Saturday off every six weeks. This promotes a fair system until private events muddle up the rota, or until a colleague needs an extra shift to cover for an unexpected plumbing or dentistry bill, or to pay rent. This week, the employees' holiday planner reads *Gertrude*.

*

Back in Gertrude's flat, the foundations of the building demonstrate weakness, fissures menace safety at each corner, the wardrobes and bookshelves slide away from the walls and the door of her bedroom vibrates loudly when a bus passes the building. The racket wakes Gertrude up early for a day off work, so she makes her way to the kitchen through the hallway. Her head swims in a fog, knickers with a loose black tank top, no bra.

'Sis!' Liam lets out his exclamation more aggressively than his voice suits – a hint of embarrassment. He is slim but with broad shoulders, his legs long just like his sister's, their family recognisable for being *so tall*. The gene that roots a surname when interactions between generations have become rare.

> *there is a twitch in my eye,*
> *a twitch, twitching*
> *like witchcraft.*

> *i rehearsed so you wouldn't see it happening*
> *me before you like i want you to*
> *see me before you*

Gertrude is scratching her eyes, refocusing until she recognises the neighbour who moved into the flat downstairs two weeks ago. She had helped the woman carry a few of her boxes because she had arrived home at the same time as a cab dropped her and all her belongings on the pavement. The unfortunate circumstance meant that Gertrude had to offer her help to this stranger, which she did amid a clumsy dialogue – eighteen months in this area; best coffee just outside the overground station; a Scottish accent – and, still, Liam slept with her. Nothing unpredictable when Gertrude has much to say about the younger sibling's attention-seeking syndrome. She yearns to know how they met and became intimate so quickly, but she waves at the woman across the hallway instead. 'Nice to see you again. Are you settling in well?' Gertrude also asks, despite her effortless attitude.

Liam tuts.

'I better go,' the neighbour says, and Liam opens the front door in agreement.

Gertrude plods to the kitchen. The room is small, the counter unimaginatively crowded with a kettle, thick with limescale, a fruit bowl in which apples are bruising and one lime hardens. A pile of plates dry next to the sink. She slides the window up, opens the top part of the coffee machine, throws the browning filter inside the compost bin, pours in fresh coffee grounds and switches the button on. The pressure releases through the loud mechanism. Liam enters the room, growling.

'It doesn't suit you. Pass me two mugs, please.' Gertrude swiftly brushes her hand through Liam's long hair, a tender gesture in lieu of an apology.

He opens his mouth briskly, but Gertrude holds her brother's gaze. The caffeinated liquid drips inside the machine: she doesn't allow him to return to bed yet. 'Okay. But can you warm up some almond milk for mine, please?' Liam asks.

Gertrude smirks in his direction, with a milk pot in her hand, and Liam grabs the milk inside the fridge. 'Cold is fine too,' he says as he shakes the bottle.

They settle on the sofa, cups in hand and facing each other, cross-legged, Gertrude's phone sitting in between them. He greets the arrangement with familiarity, and she begins reading something both relatable and indefinite, words about stars and chasing desires and worrying before changing everything again. *Your typical Aries*, they joke in conclusion. Gertrude scrolls down her phone before she starts reading the next horoscope entry out loud, which mentions an orange hat, until she stops. She looks up at her brother theatrically and picks up the pace again but with a high-pitched voice: 'You will walk into the room like an accident.' She brings her hands up towards the sky and concludes, 'Come on, look me in the eye and tell me these don't hold any truth.'

'It's called the Barnum effect, Gert.' The sarcastic tone doesn't land.

Gertrude digs further: 'I'm not saying they speak religious truth, but they give some guidance.' Her voice lowers as she gets to the second part of the sentence.

'You sound like Mum.'

If Gertrude could replace her sight with guns, Liam wouldn't live. He hides his face behind his palms; 'I'm sorry,' he whispers. He speaks seriously again: 'You're a contradiction. You left home because you couldn't stand the religious lifestyle our parents imposed on us, only to shelter into a new type of religion.'

'That's not exactly true.' She dislikes how she sounds. Liam doesn't have a clue about being estranged from a family; what being alone really means and how the feeling roots inside the body. Stomach burns, a symptom of Gertrude's hypervigilance. 'For one, astrology isn't a religion,' she says resolutely. She aches with remorse. She remembers, too: a rampant chain of movements, a rapid look over her shoulder, tight hair and running back to the hostel between two shifts to check on the places where she hid her belongings, pragmatic responses to her situation to begin with. Until all these frights gnawed away at her and her self-esteem. 'You don't understand what it's been like to be on my own,' she lets go before the words eat her alive like grief. Lonely, unseen; a muted video of someone screaming. But Gertrude doesn't share the details with Liam. Horoscope entries give her the same illusion of control as the magician that performed in the car park outside the supermarket when they were children. The man with the face painted in plaster white always chose Gertrude and commented on her hair. She loved to participate in the show – to be picked to star over Liam – but she hated the attributes he stamped on her. The horoscope entries rarely use negative vocabulary, a relief when headlines convey yet another threat for women: abduction, assault, unpunished crimes, and rehabilitation for assaulters against a narrative that asks women to be more careful. The news she read compulsively into the night in bed, on her own, at the hostel. 'Behind', 'corner', the basic language of navigation inside a busy kitchen during peak time, the words she wakes up to, in a start in the middle of the night, still, even if she shares a flat with Liam. Astrology, or the stars that prime her with recognition.

Gertrude puts her coffee mug on the table and looks at Liam: 'I started having this recurring nightmare soon after I left home. I'd wake up in the middle of the night in that stinky hostel with my ears blocked and I was convinced that there was a swarm of bees on top of my head.' Liam nods at her. 'I was there alone. I had left and still I wasn't fitting.'

Silence. Liam requires time to assimilate his sister's words.

> *look at me but don't see me*
> *abolish,*
> *don't jail me*

'I didn't want you to leave,' he answers.

'But they didn't want me to be there.'

'I wanted you there. You estranged me too.'

Gertrude hurtles back. 'I had to earn my own money so we can live this way now. I know I shouldn't have left you, but I had no choice.'

Shouldn't – a wish tempers their reality. Liam disagrees and Gertrude agrees with him disagreeing.

'But please, Sis, stay with me. And don't wear an orange hat,' Liam says tentatively.

They grin, teeth apparent, and sibling harmony is restored. She had missed him deeply when they were separated – so much so that when she closed her eyes after a nightmare, she didn't find sleep, but saw Liam smiling at her with his long teeth, making faces when they were supposed to be singing a prayer. She always laughed, and she was the one her mother picked on instead of Liam.

'Then I need your help.'

Liam looks at Gertrude expectantly.

'I have a date and nothing to wear.'

8

Mathilde and Sarah

The alarm rings early, no snoozing allowed, and Chris offers to escort Mathilde to her appointment. She informs him that he has more important things to worry about, without defining what these *things* are and their degree of gravity. Chris manages to be standing in Mathilde's way whenever he is up on his feet, while she rambles from one room to the other, her phone in one hand as she lists all the items she needs to pack in her bag. Then she stops, her thumb massages her forehead. 'I'm late,' she says. 'It takes the Tube and two buses to get there. You wouldn't guess the place is mainly visited by sick people.'

'Why don't you get ready, and I'll order you a cab?' Chris offers with a calm voice.

He is a caring man. I feel lucky. I should have checked the route earlier, but it would have meant that I had to go and I'd rather not

73

go. The letter from the hospital was instructive: time and location; what to bring; do not travel to the hospital if you have a high fever and/or a new unexplained cough; each missed appointment costs one hundred and fifty pounds to the health system. How much does an attended appointment cost? I used to wonder why they're still sending letters through the post, until I figured out that it's more difficult to cancel or reschedule a written appointment than through an online portal. They want us to come. What if I go there and they think that I'm wasting resources because I did this to myself? Some people fall sick, like Sarah did, and their care needs are more urgent than mine.

'I wanted to listen to a podcast to distract myself.'

'You can still do that,' Chris says.

'It's kind of rude to the driver.' She looks away. 'It makes me feel antisocial.'

Chris observes Mathilde, stylish in her high-rise mom jeans, a camel jumper tucked inside the waistband. She is wearing a scarf because she always covers her neck regardless of the season. Her hair is propped into a high ponytail, her fringe falls like a curtain over the frame of her glasses (her contacts are packed in her handbag). A hairbrush, a primer enriched with vitamin C and a corrector, of which the tone is called 'light bisque', a shirt made of silk material so it doesn't crumple inside her bag and so she can change before brunch. The shirt also has long sleeves that tighten closely around the wrists, as all of Mathilde's tops do, so she can hide the marks over her left arm. As for the hand, her face corrector works, for as long as Mathilde is right-handed.

Her follow-up appointment with the reconstructive plastic surgeon fell on the same Saturday of a long-awaited reunion with her schoolfriends. They had booked a spot at a popular brunch place in west London after debating locations, a tense exchange between adults who refuse to admit their priorities have shifted. Any map shows Paddington as a mid-point between Bath, Oxfordshire and various parts of London. They wish to entertain a lifelong friendship, but such meetings stigmatise their character: different obligations, means, other friends and commitments reflect on each their individual sense of self-worth. Mathilde insisted on booking the table, living up to her role in the minds of these women who have known her since she was a girl – *Mathi the doer*. Since their last encounter in person, a baby has turned six months old, there have been two engagement proposals, one job promotion and talks of a resignation, and a break-up occurred – in long-lasting relationships, not all celebrations must be a happy event.

Mathilde's trainers are the colour of sand, a golden band on the side, smart and casual, her favourite shoes. She is standing with her fists clenched as Chris approaches. He squeezes her right hand and says: 'I'm happy to put my spotless Uber rating on trial for you. Try to stay calm.' She nods and he adds: 'I can still jump into a pair of jeans. You know that.'

She nods again and fiddles for her keys.

I don't want him to come. Chris is an optimist, which is a great quality to have overall, but his rejoiced voice at the sight of the falafel stall in front of the building, him elbowing me when he finds a pound coin in his pocket and his brave smile when he returns with a chocolate bar to share, will only frustrate me. 'I don't like KitKats,' I'll pick a fight. He'll not allow himself to make one comment about the waiting time and I'll be seeking relief in complaining. He'll dare to say that he finds the wait relaxing and that 'I'm only making it worse for myself,' to use Chris's words. This is my pain. I choose how hard I want it to be.

Mathilde finds her keys, smiles back at Chris and exits the flat.

The reading rooms inside the British Library's imposed silence, and the subsequent pressure of seeing others working harder than Sarah does, give her a structure to rely on. She walks in bright and early on Saturday, a time when she yearns for a better version of herself – an entire weekend to make progress with her research.

'Good morning. I'm afraid I have left my reader's pass at home, and I really need access to the reading rooms today. Is there a way I could have a day pass or something to replace my card?' Sarah asks with an apologetic tone. The woman on the other side of a Plexiglas screen is buried in library guides and flyers while a colleague next to her stares at his phone, earplugs stuck deep and the world around him closed off. Most of the leaflets are outdated.

'Let me have a look for you. What's your name?'

'Sarah Jenkins-Bell.'

Her eyebrows frown, thick and the colour of hay. Sarah tries to read her name badge without success.

'Could you spell your name for me, please? I can't find you on the system.'

'S-a-r-a-h—'

There she is interrupted: 'Ah, Sarah with an "h",' the woman exclaims with the pride of someone who has cracked a code.

Sarah smiles widely. Such a confusion would never have happened to her sister – 'Mathilde with an "h"', she hears her say every time they need to check in somewhere or when they meet someone new. Sarah finds this detail about her sister so irritating that it has become her favourite of Mathilde's character traits. She makes a mental note to send her a text later, an anecdote to link them, but she won't press send. The day will pass, and the event won't sound as comical isolated from its original context. It wouldn't amuse Mathilde to be seen this way either. She would fire back.

'Can I see your ID?'

Sarah shows her driving licence.

The printer in the small office works loudly.

'As an affiliated student with one of the universities of London and under supervision for your PhD, you're eligible for a temporary pass.' She slides the badge made of paper and covered with a thin plastic film through the small opening. A blurry headshot of Sarah, which was taken on her registration day and before her official diagnosis, is printed on it, her name on the right and the expiry date written underneath.

'If you realise your reader's pass is misplaced, then you'll need to declare it lost and book yourself in for a new registration appointment. You can do that on the British Library's website directly, but please tick the box next to the mention of "returning reader" so they can retrieve your existing data.' The woman inhales deeply. 'Please note that we're currently seeing delays with booking appointments as the British Library is experiencing a shortage of staff. Would you like a leaflet with this information?'

The tone of her voice has changed, mechanical, a recital of good behaviours that keeps the two women at a distance from one another.

'That'll be fine, thank you.' Sarah walks away.

Will I be asked to take a new photo if I report my card as lost? I know where my reader's pass is (inside the pocket of the coat I was wearing yesterday); finding it won't be an issue. The problem is that I hate this photo of me. It's naïve. It shows me smiling and clueless when my body was failing, my secrets underneath my skin, and I wouldn't have started this PhD if I had known that it'd make me so apparently sick. I started with good intentions. Every day is the same: I wake up with harrowing pains, stiff muscles moor between my bones, a wide range of cries until I swallow my medicines with breakfast. I attempt meditation but all it does is focus my attention on what hurts, so I head to the library. It's a good act of business as usual. I sit at the same spot, on the second floor of the building, where the green desk pad is scratched with archaeologies from the previous students. I open my Word document (SJB – thesis draft 3 – WIP) and I scroll down. Up; back down. I write nothing, I think about

Kristina. I think that every time I'm about to come, my lips swollen, I wish for her to turn me around. It's vivid and unlike me, and I've never asked if we could try this together. But I want to. I had desires before we had sex. I had enrolled for this postgraduate programme feeling like a trespasser who was about to enter unknown territories, buoyant and brave enough to want to dismantle methodologies. I craved new horizons. Every day is the same: I wake up and both my life and research topic shrink, my intentions slipping through my fingers that are stiff with arthritis. I cannot possibly catch a piece of myself and stitch it back. I'm drowning and I want Kristina to love me tenderly after I have come.

It had always been obvious to Sarah that she would pursue her studies at a doctorate level. Her grades were good, the demands of reading and writing and thinking allowed her to live in her head; this was her path. Sarah's approach to problems is empirical.

It was October during the last year of her master's degree. She had arrived at the university building early enough to catch the reverberation of streetlamps bouncing back inside puddles of rain. A case of agoraphobia means that Sarah would arrive first and leave the amphitheatre last at the end of seminars, packing her stuff and making a final set of scribbles about the extra reading she wanted to do. That specific October class was taught by a guest lecturer and centred around a case study about California and the technologies the state was developing to tackle droughts. The assigned professor, who was also her dissertation supervisor, approached to ask if Sarah had enjoyed the seminar. They were enthusiastic debaters together; Sarah trusted her judgement.

'Here,' Sarah had said before reading something about the 'meditations of water' on her tablet, not the *politics* of water, but the *waterworks* themselves. The extract referenced aqueducts and siphons, forebays and afterbays, and the grand scale of plumbing. 'I can't believe this man did an entire seminar about California and water without quoting Joan Didion's "Holy Water" essay.'

'Well, this is why we need more women doing research.'

Sarah had raised her shoulders in disbelief, forcing her youth against the weight of a systemic society.

'Especially in an engineering field like ours,' she had finished, before giving Sarah a compassionate smile. Like a conjuror, her tutor inspired in Sarah a level of confidence she wouldn't have summoned for herself.

Sarah received an email the next day, no subject, but one hyperlink followed by some context and a single instruction: We need more women doing research at the engineering school. Apply, you'd be brilliant.

Didion's *waterworks*, or in this instance a study focusing on Thamesmead, a social housing site built in the mid-1960s on the marshland in south-east London. The *coughing pipes* of Joan Didion, her metaphors, a language that describes swimming pools filling up with bricks accurately; Didion's method as a reporter who denounced issues and studied marginalised communities with integrity. With her intuitive writing style, Didion defended her choices by projecting words on paper – her execution – and her investigative work.

As part of the studentship package, Sarah became eligible to rent a studio flat – 'at a preferential rate' – in student accommodation, an opportunity to expand her world outside of the family home. She wrote the application between naps, the constant demands of a body that has never quite worked as it should by capitalist production standards; an enigmatically sick child and a problematic young woman, healthy adults tell her as she keeps up with working from bed. She wrote her candidature during the rare days when typing on a keyboard granted her a hard-earned freedom in the escape room she was building with her words.

I sent the application, and was interviewed, and the acceptance letter followed through the post. It was a day for happy coincidences. Mathilde had also received a job offer from a women's centre she had approached months ago. She and Chris joined us for dinner at our parents' house that night. Dad made his usual cauliflower cheese and Mum baked salmon in foil. She had spent the afternoon making Nigella Lawson's chocolate cloud cake. We popped a bottle of Prosecco, snacked on tinned olives and Mum dug out an odd-tasting pâté, probably from a past New Year's Eve party. We had some wine from the cellar with our food. The menu wasn't cohesive because it was an unbelievable day. I was still living with Mum and Dad at the time, and Dad and I had a glass of whiskey in his study before bed. We often did while I was putting my proposal for my PhD together. I value his opinion. The next day I woke up paralysed on one side. I tried to scream but they couldn't hear me because one half of my mouth was numb. I always thought this house was unnecessarily big for the four of us. I gave up and I grabbed my phone. I started typing with my right hand, slowly, confused. I was confused because my brain was connecting the dots efficiently. I was aware of where I was and what was happening and that I hadn't woken up in the night. I pressed send to my message in the family group. My mother responded straight away – 'What do you mean you can't move, dear?' – and my father followed up to ask if I was okay. It was Mathilde, who was back in her own home on the other side of London, who told them to go check on me. The next minute, Dad was carrying me down the stairs and driving us to the hospital. Mum didn't say a word during the entire journey.

'Has your daughter been under an unprecedented amount of stress recently?' the nurse asked when we arrived at the check-in desk of our local A&E. She was calm.

'If only.' Mum spoke again with a desolation in her voice I had never heard before. She gave up putting on a show. 'If only.' 'Once upon a time,' I hear her start a bedside story, tales of the imagination, frames that edit our stories. Something unreal and fairy-tale-ish – if only I hadn't had this accident so early on in life, if only I wasn't such a sick child. If only this was an isolated episode. They checked me in.

I stayed on the overcrowded ward for almost forty-eight hours. Blood works and an MRI scan, syringes injecting fluids, stool and urine samples. Pins and needles, I started feeling in the extremities again. They discarded a stroke, and they came back to my state of angst because it was easier to say that I had made myself sick rather than admitting they couldn't find what was wrong with me. They were the doctors; I was the sick woman. I don't remember Agnes ever leaving my side, but I could smell the nicotine on the cotton of her cardigan. She is the one who insisted my bouts of fever were relevant. She said they were part of our lives, so much so that we had rituals to deal with them together. She read through every single prescription and test result, but I don't recall her asking questions.

They sent me home with a list of referrals. The white envelopes started coming through our letter box and it took months before a doctor spoke words that landed into a coherent diagnosis. You see, I'm younger than the usual age category for that type of condition. I'm a woman; they question my resistance to pain. But when they found my illness, I laughed with relief. I laughed because I had already Googled this disease months ago. I could have told them what was wrong with me, but there is no logic of consent when it comes to sickness.

Waterworks, until water drowns you.

'Good morning. Could you please give me your name?'

'Mathilde with an "h". Jenkins–Bell with a dash in between.'

'You're checked in. First floor, area B. They will call for you when they're ready.'

She follows the stairs up, her headphones still plugged in, but she has paused the podcast, her attention corrupted by the various sounds and signs that populate the corridors. Hospitals are planned to be aseptic, an unwelcoming trait for the human species that has developed alongside the concept of building safe homes for its kinds. The light, photophobia–inducing, people walking in and out of side rooms, either hurriedly and dressed in a white blouse or those who drag their feet, colourless, no eye contact.

It started with a random pain inside my ear, then a recurring stab between my ribs, and all round my skeleton. I overslept every single day, still I woke up more tired the morning after. I had no appetite, but I had cravings. Garlicky pesto in jars, spread on bread or straight from the spoon, cheesy and crunchy Cheetos, flavours that would disturb my taste buds to the point of rousing. My tongue felt numb and my mouth sour. I sat in silence, as if I was living inside an aquarium. I didn't speak about the thoughts that kept me awake at night to anyone, nor did I describe the nightmares that made me oversleep. I started hiding in the bathroom instead. Ours is small, the bath covered in dark wood and the floor made of an even darker shade of oak, no window but a powerful spotlight. There I scanned my body, my face and legs, following the conduits of my veins and arteries to find my heart again, digging out ingrown hairs and moisturising skin patches. Some hopeful mornings, I'd nourish the bags under my eyes with expensive creams that promised me time travel, determined to head out and smile. I weighed myself with the precision of a clockmaker and I soaked in hot baths. I used Epsom salts, essential oils, my skin soaring into a red pellicle, my isolation. I noticed that I couldn't articulate properly anymore, as if my sinuses were congested constantly, and colleagues asked me if everything was okay at home when I met them by the kettle. 'You look absent,' most justified with their lips sucked inside their mouths, trying to hide their curiosity. I told them about my sister being unwell and that we didn't know what was wrong with her exactly. At night, I Googled my symptoms so I could compare them with hers. Chris would be sleeping next to me, his head always turned towards my pillow, and I gambled with how I might feel the next day. Sometimes I'd find a reassuring website, I read pages of testimonies on forums, people who have been channelled from one specialist on to the other for years, the minds of women questioned by others at first, by themselves forever after. I read the names of diseases paying close attention, long words flipped my stomach with the memory of a Latin class, and when I felt at my worst, I switched tab to look at images. It was during one of these research parties that I found this American study that showed that people who carry an unspoken grief in them tend to develop an uncommon sinus dysfunction. The tears that weren't cried out are believed to be the cause. There I had identified our curse, the secret Sarah and I have kept behind our shared name since the accident. The finding was reassuring – a quantifiable wound I could treat – and I focused on that. I dug and dug and dug and I looked at myself harder in the mirror, just so I could uncover that grief that was infecting my existence. I raised the topic with Chris, but of course he thought I was making it harder for myself, that I was hurting myself. Like I always do: inflammations, lingering headaches and worsening sight – this is 'how my body responds to stress'. He shopped for compensating quantities of St John's wort teabags, magnesium sprays; he declared phones and laptops forbidden from the bedroom and fitted blackout curtains; at Christmas, he gifted me a smartwatch that monitors my sleep and oxygen levels and tracks my water consumption, because 'hydration is key', he quoted doctors. I felt humiliated in the echo chamber of my illness. I watched the graphs of my heartbeats on the watch face every evening, the inconsistent lines, the whispering voices of my ghosts. Sarah said that I was pale so I told her about the American study and the un-cried tears, and the grief I was researching so I could stop drowning inside my body. She could save herself too, I added. My sister answered with her scientific knowledge about water blockage and compared sinuses and pipes. She recommended a nasal spray she uses as if I had asked about her laundry detergent, and we kept eating our lunch. I found chewing hard; it made breathing through the mouth impossible. I was so tired, you know. I didn't mean for this to turn into such an ugly cry for attention, but I was so tired. Chris was cooking dinner. He was so excited about the fresh linguine, the Parmesan cheese and the two pistachio cannoli he had picked up at the deli near his office. He was talking about going to Sicily for the summer holiday, something about climbing up Etna, and I freaked out about not being able to breathe properly at the top. I was scared about what I could do to myself near the fire of one of the most active volcanoes in the world. The small radio in the corner of our kitchen counter was unbelievably loud. Courgettes, eggs, knives and a pan were scattered in a mess. I poured water inside a pot and set it on the stove. Chris was still talking about this rock somewhere in the Mediterranean Sea, long vegetable strips, the sharp knife making a slashing noise as it cut through the flesh. The window blurred with condensation and water pearled down the frame; boiling point.

*

What comes next is what Mathilde was told.

She was standing by the stove, threw pinches of salt into the water and waited for it to boil. Chris daydreamed about holidays and followed up with a story about work, a hybrid meeting he was chairing earlier today. He was slicing an onion while he recounted the story of his colleague losing their temper and an argument made harder by a poor internet connection. He fried the onions, which must have taken a minute or two, before he added the courgettes he had cut lengthwise. A pinch of salt, and he reached for the wooden spoon, so he could whirl the vegetables without them burning in the piping-hot copper pan. Chris knows that Mathilde likes her vegetables with a crunch. He removed that pan from the heat and set it aside; this much he is certain because he has read over the recipe again and again. He has admitted not remembering who submerged the pasta into the boiling water, not that he thinks this would have changed anything, but Mathilde has asked him to retell the night in great detail. She is adamant: she wants to understand how it escalated, because a secret about herself had brought her there in the first place.

One of them poured the pasta into the pot and set the timer for three minutes. This is when the pace of the evening quickened: the recipe had been written for cupboard pasta and Chris hadn't read it fully before setting off to cook. The fresh pasta would take less than half the time than the industrial variety – but he still had to whisk one whole egg and an extra yolk with thirty grams of Parmesan cheese. He used a fork, mixing rapidly, while he read the rest of the instructions. He wanted this meal to be good. He wanted Mathilde to have a warm dinner so maybe she could sleep. Chris mentions that he might have shouted her name amid the stress of the moment – 'Mathilde, wake up!' in a snap – and he asked her to reheat the pan with the vegetables, 'Now!' She didn't say a word. She reached for the pot with the cooking pasta inside instead, her wrist pivoted slowly towards her stomach, and she let go. She poured the boiling water over herself, the long pasta hanging over her arm like the ripped flag of the dinner they could have shared in denial of Mathilde's depression. Up, work, eat, sleep, repeat. Until Mathilde derailed this circle, third-degree burns peeling her skin off, and an emergency care unit on the way.

Chris's account becomes more uncertain as the story goes on. The pasta hanging over Mathilde's arm is the final clear image he has from that evening. After that and until they arrived at the hospital, he is unsure about the order of events: did he open the tap with cold water first? Did he take the pot away from Mathilde's hands or did she drop it? Did he call an ambulance? Did they scream so loud the neighbour heard them and called for help on their behalf? Chris has kept to himself the fact that Mathilde stood immobile and silent like a mannequin made of wax, melting before him. Her resilience to disappear into ashes that night terrifies him. Mathilde has told him that she remembers the pan dropping, the exact second when steel met tiles, but not the pain she felt. Chris cannot stop hearing the noise of boiling water landing on Mathilde's skin, his fraught senses making up the sound of her shirt crisping in contact with the heat, frying. The proof she didn't say a word. A low buzz of cold wind bursts inside his ear. He cannot listen to the radio anymore because he cries when he hears the frequency interferences. Boiling water. He threw away the kettle as soon as he came back from the hospital – it had the potential to boil more water. Mathilde's skin, the moles he likes to join as if they were constellations when they wake up in the morning, melted. Medical help eventually arrived, but Chris doesn't recall if he opened the door for them. The next thing he knows is that they drove to the Chelsea & Westminster Hospital, home of the designated burns unit in London. A diabolical disco ball, a siren on the roof. He must have put on his shoes mechanically, turned off the cooker and locked the door behind them, the gestures that keep one alive on a normal day.

Mathilde was put under the watch of an intensive care unit. Nurses put an IV in her wrist so she could be rehydrated, a dermatologist examined the skin damage, a stream of blouses walked in and out of the room, each scrutinising her. Psychiatrists and psychologists visited; Chris was interviewed by a social care assistant, a normal procedure since his fiancée had harmed herself in front of him. Had she? They had asked, only to strengthen his words with certainty. Mathilde left the facility with a strict regimen of painkillers, tranquillisers and blood-clotting medicines. The burnt epidermis was covered with a bandage and a nurse visited Mathilde at home after she was discharged from the hospital, cleaning her physical wounds and checking on her about the rest, her trained eyes on the lookout for any signs of post-traumatic stress disorder. Chris left as soon as the nurse arrived; he was afraid Mathilde would not feel safe to describe her pains around him; *I'm fine, darling, don't worry,* the passing verse that had blinded them until the night of the incident.

She calls it that. *The night of the incident.* Chris nods with a straight face. *Mathilde's nervous breakdown* is how he describes it to others.

Once the wound had healed, Mathilde underwent plastic surgery on the most affected parts: her left hand and forearm, and a patch on her stomach and hip, also on the left side. The surgeons removed the burnt areas of skin and replaced them with healthy skin tissues from her bottom. Mathilde showed little interest in the procedure, acknowledging her visitors only briefly. Sarah brought her sister a magazine with the crosswords she enjoys completing, which Mathilde did, but silently. She is normally proud of how clever crosswords make her sound. Agnes brought fresh flowers and specified that the hospital florist calls her *Agnes* now. She shared the kind of gossip that should have entertained Mathilde, but the conversations thinned into a monotone monologue. Mother also rescheduled daughter's wedding. The event was due that summer and was pushed back a year. Chris sat quietly next to Mathilde, holding her right hand for as long as visiting hours allowed him. Mathilde's father only came once, but tears fell down his plump face and he never returned.

This is a story from last year.

*

On this Saturday morning, Mathilde is sitting back in the waiting room at the hospital for her follow-up appointment. Posters list signs of cancer; misguiding photos of apparently healthy children and adults to raise awareness about diabetes; telephone numbers for support lines and flyers about charity sports events are stapled to the walls.

An old woman approaches the reception desk, her voice sounds on the edge of breaking. She is convinced that everyone who has come in after her has already been seen and gone home. The receptionist assures her there is more than one service affiliated to this waiting room so the order in which people arrive is not relevant.

Two young men walk in, one has only his right eye open, a plaster at the top edge of his nose, and a consultant asks them both to wait. The doctor goes to find a nurse; they will fit the injured man in for a scan of his head between appointments. He asks if he can go to the cafeteria; he says that it has been 'a long night' and he fell asleep with his head resting against a wall. The eternal dilemma of who deserves to sleep soundly. The member of staff says no, he must be present when they call him for his turn, otherwise he could cause further delays in the service. His friend comes up with a strategy so that they can go and fetch food despite the restriction – he will go first and then, when he returns, they will exchange roles. This way one of them is always in the waiting room, he explains. They are quiet for a short minute. One of them comments that there is no phone service inside the hospital so they can't communicate, which is problematic, and so they continue to debate vocally despite the echoes inside the small, windowless waiting room.

Mathilde smirks for being nosy. She checks her watch; the numbers disappoint and she endures each one of the passing seconds. She sighs.

A nurse appears at the corner of the corridor: 'Mathilde?' She gets up. 'You okay, my love?' She doesn't have time to respond. 'Sorry for keeping you waiting, love,' the nurse adds.

The wounds are clean and her immune response to the transplant is encouraging. She should be grateful; she hears the doctor advising her. Mathilde blinks.

I haven't cried yet. I recognise the way they all look at me. Chris, Sarah, Mum. I know they are waiting for me to burst, but I need to find the source of the blocked tears first.

9

Gertrude and Mathilde

'The date is today. So, are you going to help me pick an outfit?'

Liam answers Gertrude with three questions: what does he do for work? Where does he live? Where is the date taking place? He meant to add a mention about his sister enabling the shared location feature on her phone, but he doesn't want to sound controlling. When they were younger, Liam had the upper hand over his sibling, bossing Gertrude around the house and playgrounds. He was a charismatic child with his uncombed hair and knock-knees.

'He works in wealth management and he lives in Pimlico.' Gertrude pauses to let the information sink in, allowing her brother to enjoy the irony of the situation.

'You're kidding me. Gert, why do you do this to yourself?'

She grabs his hand and says playfully, 'We're going for bottomless brunch near Paddington.'

He shakes his head with over-reaction. 'Why would you go to Paddington? And for bottomless brunch? What if he's bad company? You won't even have an obvious end point.' Before Gertrude can respond, he adds: 'I predict that he'll be bad company.'

A pause. Liam could stop here, but he must say it. 'No horoscope needed.'

'The venue is near the canal so I can push him in the water if I need to end things early.'

Liam jumps up from the sofa and walks towards Gertrude's bedroom, rambling on about something with the occasional words echoing – *finance, bankers, twat* – while Gertrude follows him. She stops at the bathroom door, but he carries on along the hallway. Gertrude gets into the shower, leaving the door ajar so she can hear Liam mumble from a distance. Her own mind drifts away as the cold water submerges her hair; the thickness of it falls heavy over her forehead.

> *whatever the linguistics*
> *they/she/her/them*
> *i am left with the one body.*
> *gertrude,*
> *an ungrateful guest*

In the bedroom, Liam checks the weather for the rest of the day and scans through the restaurant's menu with the sticky nonchalance of a teenager who has refused to grow older. When Gertrude returns, she finds her brother has layered a selection of clothes over her bed. She is wrapped up inside a bathrobe, her hair drips on the carpet, her eyebrows are high; she disapproves of his selections. Each clothing combination forecasts an inanimate version of who Gertrude could be today.

'Wait a second and let me explain.' Gertrude nods; Liam continues: 'The flowery green dress is celebratory and cute, inoffensive. The long, fluid dress is elegant and makes you own it: red lipstick, the lengthwise stripes will make you look tall and impressive. The fitted petrol jeans with the oversized white shirt tucked inside is a classic. The shirt is mine by the way, so please get yourself a white shirt for any future dates with the banker. Also with red lipstick to make it feel more datey and the result is smart and casual. You're challenging him about how things could go. Curly, wild hair with any of these, obviously.' Liam speaks fluently; words flow easily, linking the public and private facades of his identity with a humorous candour. It exasperates Gertrude, but with a tendered devotion – like a sibling.

Gertrude squeezes her hair first, then blots it with a towel, her eyes switching from one outfit to the other. 'There are so many things wrong about these outfits,' she says firmly, before lowering her voice a few decibels, 'and I'm not waxed.' Liam removes the floral dress from the bed, and Gertrude burns with a contradictory self-awareness about the comment – she resents that it bothers her not to be waxed and she hates to have told her brother that she hasn't waxed. Unruffled, Liam slides the hanger around his forearm, playing butler for his big sister. A silence, then Gertrude adds with confidence: 'Can I please borrow your shirt?'

'I knew it! Of course you can. Just don't order the bruschetta with tomatoes.' She hands the other dress back to him, disclosing her confusion as she does. 'I checked the menu before letting go of my own date shirt.'

A sharp laugh escapes Gertrude. 'Shut up and let me get ready. I'll come to say goodbye on my way out.' He tidies the two dresses back inside the wardrobe and walks away. 'And, Liam.' He stops to look back at her. 'Thank you.'

Gertrude passes a styling mousse through her hair with the help of her fingers, then she applies a moisturiser on her face, followed by a light BB cream. A touch of mascara, the mixture dry and the result patchy. She dislikes make-up – lipstick aside, because the red paint on her lips gives her confidence, eager to speak so she can flirt with the shape of her mouth, the gift of her white teeth and the red of her hair, her radiant being. A splash of deodorant; she doesn't own perfume. A skin-coloured set of underwear, and then she dresses. Subtle earrings, two small golden hoops for the first piercings, then a red, single fake diamond stud for the second one.

She says goodbye to Liam, thumbs up from under his duvet, which gives her a boost of energy; in white trainers and a leather jacket, Gertrude passes through the front door.

High-rise buildings with large window panels line the Paddington Canal. The architecture of the neighbourhood argues in favour of efficiency and modern life – markers of history have faded away, almost like a ghost town populated with people who don't live there but merely transit. Coffee shops advertise seasonal drinks, glossy bars list pizzas with creative topping options on their menus and restaurants feature minimal designs. The pace, a streaming flow, has stolen the possibility for habits to root in Paddington.

The venue where Gertrude and Mathilde will cross paths on this Saturday is a testimony to what London does best, it is always being reborn, repurposing buildings to accommodate new trends. The structure forms an imposing block, thick and beige bricks, an old factory in which windows were fitted throughout – black steel frames embracing each one of them. A high ceiling and warm air, the sunlight streams through and plates of food are juggled between waiters' hands and guests. Large glasses of Aperol Spritz shimmer on most tables and pots of hanging plants are hooked onto the aluminium beams, strings of nickels and curly spider plants, bottles of white wine sit inside silver coolers. The rare beer, golden fizz. The noise is suffocating and so is the heat, but the restaurant has earned a reputation and they don't accept walk-ins anymore.

Mathilde arrives last. She hands her jacket to the front of house and joins the table, where she reunites with her childhood friends and mumbles a vague excuse about the washing machine leaking and flooding inside the kitchen, an apology for being late. 'What shall we drink?' she asks jovially.

They understand not to ask questions.

A bottle of rosé arrives next, Côtes de Provence, a bucket of ice cubes on the side, and a homemade organic lemonade in the guise of a pregnancy announcement from one of the friends. The mood is light, questions fuse one after the other, so the headlines are touched upon, but little attention is granted to the details that shape specific responses. These are relationships that have suffered the unavoidable experience of growing up, of meeting new people who share more interests as adults through work, hobbies and, lately, mums' groups. It has taken years to work out new boundaries between them, and they often fail to articulate them promptly, ending up disappointing one another, feeling wronged or misunderstood, the emotional attachment they resent and the memories they gratify. A lifelong friendship on the one hand, but the whims of daily life on the other.

The food arrives and the meal begins. Crab Benedict, a generous and zesty hollandaise sauce, the bright yolk breaking through and reminding them of the quality of a simple pleasure: toasted muffins. They speak about what they have been watching on television, they exchange podcast recommendations. An old classmate has started an independent show where she comments on the diaries she kept from the ages of thirteen to sixteen. They admit listening to new episodes promptly, even though they get chills at the thought of hearing their names through this revelatory voiceover that sheds new light over the years they have worked hard to romanticise. Smoked haddock and shrimps for the wild rice kedgeree, with another soft-boiled egg on top; some grimace at the smell of fish while others' mouths fill with saliva. The conversation moves on to holiday plans; Greece, Italy, the promise of sun and the dream of swimming in wild waters. Mathilde excuses herself, she must go wash her hands.

A spiced chickpea, cauliflower and baby spinach salad complements the brunch spread. Coconut yoghurt dressing, tahini and sunflower seeds, the dish that makes everyone an ally around the table.

'Girls, ten o'clock on your right. Be discreet. I bet she's waiting for her date,' Mathilde says as she sits back at the table.

The group of friends have always indulged their interest in the tables around them, and the stories they might tell.

'The location is a wild choice. And it's definitely a date – I spotted the retouch of lipstick earlier,' one adds as the women start eating.

A man joins 'the woman with red hair and long legs', as she has been labelled by the group of friends, and they review the pair's matching outfits of white shirt and jeans combo. Between mouthfuls of food and quick approving comments about the toppings, they agree he is a catch, his skin smooth and his shave clean. They can't hear what the couple are saying, precisely, but one of the friends reported that the man had asked about the woman's journey to the restaurant – she had heard on her way to the bathroom – and this confirms their suspicions. It is a date.

Another bottle of rosé for the table, an extravagant fountain of chocolate, strawberries and waffles is wheeled in for dessert, momentarily lifting worries away from the women's minds. The sweet bomb brings back memories; they describe past summer camps, past nights out, past boyfriends, past house shares – despite the occasional update on the table next to theirs. They fail to be subtle when he puts his hand on hers; the thrill, the novelty of desiring someone new.

The meal drags with an order of coffees and teas, the caffeine kick inviting them to circle back to the present tense and their respective families – concerns about their mothers' health, retirement plans and the latest embarrassing thing one of their elderly uncles said at a family dinner. The distraction of a stranger's life fades.

They split the bill equally and they leave, but not without a catwalk of complicit smiles to the dating pair.

Gertrude walks along the Paddington Arm of the Grand Union Canal. She marks a brief pause in consideration of how easy it would be to disappear into the water before quickening her pace. She steps inside the restaurant.

> *i have been told to love,*
> *that i should love to be loved*
> *because sex and romantic feelings align,*
> *but i wouldn't want to touch to be loved*

Gertrude has had one relationship so far. It coincided with the short intensity of a youthful summertime: she remembers outfits more accurately than activities; she wore dungarees at festivals and loose suit trousers she bought in a vintage shop for a picnic in Greenwich. She went to demonstrations to defend causes she didn't care for as much as she said she did. There were large buckets of popcorn for a fix of normality and midnight pasta to fall in love with how good a person can be – until they broke up. Gertrude had said a definitive no to sex.

> *'I am sick to death of this particular self. I want another.'*
> *i read the Woolf, once*
> *Orlando, Virginia,*
> *my archive*

She fell through the looking glass. The vivid years of puberty bled like a plucked ingrown hair, inflamed and scarring, setting the scene for future repressions. She looked at the others, passing handwritten notes on small bits of paper through the classroom, running around ping-pong tables after lunch, spending evenings at the cinema, dating and talking about French kissing at the school gate the next morning. Gertrude stood, bizarre and shrinking. Her schoolmates amended their relationship status and their pronouns on social media with the self-sufficient confidence of typing 'I' on a keyboard.

i, gertrude, exist
so honest, but
dishonest before you

Gertrude lifts her phone up so she can check her lipstick – a selfie. She deletes the photo. She fiddles with pins so her hair behaves. The waiting time has narrowed the room down.

Her work schedule means that she is off work on Mondays and Tuesdays most often, forty-eight hours when London becomes tragically unanimated. Cafés minimise their opening hours, the office crowd demonstrates enthusiasm for the gym. Gertrude downloaded one of the three recommended dating apps to pass the time. Between swipes, she switches tab and buys scrubs obsessively – aloe vera, sugared strawberry, delicate bergamot and honey – chemically constructed perfumes to wash off her dilemmas. Then she can message strangers. Remember that Gertrude responds to facts better than to feelings: she approaches dating app profiles like case studies for the archetypes she fears. A modern and privileged form of self-harm, an applied method to question the veracity and therefore the validity of her experience.

Then she said 'yes' to investigate how the word would affect the equation of her being.

Saturday in Paddington, Gertrude has a date.

The introduction is shy: small talk about their respective journeys to the venue and the number of platforms in Paddington station. They debate a figure and can't agree if there are platforms upstairs too. The last time he took a train from there was to go to Glastonbury and they briefly digress about the last edition of the festival. He says something about not being able to charge his phone at the camping site so he can't show her a photo to illustrate what he meant about the grass being burnt – a dystopia, they still agree – and Gertrude asks him if he has noticed there is no phone signal in front of the kiosk between platforms 8 and 12. He smiles and asks her what she thinks causes this black hole. 'Ghosts!' She surprises herself as she settles into the pace of their conversation – simply another human being; the imagery of dreaming a stranger into a real person has ended.

Gertrude asks him when he moved to London. The question makes him flippant, so she moves on quickly, picking up the menu and wondering about food. 'First,' he says, 'are we going for white or red wine?' She chooses white without thinking twice; Gertrude is wearing Liam's white shirt. She scans through the alcohol percentages as a safety measure, and points out the Pinot Grigio. Twelve per cent; organic production, the promise of refreshment with the crisp almond finish listed in the description that is to Gertrude's taste. He agrees and they start talking through the menu with tentative tones shadowing their voices. The nervousness linked to ordering food with someone new weighs in and they fall silent without meaning to, both debating their choices introspectively. Gertrude remembers a flying remark about his vegetarian diet earlier on – a text he had sent on the way back from the gym. But is he a pescatarian? More

103

people seem to know about the word 'pescatarian' than they are inclined to use it, and this lack of clarity annoys Gertrude profoundly, especially when she is cooking in the kitchen at work. This is misleading, a threat. A label. She notes the attention with which he is reading through the menu – indecisive, marked expressions – and she doubts. There are only two vegetarian options listed. She can't find the bruschetta Liam mentioned earlier.

She craves the sticky beef short ribs, iron served with a side of slaw to relax her jaw. A phantom panic haunts her; imagine the scene: Gertrude wolfing down the ribs with her red hair and pale skin. Androgynous and voracious Gertrude who bewilders strangers – beautiful Gertrude, a wax doll. She smiles to herself. She considers the fried eggs (served with chorizo, chilli beans and sourdough bread), a strange dish albeit a brunch classic. Gertrude snaps the menu back on the table.

'I'm going for the short ribs. What about you?'

'Falafels for me. And two glasses of Pinot Grigio, right?'

She approves, they order, another short silence winds through the table, which is dressed in white dinnerware. It is the type that is required to readjust; a good silence. The conversation restarts, and they begin talking about themselves, initiating a dialogue from their respective weeks to their work, mentions of friends and family. The food arrives, and mouthfuls force them to pause between sentences.

'Can I ask?' He meets her eyes; she nods expectantly. 'How

come you're called Gertrude? I haven't met any other girl called Gertrude in the UK before.'

Girl. Her cheeks redden. She takes another sip of her wine before she confesses: 'You got me worried for a second.'

'What did you think I was going to ask?'

'I don't know.' She is fiddling with her napkin. 'Something revealing about me or about my parents.'

His face flushes, red and endearing.

'When my mother was still cool, she studied in Paris for a year. She became obsessed with Gertrude Stein, obviously, and she thought it would be a great idea to name me after her. Something to do with women's empowerment and all that jazz.' She rolls a breadstick between her fingers. She cannot help but add: 'She has changed her mind about most of her old opinions over the years, but I have to put up with the name.'

'Parents should think harder when they name their children.'

'It is a whim for life,' she says absently.

'Please tell me your brother is called Pablo.' Their eyes meet again with the strength of curiosity. A tease, Gertrude bites into the breadstick.

A hard, audible crunch.

'Of course not. He got away with Liam.'

'I bet he's not as cool as you though,' and he puts his hand over hers softly.

'I wish, but I'm afraid he's the cool one.'

'Younger brother?'

'Gen-Z type of young.'

'Ouch!'

They drink.

Gertrude continues: 'He was still in bed when I left the house earlier.' She doesn't tell him that Liam helped her dress for the occasion. That she read her brother some of his texts; 'arrogant', Liam had commented.

'Well, look at us. Up and drinking: you're the fun one.' He marks a pause. 'My brother still lives with our mother back in Berlin. He is studying international economics and policies at university. I'm not quite sure what his degree entails to be honest.'

'Are you not close with your brother, then?'

'We don't live together, but we get on.' Gertrude distrusts the construction of his sentence – *no, but*. He asks if she wants another glass of wine, a signal that their conversation has become too personal, to which Gertrude agrees as he lifts his hand up in the direction of the waitress. Gertrude smooths him back in with a story about the time she travelled to Berlin with two friends for a long weekend. Two summers ago, a few weeks before she moved to London. They queued outside of Berghain for hours, until they reached the front and smiled at the bouncers and were allowed inside despite having lost faith somewhere along the line. Gertrude details people's outfits with a sparkle in her eyes. She loved dancing at Berghain, one of her most treasured nights out, the music differing widely between rooms and the freedom she had seized for herself, navigating her body with the lightness of a feather and the precision of an archer. Inside the venue, she discovered a new layer to the concept of desire. There, she tells him, she had ownership over the signals her movements sent out. She wasn't posing to please the lens of others, but her actions matched her intentions — she felt entitled to do that and the crowd was receptive. She had felt safe, dancing, sweating, reaching that thin balance between letting go of her thoughts and controlling both her legs and arms so they could move in line with the rhythm of the music. She remembers that the next day she painted her nails the colour of sunflower petals, hopeful. She had nonsense conversations with strangers while waiting for the toilets, about sex, politics, hair dyes, miniskirts and even the sweet mango fruit; she met someone who had the same date of birth as hers and they whirled together, the best dance she had ever shared with anyone, wild but coordinated, like a cosmic swing with herself. The rest of the night was without speech, the language of bodies talkative, insomuch that there was something fundamentally primitive attached to the imagery of her partying in Berghain. The first time she was happy to meet expectations, a night freed from assumptions. She had established a new bridge between her body and the conception she had of herself; minds and nerves, appearance and senses, they had agreed in the space of one night out. *This* experience had more political influence on her than any books she had read before, any conversations she had had or documentaries she had watched — *this* she had *felt*.

Gertrude's smile breaks wide and contagious: 'As if my

body could speak, finally.' She ends her longest monologue since they met.

'I've never been to Berghain,' he says shyly. 'And I'm a terrible dancer, but I can relate to what you said.' He explains that he attends life-drawing classes on Tuesday evenings. He started a few months ago prompted by a phone conversation with his mother. He had told her about his week, which he had spent between the office, the pub with his colleagues and the gym. He had spoken candidly, and she replied good-heartedly: 'That's all you have to tell me?' That was it, he confesses to Gertrude. The size of his life had made him feel awfully sad. So he found this class that takes place at the back of a pub. He describes the model that stands before the group, someone new each week and who stays still before the students; immobile but dressed, and the vulnerable exposure that drifts between the observers and the poser.

Gertrude snorts; he stops.

'This is not the same.' She yearns to hurt herself for having shared the story of that night with him. The account doesn't contain the same freedom once it has been spoken out loud. 'If anything, this is the opposite scenario.'

'What do you mean?'

'You went to find someone to pay so you could feel better about yourself.' She takes a sip of wine. 'You're talking about a hobby, but I was the model until I freed myself.' *Hi, I'm Angela. Are you on a date that isn't working out? Does it feel a bit weird? Go to the bar and ask for Angela and the staff will call you a cab without causing too much fuss.* She read this on a poster in the bathroom when she arrived at the restaurant earlier today, a reminder to be scared as a condition to stay safe.

'Jeez! It's just a drawing class.'

She brings a piece of meat to her mouth – chewing and swallowing – and makes a point of looking at him as she does. His plate lies empty before him.

'No, it's a power play.' Her ear lobes burn with the fire of anger. 'Trust me, I can spot control when I see it in action.'

He cringes before he draws back; his gestures reveal his desertion, the intention to impose a distance between them. The moment is necessary to appraise this new tone in the conversation.

He responds calmly: 'I was just trying to find a connection between us.' She is taken aback. He persists: 'Instead I clearly touched a nerve, but I'm struggling to see your point.'

'Well, I don't understand why you thought there would be a connection between the two stories. It might all be entertainment for you, but that night at Berghain wasn't just a night out for me. It's when I became aware of the connection between my body and my identity.' A sip of wine. 'When I understood that all the things I had been warned against all my life – *don't dream too big, don't disagree, don't go out on your own* – were meant to ensure that I wouldn't break rules. And not to keep me safe.'

She downs her glass of wine. 'They also warn you against drinking too much on a date with a stranger.' She looks back at him in the eyes.

She thinks that he is scared.

'Do you want some dessert?' he asks.

'I do want to continue this conversation.' Gertrude's pupils are the colour of lava. 'And I can always eat ice-cream,' she adds. Gertrude is both a sweet tooth and the type who negotiates.

'So can I.' He orders one scoop each of the mint chocolate chip and stracciatella flavours. One bowl and two spoons – Gertrude throws hazelnut in at the last minute. The waitress refills their glasses with water and walks away.

'Women always have to compromise.' Gertrude restarts the conversation; he sighs discreetly. 'I started with sharing something personal: a night out when I was safe to enjoy myself. I wasn't afraid, I drank and I took drugs and I danced on my own. That is, an occasion when I didn't feel any pressure to act in a certain way for my security as someone who broadly ticks the box as (her voice drops a decibel) *an attractive woman* in a public space. You said that you can relate because you started a drawing class after feeling sorry for yourself.' She pauses to take a sip of water. 'I wish I could just go to the gym and get strong, or go for a run when it's dark after work without being afraid. That I could go to the pub without triple-checking my outfit is appropriate before heading out. There is a radical difference between how you and I negotiate leisure, and that is the consequence of our genders.'

'But you're the one who is making this about gender.' He turns his head away, hopeful to catch sight of the waitress.

'I wish the universalist line worked in practice. You can't deny that female is the gender that must make efforts. The effort to smile, the effort to fit into a certain size of clothes, the effort to please – constant efforts.'

He opens his mouth, then he closes it. Gertrude frowns, and he speaks: 'I was thinking about this German word ... It means making something worse by trying to fix it.'

Silent break.

'Look, all I wanted to say is that recently I got into life drawing and I never thought I would. I'm sorry if it made you feel threatened or undermined in any way.'

He says the second sentence more quietly and not meanly. Then he concludes: 'Circling back to what you said, this is me making an effort to be happy.' He is biting his lip.

Gertrude isn't listening to him anymore; her heart is in a storm. She tightens her hair bun; *smile, love*, the men at the pub tell her. Be diligent, fearful. Laugh, smile to defeat a dangerous situation. To make things *feel right*. Gertrude relies on the pattern as much as she denies it, its ease working a pathway inside her brain like the lyrics of a summer hit – repeat, repeat, so you don't have to look at yourself in the mirror. So you can make it to tomorrow safely.

The waitress returns with their ice-cream, and he dives in instantly.

'Hunger' plays through the stereo and Gertrude welcomes the coincidence to divert their dialogue: 'Have you listened to the new Florence + The Machine album?'

'I don't know her.'

He wouldn't know them. 'Which bands do you listen to the most?' She asks the innocent question. The brunch had started well with mentions of trains departing from Paddington in the direction of Glastonbury, fun and sexy, until it spiralled, bottomless.

i, gertrude, off-putting

They wade through the ice-cream quietly, the texture melting already. Their resolute appetites make Gertrude sick – it appeals to the avaricious side of the human heart she finds pathetic. When the bill arrives, he suggests they split it equally. Gertrude adheres to the principle (and she would have suggested the same if he had not), but there is something about the added tone in his voice, the stretch of his arm as he throws the receipt back in the middle of the table, an extension of his opinions. He pronounces the number owed out loud. *Forty-five.* A frisbee to a dog; he calculates his actions, showing her his truth, stealing their argument. To disagree always comes with a price. Forty-five pounds at the end of a meal consumed trading in privacy. The scenario amuses him as it unfolds; for Gertrude, twisting gutfeel.

They each pay their share and part ways at the entrance.

10

Sarah

Frustration inhales Sarah's body. Her stomach gurgles but she still hasn't written a word. Her legs sizzle from having sat on this chair for hours, her blood not circulating, ideas frozen in her head, a warm forehead before long exhales of paralysing panic. *Am I intelligent enough to write this paper? I'm a waste of space. Do people know about Kristina? There is nothing to see. Is Mathilde okay? I want to hear her burst out laughing like she used to when we were kids. Does she hate me for the secret we keep? But she made me swear to keep it safe.* Sarah stares at the blank page – her doubts forbid her to function.

It hasn't always been this way.

When they were children, Mathilde was the sensitive girl, careful with her dolls, while Sarah played as carefree as a kid who hasn't yet been warned of dangers. She spent hours squatting over ants and insects at the bottom of the garden, counting their legs and studying their behaviours. Sarah was an avid reader too, mapping the world she couldn't travel, finding the friends she didn't meet in real life. Each year when winter stormed with viruses, Agnes kept Sarah home because her fragile immune system couldn't take the exposure – so her daughter made the house a playground. Her father disagreed with the protective approach, and the tension between both her parents made Sarah cling to her best behaviour. *My illness conditioned our household.* Agnes refused to home-school her daughter fully, though; Sarah needed social exposure. 'Winter is one of four seasons only,' she repeated vehemently. Sarah devoured mythological tales – verses from Homer, retellings and modern takes, Virgil – and she drew phoenix figures obsessively. She is drawing one just now, on the printout of an old essay. *I needed to believe that it's possible to die more than once so I could motivate myself to grow up. To regenerate. I backed up my conviction with scientific facts and I do the same for any ideas I birth. It's easy to make up your own realities if you keep within a narrow social circle.*

If you received a death sentence tomorrow, which life events would come back to haunt you? The human heart sinks in sorrow at hopeless times. *I can picture the lake and I can't help but wonder what would have happened if Mathilde had watched over me?* Sarah gives the phoenix feathers, a gift from the animal to cover scars, a feature that can be used to lay ink on paper. *Until she left home for university, Mathilde used to paint with a joy only creativity could nurture. I sat underneath the easel, and there I would sketch magnified details (the fabric pattern for the suit of her characters; the fish scale for her sea creatures), sample colours and study*

114

forms for her still-life paintings. I passed the tubes of oil paint on to her as well, her dedicated little sister. Mathilde complained about her nails splitting and Mum bought her gloves; she mentioned needing a clearer light and the easel was moved to the library upstairs. I would pass the wrong tube to Mathilde often, dropping it because of my poor coordination, spoiling the wooden floor. Agnes asked me to think harder before doing. Mathilde gave me complicit smiles: 'Always so distracted, Sarah bird.' Only pencils are allowed inside the reading rooms at the library and this rule suits Sarah's process. *Would we have evolved organically from the children we were if we hadn't lied?* She can erase pencilled lines, rewind and reset.

A past, linked event: Sarah and Mathilde went to see the Pierre Bonnard exhibition. The Jenkins-Bell family have a membership to the Tate Modern, where Mathilde and Sarah meet occasionally. The sisters take the Friday off work and launch the day with breakfast at the members' café, where the view plunges over St Paul's, the imposing caricatural London dome. They order the syrupy lemon and poppy seed cake, a tea for Sarah and a flat white for Mathilde. They comment on the surroundings made of aluminium, steel and concrete they find ugly until summer makes the materials brighter and softens their taste. The Millennium Bridge stands as a signifying mirror over the Thames. They start the visit with the temporary exhibition, walking slowly and as a duo so they can comment as they discover the brushes and lives of artists. They head to the permanent collection afterwards, among which they disperse, walking fast and slow, anti-clockwise and back, depending on their mood and what lens they choose to use to render the day's world bearable.

Sarah rarely asks Mathilde how she is directly, nor does Mathilde ask Sarah. They have an inherited faith that ignorance is the most efficient strategy to tackle pain. For this, Agnes is to be thanked. But there is a difference between not asking the question and not wanting to know the answer – a form of discourse they have practised over the years.

'Why did you stop painting? You were so good at it,' Sarah asked Mathilde as they paused in front of one of Pierre Bonnard's standing nudes.

'Because paintings are like frozen opinions,' Mathilde responded.

'I'm not sure I understand,' Sarah admitted, her eyes brushing over the large canvas before her. A window and sink next to a single bed, pink sheets; Paris, its infamous studio flats that are ingeniously compact and restrictive for a human life, hidden underneath the roofs of Haussmannian buildings. A woman stands at the foreground, her lines defined, naked but wearing a short bob. The colour palette suggests memories of springtime; Sarah scaled the space between each detail so she could understand how Bonnard had allowed layers of perspective into the painting, the artist chaperoning a viewer's opinion. She was attentive to the dynamic of its artefacts, the bottle of perfume in the corner. Possibilities, the romanticism of a city elsewhere; there was nothing fixed about this painting.

Mathilde didn't explain her reasons, but she said: 'I'm

nauseous at the thought of painting something. I'm not a child who lives in her head anymore.' Sarah won't forget the strength with which Mathilde had squeezed her hand, then she added: 'I'm too scared of what people would think.' She stepped away from the painting, and Sarah started seeing the billions of small dots that agglomerate to draw the lines of a cohesive shape – message delivered.

In the Jenkins–Bell family, silence is the condition of their union. A performance; the first act in Sarah's play of a life with chronic illness was a period of mutism when she was six years old. 'A form of social phobia,' as the family's general practitioner had justified Sarah's refusal to talk in any circumstances. Agnes called Sarah's state a tantrum, *an evil eye*, in the mind of a mother who heads a family whose members she has educated to be socialites. Mother disqualified the experience as an isolated event in their life and called any further investigations off, until Sarah's father missed the sound of his girl's brittle voice enough to contest his wife's opinion. He didn't care about domestic matters, until he walked into a home that remained firmly silent. The walls were cold, a still life without paint. He took Sarah to a private clinic, and she was referred for both an ENT check-up and a psychiatric evaluation at the affiliated paediatric hospital. The waiting room offered an expensive choice of wooden toys, teas and coffees for the adults, and a drizzling caramel cake loaf to slice between generations. The recipe was rich and made teeth rub like old coins. Paediatric nurses baked sweet treats, but they never lied to Sarah before

117

hurting her, and they used the language of adults to explain procedures to children. The results were inconclusive in that medicine couldn't find anything wrong with Sarah – no signs of early deafness, healthy nose and throat – and they dismissed her case to the psychiatric department. It was on the ground floor, as if it needed to be the least demanding place for patients possible, a simple walk-in, and there they started questioning Sarah. Her choice to keep Mathilde's secret was unchallenged because nobody asked what had happened. *They think they did, but they didn't want to know.*

Sarah had almost drowned during a family holiday in Wales the summer before she stopped talking and, despite being a *child* (she'd mimic the tone of her mother here, crisp and grating), she understood the event would be one that sealed lips as soon as she woke up in a hospital bed. She was swimming in the lake at the bottom of her grandparents' garden, like they always did. The weather was brilliant, and Sarah had grown strong enough to remove her water wings; Mathilde had supported her sister when she begged their parents to let her swim freely – 'like the grown-ups do'. Mathilde promised to look after Sarah – she was the bigger sister; she had had a full year of swimming lessons with school. The weather was brilliant, and Mathilde wanted to tan before going back to London. Adolescence was tickling her self-worth and she had braces fitted recently, boys to chase and girlfriends to entertain, the busy life of a teen-ager whose world gravitates around their feelings. Their bodies were spooned together inside the small hospital bed,

Mathilde muttering into her sister's ear, braiding her hair softly. '*Once upon a time, there was a phoenix with a belly made of fire and feathers the colour of rubies, and it jumped out from underneath the water inside the lake at the bottom of Gran's house and flew high in the sky . . .*' the story Mathi told me goes.

'Cross my heart and hope to die,' Mathilde murmured, before adding: '*Say it too, Sarah bird, so I know we are sisters.*' *Cross my heart and hope to die* – Sarah responded and never told anyone that Mathilde wasn't in the water with her that day. That she saw death at the bottom of the lake instead of her sister.

On this Saturday at the British Library, Sarah sketches, scrolls. She reads over emails she sent weeks ago, interrogating the words she used and the tone that comes through, cold and out of context. Sarah understands that most human conditions are invisible to the majority and preserves her privacy by keeping herself out of others' business. She scrawls, burying the phoenix figure under the weight of her pencil. There are the stories Sarah keeps secret so they can't be stolen from her. Harder and harder, the piece of paper tears, pencil stains her skin. When she isn't afraid of judgement, the conviction that she only deserves bad things limits what Sarah thinks she can do.

Cross your heart now and keep my secret close. This is the account of the night Sarah slept with Kristina for the first time:

Freshers' week was ending, and we had just crossed the finishing line of a pub crawl in Clerkenwell. I had been going to the same university in central London since the first year of my bachelor's degree. I'm a regular at Koya bar where I eat bowls of walnut ramen and I visit Dillons Coffee at the Waterstones on Gower Street weekly. There wasn't much to report from that specific week – I ate a cinnamon doughnut from Crosstown Doughnuts, and I bought reduced sushi after 8.30 pm at the Itsu on Warren Street on my way home – until the last night. I went out with my colleagues because I had promised Mathilde and Agnes that I would try harder to make friends and to be happy the way they wanted me to be. Cole Bleu's 'u' had come up on the stereo. The room had narrowed, and I caught sight of Kristina dancing at the end of the passageway, her wide smile and slightly crooked nose, the burlesque forms of her shoulders and hips. The walls closed and Kristina's movements slowed down with the beat of the music. We knew each other from meeting up in her office to discuss my research proposal; she had agreed to supervise my PhD on the same week I contacted her. It was as if the music played for us that night at the club. I listened to the lyrics and I followed Kristina's provocative stare, consistent and certain. I approached and we started dancing at a reasonable distance. I was conscious of the public around us, testing the agility of my feet, touching, teasing, my desire building up. The song blasted with wonders. Then came waves of her perfume, an acidic touch of zest, an expected scent for one so sharp, and we danced together.

With a banging headache, the bedsheets pushed away into a ball at the bottom of Kristina's bed, Sarah woke up the next day. The flat was new, electric white heaters, whiter walls and floor-to-ceiling windows. The view dived down into the canal; Sarah was bending over the balcony when Kristina approached, the tone of their intimate after-party still to be announced. *Sweet*, she likes sugar in her coffee.

'I told you you'd appreciate the view.'

Sarah didn't remember but she nodded that she did.

They were standing next to each other on Kristina's balcony. There was the Olympic stadium on the right, the red observation tower – 'with the slide!' they both exclaimed – and the Olympic swimming pool where Kristina practises her crawl strokes three times a week; the busy roads and bridges, asphalt and grey clouds; the surrounding wetlands, all the way to Walthamstow on the left; a wader was feeding at the bottom, next to a canal boat, its long beak made to pick worms. Sarah had wondered why they were travelling down from the north now, but Kristina interrupted her. She had put a finger in front of Sarah's mouth.

'These are redshanks. Listen to their "tyu–lu–lu" song as they fly.' Kristina pointed at a group of them. 'They are making their way along the river Lea, from Tottenham Hale down the Hackney Way.' Then she removed her finger, passed her hand behind Sarah's ears, stroking down her arm and intertwining their fingers. 'Do you want to go hunt for them?'

Sarah nodded again. *I'm Sarah bird, I thought. We kissed; she didn't let me rest from the blow. We fucked. We never went out to hunt redshanks, but I have had this recurring nightmare ever since I started sleeping with Kristina, where I wake up with my feet feeling wet. This is the thing with consent, you know. I wanted it. This is the problem with consent, the blurred line that defines the concept. Like a phoenix, the definition of consent doesn't hold time accountable and regenerates so we can be born again, and again.*

11

Cloe

Only one of the two seats inspires comfort. Decorated with cushions and made of a stiff linen fabric, the seat falls low and offers high back support – Colette's disregarded reading chair, until she must make a point by getting out of bed. A small coffee table wobbles between them, a cheap wood imitation painted in white to cover the top, which saddens Cloe deeply, so deeply she finds it irrational. A plastic stool on the other side for visitors. They settle. Colette's traits have narrowed, a physical demonstration of her humiliation after having had to sit in a bathtub, naked, waiting to be washed; she insisted that she wanted to stay in the reading chair after the shower. Her back straightens; she fights for her dignity.

'Have you visited your mum this week?'

Cloe shakes her head; the lines that form a butterfly

tattoo fly behind her left ear as she does. No, she hasn't visited Héloïse.

Colette stays still. 'Have you called her?'

Her butterfly tattoo reappears as Cloe's body language betrays her silent self. She has called her mother.

'Cloe, ma chérie, what will you do once the voicemail is full?' Colette hasn't applied lipstick again after her wash, her lips are thin, their texture soft and her mouth small, just like her daughter's.

'I don't always leave a message,' Cloe says shyly, before adding, with gained confidence: 'And if I needed to, I have both her phone and password. I would be able to empty the message box.'

Colette's eyebrows frown. They are thin, too, of a light brown shade. Her entire face is wrinkling, which gives her a strict appearance. She reaches for a leftover, halved biscuit, her face releasing while a crumb sticks in the corner of her mouth. Her expression has softened, yet she has more to say to her granddaughter.

'I don't understand why you wouldn't visit your mother instead of calling her. I would like to know if the pansy flowers we planted have matured well.'

She pauses and they both peek out of the window. They chose wild pansies because they flower in winter, Héloïse's preferred season, the purple petals that symbolise a passing love, bright colours and heart-shaped; a hopeful plant. But Cloe never went back to the cemetery after the funeral.

Colette goes on: 'We need to prevent moss from building

up on the memorial with all this rain.' She sounds frustrated, short of breath, as she asks her granddaughter to fix this. Cloe ignores her grandmother purposefully, her spine locked, and her focus set across the window and over the garden at the back, so Colette attacks: 'And it's not even the case that she recorded a voice message of her own. I checked this myself. It's the generic one from the network provider.'

They look each other in the eyes, the coffee table between them, crippled by the arrested history of their family. Cloe fades to grey, but Colette is firm. She knows her mother won't pick up the phone; she dreads not hearing her voice ever again. The impulse comes when she needs her mother's opinion about a decision she must take or, most regularly, when a funny thing happens at work – simple life moments that remind her she has lost her best friend. Then there are the days when the cloud of grief blows up, a stubborn downpour, and she dials the number because she can't accept that Héloïse evaporated into a sticky mist. She was the symbol of life, her mother, cracking jokes and lightening the mood in every single room she entered, resolute to live and unafraid. Cloe bewails the sadness that overcast the farewell ceremony they hosted for Héloïse, she who didn't talk about dying so she could keep on living. Héloïse opened a bottle of fizzy wine she titled Champagne for any occasion, with her goûter most often, a piece of apple tarte Tatin and a glass of bubbles at four-thirty on Saturdays. Her voice was deep and her laugh unapologetic; she made most people uncomfortable, the single mum who exploded the nuclear family, leaving

Cloe and Colette behind, surviving inside a cloud of their mother and daughter's echo.

Cloe misses her mother every day, therefore she calls Héloïse's old mobile phone every day, a simple equation for her survival. On this ordinary Saturday, Cloe refuses to step into her grandmother's purgatory. Instead, she daydreams about showing Colette how much more she hurts in comparison to her – oh, yes, she does. She agrees a child should never die before a parent, but Colette's pain is tagged with an early expiry date as she flirts with her own death sentence. Colette, she sprints with her grief; Cloe's existence is cursed by the ghost of her mother.

They stay silent.

The clock, which is attached to the wall, rings at five o'clock daily. A nurse enters and they start counting pills before a tray is wheeled in with Colette's dinner. The two women settle Colette back in bed, her shoulders high, and a folding board comes in front of her; granddaughter ties a napkin onto her grandmother's nightgown collar. The process is slow; tenacious but with a weakened throat, Colette swallows one pill after the other, a circular formula from the source treatment on to the consequent meds prescribed to heal the ills the first round had triggered. Liver, thyroid, guts, organs shut down before the eye of the cyclone and Cloe forgives her grandmother.

They start a game of guessing what will be on the menu while Cloe unwraps the cling film that seals each plate. Habits die hard, so they complain about the saltless bread before sharing memories of meals on the balcony in Cannes. A time when sentences were shadowed with breaths of garlic, Colette's famous aïoli, their fingertips sticky with prawn shells and the bin bags breaking open under the weight of mussels; new potatoes, halved and cooked with butter and parsley, salade niçoise but with anchovies; baguettes from the one bakery, éclairs au chocolat for dessert on Sundays. The Paris–Brest they knew Héloïse ate on her way back from the boulangerie without telling anyone. Hazelnut, Héloïse's favourite nut. This is the note on which Cloe leaves Colette, the details that author the testimony of their surname, signs of Héloïse's existence before the year when one diagnosis preceded another with the torment of a thunderstorm. Breast cancer first, spreading into the lungs then the brain, palliative care, life support and say goodbye. There are images that won't leave these two women, the pains of a body pacing through the last minutes of a lifetime, and only in a pair can they manipulate nostalgia to replace mental photographs with a smile on Héloïse's face. The stories Cloe and Colette tell; Cloe's unanswered phone calls and Colette's nightmares, the stories they keep close also.

Cloe drops her lips on her grandmother's forehead, clears the food tray and places it back on the trolley outside of the bedroom. A final stop at the door frame, Colette sends Cloe a kiss with her hand and Cloe closes the door behind her, until next week. For now, Saturday evening awaits.

PART 3

Sunday Afternoon

12

Cloe

Twenty-four hours later, the afternoon light floods Cloe's bedroom. Sunday. Her muscles ache with dehydration, lowering the tension that has possessed her like an aftertaste at the end of a meal eaten without appetite, and she sits at the end of the bed. Seemingly random memories come in waves: the colour of her first pencil case at school; the glossy nectarine fruits she bit with her full teeth; the mandalas that decorated the serving bowls on the lunch table in Cannes, turquoise and navy, and those she drew with her compass, its needle effective to bind blood pacts with schoolmates; the pencil sharpener in the shape of a miniature globe. During a summer holiday, she had befriended a girl with long braids at the beach – they snorkelled together. Days spent in water, skin stinging with salt, hair wet and compact, they found rusty bracelets and empty shells. 'Ma Préférence' by Julien

Clerc, Héloïse's favourite song. Are these inconsequential? She has stood up by now; she is undressing. She stops, in underwear, and with her back to the window. The carpet is soiled with hair balls, the bathroom is located behind her; she wants to shower. To wash away her blackout, to free her aura from his smell, an estranged body. Yeast, overnight ashtray, rain breaking after a heatwave, acidic smells that uproot her from the trail of reason. If there is one take-away from the evenings she has spent cross-legged on the sofa, balancing bowls of either instant noodles (seafood or spicy flavours) or cereal (Frosties), this is the one rule. *Do not shower if you have been a victim of sexual assault.* The rule girls are taught in passing when they watch procedural TV shows leisurely. *What if I'm only suspicious? I want to write myself off with water and soap. Erase before making myself up again.* An everyday gesture through which untold stories flow through – a probability can become a statistic in the span of a life's event. Listen to Cloe.

The shower room is where our tongues loosened up. We shared a sense of self-pity, an unfair spread of body hair sprouting across our bodies; our fringes dropped like slugs on our foreheads; naked, we were confused. We described him as generous and dedicated, but with a short temperament. He was disproportionally ambitious on our behalf, us his team of brave girls, but with a passion for swimming and the strokes he was training us to perform. Something honest and pure. There was a division between those of us who were thought to be favourites, those who were clear favourites and the ones who dropped out along the way. We made alliances and it led us to a collective silence, while we won one competition after another, as a team doing relays and individually, for some of us. We were allowed granitas on the occasions when we won – bubblegum, peach, strawberry flavours, served in tall plastic cups – sweetener, crushed ice, always from the same truck, before we took a cold shower. We returned to the pool the following week to pick up our training routine. A repetitive pattern we couldn't break because truth is close-knit with authority. Brittle nails and tender skin, the damages chlorine caused to our bodies. We were focused on our ambition of becoming athletes: we aimed for the podiums.

Cloe distrusts the workings of the penal process when one 'thinks' that they 'might' be a victim. Her questionable state of uncertainty – sentences like 'women require teasing in order to desire', ingrained in popular culture and filtering through real conversations – prevent her from seeking help. The fear that asking for help would launch a crusade to haunt her person precludes her from coming forward. Cloe has researched the question before – online, with tentative questions to friends, on screen and in books – and she concluded that the system relies on the victim to demonstrate that they are a victim indeed. And victims have a reputation for being liars.

It never felt big enough to report. One slap, a reddened cheek; one caress, not so tender, a little uncomfortable, but so were the various squats and plank exercises we did when we warmed up next to the pool, our swimsuits not fitted to accommodate such body movements. Cold, goosebumps, vulnerable bodies. Our sportswear, the heat, the water, and the dedication we put in to building muscles. We were

131

trying to show our strength; we couldn't say we were victims to the adults. We heard that our friend L. talked to the nurse, and she was told to toughen up. Don't call me out – I'm aware that I'm using her initial only, but privacy matters in this story. L. switched to judo classes that same year. We didn't receive an explanation and the other parents didn't want to offend our coach with questions – they raised eyebrows but lowered their gaze. Application forms for scholarships always require a recommendation letter; do you see where this is going? This is when I understood that a hierarchy of authority applies to adults as well.

We loved the practice of our sport, immersing our heads under the water, being light-headed inside an abrupt, silent bubble, hitting the surface so we could hide beneath it. Caps closed our ears tight when we swam; our brains recorded the distances we covered each time our toes touched the end wall, an acquired reflex. Push, flexing knees and extending legs, wide and stretch and wide. We owned our freedom, the embarrassing noise of our flip-flops at the end of a race, a genuine smile upon grabbing the edge of the pool on the other side of the lane, the sound of our hands cutting through water, a splash, our forceful act, swimming and the performance of our bodies.

The silence in her studio flat is pressing, punctuated by Massimo's occasional yowling, the animal determined to punish Cloe for her late return this morning.

We kept a poster of Rebecca Adlington in the main changing room. Rebecca who broke the nineteen-year-old world record of Janet Evans in the 800-metre final at the 2008 Summer Olympics. We worshipped Rebecca Adlington. Her freestyle moved us so much we memorised every detail we could find about her: height – 179cm, weight — 70kg, medal records, all the way until the year in which she retired, 2013, aged twenty-three. Life is short, so we understood. We turned a blind eye when we stumbled upon comments about her nose shape and her physical appearance, rumours of a rhinoplasty that distracted the press from Adlington's results. You see, it wasn't a question of agreeing or disagreeing with their views, but we feared this could happen to any of us — being singled out for our physical attributes and not for our athletic accomplishments, to be seen this way. We lifted more weights, and we clocked up more lanes. We made sure the texture of our hair, the shape of our shoulders and the arcs of our legs were fit and beautiful. We never agreed upon a definition of beauty as a team, but I still pay close attention to my nose when I apply moisturiser. We watched videos of Adlington's races in slow motion, pausing and zooming over the placement of her spine and of her hands. We researched her training so we could achieve what she had done, matching her method, her speed and her athletic body. Our vision was like tracing paper — we craved to grow up, to evolve from our status of girlhood into being recognised as performing athletes. We had set our minds to fight our destiny, an affair of hormones and breast development, these slowing attributes. Our 'buoys' the boys called out in the car park outside the leisure centre. The benches were made of stone, like graves, and they sat on the back edge with their feet resting on the seat. They smoked with pride. They turned green with envy each time we won another competition; the pool was our pitch, where we orchestrated the rules and set the bar high for performance. I want you to know that my team was consistently faster than the male swimmers who competed at equal levels. We always have. Our muscles enlarged, our shoulders widened, fast fast

fast, and we earned our strengths; we loved glittery eyeshadows, also, and having our hair done. Our growth was a storm of confusions and contradictions – our teenage years. There were pills that could slow down the virus of puberty. They would enable us to preserve the body shape we required to meet swimming's needs undistracted; discipline and the glue sticks we used to keep the sides of our swimsuits closed against the edges of our hips. Long bodies toned with pride. We learnt to protect our ambitions against the expectations they set for us, but we were fighting the wrong monster. I wanted to be seen for my worth, and so did my comrades. We wanted to swim. Do you understand? We were girls and we hadn't been taught how to say no. And, maybe, you should accept that we can still be victims; victims who didn't say no.

Cloe pets Massimo, his rebellion calming down under her stroking, while her right hand is clenched over her phone. Firmly, she refuses to look for the truths she doesn't want to recognise: the present achievements of the other swimmers in the team; her mother's phone number starred as a favourite, the number of times she has called displayed in brackets next to it; her search for the unknown number, herself, and her actions.

I would have wanted the attention. Enjoyed it even, I regret.

Cloe, would you like to come into my office? Coach asked, and I said yes. He told me that I was brilliant, my progression was fast and exponential, my measurements were healthy, my drive was high. I smiled, feeling touched and thrilled. I was grateful that my hard work was being acknowledged, so when he added that I would need to start staying late at the leisure centre a few times a week, I said yes too. I needed to train harder to become the best — I never wished to be good. I had seen some of my teammates lingering on before. I had been envious of their opportunities — their head start — and I ignored their warning looks, blank and empty. I'm innocent; all I wanted was to be admitted into the elite group. B. squeezed my hand the first evening. I saw her signals as a shared joy; B. started swimming the same year as me.

Before you judge Cloe, consider that she was taught that adults are forbidden from touching children this way, and so were you. That adults hold truth and children manipulate the truth to seek attention. Keep in mind that the order of society dismissed the possibility of the event before it happened, so it couldn't be conceptualised and become an issue.

The other night I was sitting on the sofa, staring at the TV, spooning Frosties into lukewarm milk for dinner. My favourite when the spice of noodles stings. Past ten, the second programme kicked in, an investigative documentary about a group of teenagers who got sucked into a prostitution network after they took on what they thought was an innocent summer job. One of them wanted to buy a new iPod Shuffle. I also had one and, at the beginning, I didn't think much of the show because I've consumed enough television to be accustomed to producers' sensational inclinations when it comes to retelling women's stories. I kept watching like a voyeur who wrestles with the narrative of influencers versus the reality of followers, chosen words that portray sexuality as a dirty act of self-complaisance, all these stories that bury my truth with their tragic ending. That soothe your ego in telling you that if I survived, if I function even after, it wasn't as bad as I say it was, or that maybe I wanted it too. The teenage girls from the documentary were supposed to sell fries, their parents said to the camera, sitting on a black leather sofa, their shoulders touching softly, a close-up on the T-zone of their faces – a modern confessional. This is the moment I knew that I should switch channels: a trigger warning of my own. But I could not tear my eyes away. I watched for the full ninety minutes: the journalist was obsessed with commenting on how close the girls were, friends in real life – since childhood, he insisted – arguing that their sorority caused their peril. A clumsy montage featured text messages and handwritten pages from the girls' diaries, doodled hearts and scribbled promises for life, a soapy yet suspenseful soundtrack. He was similarly obsessed with describing the girls' bodies, their outfits and smoky eyeshadows, their actions he qualified as childish and impulsive, their relationships and impudent smiles, the 'naivety' with which they stood two feet into their fate: sexual assault. It was only after I had switched off the TV that I realised that I still knew nothing about the assaulters. The focus was on the girls and how they became victims – as if they had agency – as if the audience had a choice to believe otherwise. Nobody else bothers questioning the source of a problem, but I care because there hides the origins of my name.

Have you watched a similar documentary before? A voice-over redefines consent in the name of victims – *Women must negotiate consent; say no, even when they are unsure if they would like to try. There is no trying something new without consequences* – and makes you complicit as you assimilate the information.

With actions, come punishment. It's dangerous to think otherwise. But what this journalist, or anyone else, doesn't know is that I had made a pact with B., and with the others too. We agreed that not one of us would talk. We were stronger in number, and we were going to the nationals. If we started talking then we would be put up against one another – and there would be no surviving without our pack – us, the victims, they would have underlined our status before teaching us how to lie. We were a team of girls who wanted to be seen for our worth. We knew our truth and how to keep it close so they wouldn't use it against us.

Cloe stretches. She slides her wrists along her bare legs, on which her skin wears two tattoos, one on top of each knee, two compasses featuring symbols that echo the personality of her parents. Sharp edges, the fleur-de-lis and a bee for Héloïse; a panot, a lizard, the cardinal points to trap her father, Francesc. Her blood has frozen inside her legs, she is light-headed; she must leave the house or the place will also be damned.

Until hiding made me rot. I should have spoken up; the rest is my punishment.

Cloe keeps a photo of her parents inside a drawer. They pose oddly in front of an olive tree, their stances wide and their arms crossed, hiking backpacks, a cap for her mother and a ponytail tied up at the back of her father's head. They seem free of worries, happy. Cloe closes her eyes firmly as she opens the chest of drawers and grabs the first t-shirt her fingers touch.

Francesc, her great disappointment, his lack of bravery, thus his departure. 'For love', as soon as Héloïse fell sick, sicker by the day. The body he refused to witness going through degradation, his absence from Cloe's life ever since. A man who wasn't robust enough to see life end. Cloe has called Francesc too, but the ringer cut short with an automated message: the number is not recognised.

Do you think that I'm contagious?

Men can leave without looking back; women carry history on to the next generation. *Dad, Coach, the strange man from last night, they get on with their days and I wear scars, stitching, crafting a life of my own.* Cloe jumps into sarouel trousers, dark green, a denim jacket, and walks out of the flat.

I am. I'm contagious.

13

Sarah and Cloe

A soft layer of dust covers people's hands, the air merciless before a thunderstorm. The morning rain cast the clouds away, and the late afternoon paints the sky the colour of lavender; Londoners slow down.

Usual spot in 5. Kristina texted Sarah just after she had left the reading room.

Her eyes burn for what she cannot see, her skin stretches under the all-consuming heat, and she shuffles to the third floor. She climbs the steps, one after the other, marble staircase and walls styled with gold stripes. She reaches the maps room, where the cartographic collection resides. Large tables have been arranged in the middle, their shape flat and long to accommodate the history of the world and its continents. The location is unpopular. It smells fusty in there and Humanities on the first and second floors steals the show, the desks more intimate and the ceilings higher, and stylish readers attract look–alike peers. But Sarah doesn't enter the reading room; she continues ahead instead. There she steps inside the only room whose door can be locked from the inside and by anyone in the building. She pushes the bolt shut behind her.

A snap; she waits.

A knock; Sarah stands still. A second knock; she opens the door.

'So, will you teach me French now?' Kristina pushes Sarah towards the side of the room as she says the words, her breath close to Sarah's lips. The pale oak door stands behind them, and she locks it again.

Sarah extends her arm in front of her, her palm open at the top of Kristina's chest. She stares, the sensation of her rib cage underneath. 'Tina, stop. Can we talk first?'

'Talking is good.' Kristina puts one foot forward. 'As long as you teach me a new language, like you said you would.'

A pinch stabs Sarah in her stomach. *Like you said you would.* She doesn't remember making such a commitment to Kristina. She would have promised anything to Kristina if she had asked at a precise time – when the sky has a cobalt blue colour; when their bodies rest naked and the sheets are filthy; when pleasure numbs her tongue and constructs a lie so she can have seconds.

Sarah had spent her third year of university abroad. In Montpellier, the capital of the old Occitanie region with its white bricks and alluring squares, the warmth of a

Mediterranean city. She danced often that year, with students who had travelled from Sweden, Poland, Scotland and Ireland, eating pastries for breakfast until she craved porridge. But she wouldn't be able to teach Kristina the French language.

'Tina,' and Kristina steps forward once more. She starts kissing Sarah, rough and warm – ear, cheek, neck. Since the day they met in person, in Kristina's office when Sarah was defending her research proposal, Sarah has been intimidated by Kristina's fluency of movement. On emails, she thought the upper hand was on her side, the native speaker of English between the two, until it became physical and Sarah fathomed Kristina's coordination as an extension of her confidence. Sarah calls Kristina 'Tina' because you have guessed who sings her favourite karaoke song. It was their second date. They started with a drink, standing outside a pub in Bloomsbury, before a dinner of fluffy pitta bread, hummus and falafels with sides of green and garlicky beans. They reviewed the world around a pint, and they talked about themselves between mouthfuls of food, teasing their curiosities for one another, then ended up in Lucky Voice in Soho. The stairs heading down to the basement venue are narrow and painted in black, but the entrance logo is bright pink – always a good sign. When Kristina announced she was going to perform 'What's Love Got to Do with It', Sarah shouted back at her in disbelief. She didn't want not to be attracted to this woman she had just met. Kristina pressed play on the karaoke machine and Sarah sizzled.

Kristina wasn't a good singer, but she had charisma. Her Tina has charisma.

Kristina is unbuttoning Sarah's shirt, who mumbles something about her poor language skills. Her voice fades, babbling words about not wanting to teach her anything. She used the verb *talk*; she wants to talk.

'You don't have to teach your supervisor anything,' Kristina murmurs in Sarah's ear as she lifts the shirt off her shoulders and arms. Sarah makes the last movement, bringing her elbows up so her hands can pass through the sleeves. 'You only have to keep working hard,' Kristina adds. She kneels before Sarah; they both undress, they demand. They find relief, the order in which motions take place doesn't matter anymore.

She doesn't touch me like I'm sick. She doesn't consume me like I'm contagious. Under her hands, I'm alive. I touch and I feel and I make her feel with my touch. At the tip of her tongue, I can speak my truth. I wear Kristina like velvet, an elegant material that is hard to take care of, durable but not breathable, a constant negotiation between wanting and doing.

Kristina leaves first. The door catches behind her, silence shrinks the room, particles of dust are caught in the light. Sarah glances around, from left to right attentively: the decor is minimal, empty shelves cover the wall on the right side of the door so users can dispose of their belongings safely. A blue notice is taped on the end wall, on which a brief definition of the concept of 'multifaith space' – *a room that combines the plural needs of religious practice as well as pragmatism* – is written (*such a facility can be found in hospitals, universities and airports*). Shame – the immorality involved in her activities in that room – has translated into Sarah knowing every inch of it, where scratches and stains the size of flies spoil the white paint, the section of lighter wood on the third shelf, where the sunlight lands at noon. Sarah has studied the room with the precision of a trespasser who must prepare to escape should they be caught. She finds gratification in that transgression too – a form of ownership, an unethical behaviour. *I carve my own pleasure*, Sarah tells you as she sits on the floor, hot and cold, sweating.

She will see Kristina again, her supervisor, their monthly mandatory catch-up and the calls in between. Sarah stays still for another minute. *It was good*, she curses herself inside the prayer room. *Sex with Kristina is good*.

Sarah's consent is about the consequence of wanting (something other than what is asked of her).

On the same street where Cloe lives there is a primary school. She worried about the noise before moving in – classroom bells and pupils playing tag, walking through the gates in groups, quests for fizzy drinks and sweets at the corner shop in front of her house.

Life carries on instead: girls laugh heartedly, attach sportswear bags to the handlebars of their small scooters, ponytails swinging. The living-room window, its descending view over the pavement, made Cloe fond of staying home. The dynamic is different to the one of a place like the town where she goes to visit Colette – short buildings and one street to thread life paths together – Cloe can catch everyone's whereabouts from her flat, but she doesn't mingle. She settled into the role of an observer and she retreated. The comfort of silence cast a spell on her relationship with reality – she thinks harder than she talks, a language nobody can translate on her behalf. She works as a copywriter for a marketing agency; she subscribes to a food provider that delivers her shopping each week to her doorstep; most cinemas have launched an 'at home' service, she adds in a quick run to the convenience store across the road for her fix of popcorn and the fizz of Coke. She hunts for the vanilla flavour in honour of Francesc, who downed cans of the drink and praised its floral taste as high as his beloved Catalonian hills, a low life under a high sky he missed dearly and vocally. The week passes in a gulp; then Saturday arrives, and she travels to see Colette. When the night falls, she returns to London and she heads out to dance.

Repeat, another week. Repeat, until disruption.

Sunday, a hangover. Last night, Cloe went to dance at her favourite club. The occasion fell on a friend's birthday, but she would have headed out without the excuse. Nightclubs remind Cloe of the pool: fragrant and chemical and challenging. Dancing is the closest she has got to swimming again, flexing and stretching, a lane of her own.

Did L. expect me to join her when she denounced him? Why didn't she give me a heads-up? Did she want us to escape together to the judo team? We often spoke about the importance of knowing how to fight back. Am I a coward like my dad? Genes simmer on a low heat, until heredity boils over. I was invited for a screening after Héloïse's diagnosis, a blood test to find out if I have mutations in my DNA that could increase my risks of contracting breast cancer. I haven't booked it yet. What did I do last night? These wounds, my bloodline, they are linked.

We had gone away to attend the final gala of the year, travelling on a Saturday and competing on the Sunday. It was the final performance that could allow us to go up one division. Our parents had signed a declaration to allow us – their underaged children – to travel without them. Legally speaking, they had placed us under the supervision of the swimming club; with the admin officer and our coach, namely, two adults for ten girls. We were staying in a hotel near Canterbury; the rooms were simply decorated, the carpet the same grey as the feathers of a mallard, white bedsheets, and the wallpaper grey too despite the occasional burgundy stripe; the bathroom was windowless, the only light coming from inside the mirror, illuminating our bloodshot eyes and pale faces. We each shared a double bed with another team member and our rooms were lined in a row along the corridor. A TV monitor was fitted in each room; we had gathered in one of them together as soon as the curfew had passed – Cadbury's Dairy Milk Buttons, Bounties, cans of Diet Coke spread over the bed, a bottle of Smirnoff vodka hidden underneath the mattress. He never came in. We dipped the tips of our tongues in the alcohol, the taste revolting. We passed the sweet treats around, talking about our dreams, standing at the top of a podium at the end of the solo section of the gala, recognised as the winner. We entered the competition the *next day and one of us scored second in the individual ranking, while our team came fifth. I wasn't defeated because what happened next overcast everything else. After that day there was no swimming, no 'team Larks', only drowning. What had made us proud, now made us shameful. We were bound by our silence until they made us put words on what we wish had never been defined. On gestures that should have stayed a rumour. On feelings that were justifiable only if they remained ambivalent. On actions we wanted to be meaningless so they wouldn't soil our future lives. Words that were ordinary became surreal, the literacy of punishment.*

When we boarded the bus after that final competition, he wasn't there to count our heads. The driver didn't take us back to the car park outside the training centre where our parents would normally be waiting for us. We were chaperoned into a long corridor instead, the neon lights bright, brighter than my pupils could handle, the consequent dizziness terrifying me, messing with my thoughts and therefore my storyline. We were thirsty and they separated us. This is when our shared years ended: no return to the changing room, no more collective shopping list for beauty products, not another training session. We had to become adults by the time we reached the end of the corridor, but we kept being a good team. I denied everything. What remains unsaid, doesn't exist. The end of our innocence; it wasn't him that we defended, but ourselves.

My body has never been the same since. I need regular breaks to visit the bathroom, my collarbone is bent, my bony wrists crooked from the clenching, anger and remorse, two emotions that I must hide. I would still deny everything today. This is what consent does; the dark side of wanting. Keep my secret close while I stay for one last dance.

The microphone goes on, a voice begins the countdown to five o'clock, when the library closes its doors on Sundays. Readers are invited to return books to the librarians at the counter, where they can ask for borrowed items to be kept aside for up to five days. Visitors are channelled outside with less warning.

Sarah walks into the lift and goes back down to the basement to pick up her belongings. The journey is short, an intense couple of seconds with her own guilt: Kristina's hands, the length of her fingers and her clumsiness, the size of her pupils and the intensity of her stare – a bell, she walks out. She types the number 2704 once, then a second time, and she gathers her stuff. A compliant student, she zips her jacket up to her chin, packs her laptop, sets her headphones for the commute, checks that her contactless card for the bus fare is easy to reach and leaves the building.

The sun has grown shyer with the evening; the wind blows. The back of her neck tickles, her hair cut short – Sarah has misplaced the scarf Kristina brought back from a week-long academic conference and had gifted her. They had spent the evenings sexting, something Sarah had never done before. She found playing with words and the projection of her desires more pleasurable than she had thought she would, and the distance brought the two women closer. Bright yellow with the motif of a tiger covering most of the fabric, the design doesn't suit Sarah's style. Sarah reckons

Kristina had bought it for herself until Sarah made a sarcastic comment about Kristina having failed to reward her for being *so good* while she was away – and, magically, Kristina had a present for her. The scarf has become a sign Sarah must see to restore her self-esteem; a collar she can untie when she is the one who always stands naked first. *Kristina cares more than she wants to show me* – does she? The lost property office has closed already; a sweat breaks on Sarah's forehead. A scratch inside her nose, a weight over her chest; she wasn't wearing her scarf when she took the bus on Oldfield Road after lunch.

Cars drive faster, the light shines brighter. I spin. The birds sing and I'm heading back to the pub.

The music stops abruptly. Phoebe Bridgers' 'Motion Sickness' is interrupted by a monotone ringtone, and Cloe has guessed who is calling before looking at her phone. There is safety in her current setting – Sunday afternoon, walking in public in north London, young parents are running errands, buggies and defeated football supporters share the pavement – a missed call, a text.

Hey. Just let me know if you got home safely, ok?

Touching up her lipstick, a toilet break, a round of shots. Cloe doesn't respond. He calls again, she picks up and his tone is different than she expected – cautious, the approach of a new swimmer who is testing the water.

'I'm sorry for being so insistent, but you were so wasted last night. I was worried about you.'

She feels dirty.

He continues: 'I wanted to get you a cab, but you wouldn't let me.'

'Are you a friend of Lucy?' Cloe asks slyly.

'Yeah. Well, a friend of a friend. We had been dancing together for a while, so I felt responsible for you. I just offered to give you my sofa until you felt well enough to go home.' He speaks fast.

Cloe hadn't asked for details; his assumption flusters her. She gathers her response, but he has the advantage of memory. He cuts her off, talking about the music, the pricing of the drinks, the photo booth, the crowd; his discourse is punctuated with casual 'mates' to distance any intimacy. Then he threatens her: she should be more careful next time; she could have ended up somewhere different, with someone else, someone who isn't as well-intentioned as he is. The literacy of abuse, an exercise of power play and denunciations; lies, manipulations, the turn of the screw.

'Pretty wild. Do you remember around what time we left the club?' she asks. She knows she had wanted to leave early.

'No. Sorry, mate, turns out I was quite wasted too.'

She doesn't respond and his tone switches, looking to be reassured: 'But we had fun together, right?'

They will ask you why you did not come forward. Even Héloïse had asked: If you were a victim why would you not say something? She proceeded with a list of scenarios, awful, awful scenarios. They will go through your records, and they will see that you praised him publicly, they will call you out on what you said and your words will be taken out of context. They will remind you that you had agreed to stay longer after the usual training hours, and willingly so. They will read you back your previous statement from the time when L. came forward, only a year before. They will lay out your discrepancies and frame you as a maniac who is looking for attention. They will say he upset you because you weren't a good enough swimmer and that you are taking your revenge. Héloïse became pragmatic, mother protecting daughter, as she justified her plan of action: we must consider that your results haven't been good this season. You will quit tomorrow, Cloe, and leave this cochon (Héloïse had used the French word for pig intentionally) *and all he could entail for our lives behind. Trust me, you've got too much to lose in this story. Pigs scream the loudest when their throats are cut. If you don't say a word then this will simply turn into a bad memory, something that made you stronger, instead of the thing that will define your future life as a woman. Do you hear me, Cloe? This is how you will find your justice, by making your own peace and saving yourself. Not one form of official punishment will do it for you. Trust me, Cloe, I'm your mother.*

Cloe replays Héloïse's diatribe in her mind, the gesture of her hands that punctuated specific words stamped inside her brain – *usual, maniac, revenge, cochon, woman* – as she had managed the family's response. Francesc was oblivious to the situation, his mind focused on keeping his tapas restaurant on Green Lanes in business. He called the place Núvol, 'cloud' in Catalan. Héloïse stressed how hard her father was working every day, reminding Cloe of the difficulty of earning the confidence of the bank in a country where one isn't from originally, the careful and tight profit and loss equation the family relied on. Her parents had made the decision to raise an only child, so they could afford the best for Cloe – an education, practising a sport at a competitive level – and they could not allow their daughter to jeopardise everything they had built as a family. To be problematic.

Problematic. Or poisonous?

Héloïse had always been Cloe's greatest champion, driving her places, preparing packed lunches of sandwiches, devoting her time selflessly, motivating and boosting her ego, balancing her duties as both mother and life coach. Héloïse's behaviours betrayed an uncharacteristic fear, and that day is when Cloe learnt submission and survival often come in a pair.

The circle completed, Cloe had followed her mother's instructions, and so another generation stayed silent. Cloe publicly denied having been sexually assaulted by her coach and declined to comment further. Her mother – her legal guardian – countersigned her declaration. Cloe quit swimming and the case was closed since most of her teammates refused to join the prosecution, a lack of evidence and no funds to afford a lawyer in the case of the only girl who came forward. For all Cloe knows, he could still be training girls somewhere. Food intolerances, pelvic cramps, night terrors, the sore testaments of her body.

How would anyone trust me now? Years later, a no one, an attention seeker.

He asks her if they had fun last night and Cloe says: 'Yes, yes I did.' A gust of cold air makes its way down her spine, acid fires up her throat, a fog settles inside her brain. She returns the phone to her pocket. Cloe draws in a deep breath to escape the cage of her thoughts and keeps walking up Oldfield Road, until she steps into the local pub.

14

Gertrude and Cloe

'"True Colors"! By Cindi Lauper. That's a fun one,' Gertrude says as she peels potatoes. The portions of roast have nearly sold out and afternoon hangovers beckon across the pub. She is making chunky chips, a crowd-pleaser at the end of the day.

'What about mine? 19th August 1984.'

A short wait. The staff roams around the kitchen – the sinks overflow with soapy water and the large oven is warm enough to preserve the last cuts of meat at a safe temperature – until Gertrude breaks through, enthusiastically. 'This is a really good one: Ray Parker Jr.'s "Ghostbusters"!'

The room melts with approbation, the efficiency rate in the kitchen slows down, but the mood revives ahead of the evening shift. Phil leaves early on Sundays, as soon as the lunch rush is over and when stocks for key ingredients run low enough to forbid him from cooking something else.

A collegial atmosphere reigns inside the kitchen: Gertrude on potato duties, the sous-chef carries on inventories in preparation for the following week, the kitchen porter washes up utensils and appliances.

Stefano returns from the locker room. 'So, do I get to know what the number-one song on my birthday was before I go?'

He is looking at Gertrude with his typical, semi-closed eyes. His lips are pinched, the promise of a future smile, flirtatious the way friendships can handle temptation. Without a drop in her gaze, Gertrude puts the potato peeler aside and grabs her phone. 'Of course,' she says, and she enters the data on the website. She doesn't need to ask Stefano for his date of birth.

She taps her foot on the ground, a smirk on her face: 'Obviously yours is "Vogue" by Madonna. Here you go, that's your "fun fact about myself" for your date sorted.' Gertrude consciously looks him up and down, reviewing Stefano's outfit. He hadn't *really* told her why he couldn't stay longer today.

'How gracious of you.' Stefano rolls his arms down and bows before Gertrude theatrically. He knows such a gesture will annoy her, so he softens the movement with a final, complicit wink; he turns his back and waves to the room as he walks out.

The rest of the kitchen staff says goodbye too.

They are quiet, which puts Gertrude on the spot. She has heard the rumours their colleagues entertain about her and

Stefano. She panics and overshares: 'I also had a date yesterday. I bet his birthday song was,' she snaps her fingers, a tut, and she hums.

'Carly Simon,' says one of her colleagues.

'That's it! He was vain.'

'Well, you are talking about him,' her colleague responds. Gertrude exhibits her disapproval.

'Come on, don't leave us hanging like that. What does he do? Where did you go? Will you be seeing him again?' the same colleague asks, his hands deep in water, foam climbing up his elbows as he scratches the heavy-duty kitchen pans. They produce a bloated and distant noise, underwater.

No, she doesn't want to tell them about him. She has given enough information away in the hopes that her colleagues will see her as someone other than 'the sad and lost girl who works at the Oldfield Tavern'. She wants to show them that she chose to work here and that at the end of her shifts, she doesn't stay behind at home while Stefano goes on dates. She goes out too and she is not afraid. Yet, she cuts the conversation short: 'He was an entitled idiot and, trust me, I'm not seeing him again.' The end; they pick up their tasks again quietly. The potatoes, peeled and rinsed, have a soggy texture under Gertrude's hands. She chops the chips fast, the line of her knife fluid and her approach to the blade controlled. Empowering – chop, chop, she throws a batch inside the fryer; empowered, she chops, chops, chops, another load goes inside the heated machine. The oil crisps, the sound of fire, her burning skin, and she shakes the baskets vigorously.

can't they see?
what they think of me
what they make of me
is the product of their interpretations,
not my identity

Gertrude has become the link between domesticity and the kitchen space at the Oldfield Tavern. The floor is female, but the kitchen bends around the male gaze. She cannot bear to hear another story about one of her colleagues' grandmothers. Enchanted tales of how the elderly woman peels apples in one go, keeping the fruit perfectly round for them – they say this as they show Gertrude how to hold the peeler more firmly, so she will peel potatoes more thinly – or the grandmother who prepares beans on toast. Self-indulgent, heteronormative desires dominate inter-actions at work: her colleagues second-guess her opinions and her reasons for working here. She cannot have chosen it for herself, they assume. She smiles – *smile, love* – most of the time, then she walks to the sink, an industrial model with its bottom low, she runs cold water through the tap, and she considers submerging her head in the water so she can scream. Louder. So she can be heard for the words she means to speak.

bees buzz in a swarm
echo inside the labyrinth of my body
and back,

in a swarm,
like dream catchers, i freeze
when i want to run, fly, swim,
or dance with myself

A member of staff – a man about her size with a round face and glasses of a similar shape – greets Cloe with a smile she doesn't return. The soundtrack of others having a good time kicks in and she settles on a stool at the bar.

Fumes and babbles filter through the kitchen doors, a few leftover plates of congealing meat sit at the corner of tables, wet dogs and beer kegs are dotted around the place. The unpleasant melody of a bell echoes in her head – *But we had fun together, right?* – Cloe wants to be at the centre of the action and for everyone to notice her, should she require to show evidence tomorrow. Tacky and heavy, she can feel the bedsheets in which she woke up this morning slide down her legs.

The bartender slips a menu next to her and taps his fingers against the plasticised cover to catch her attention: 'Just give me a shout when you're ready, okay?'

'A Bloody Mary, please,' she responds. He reaches out for a shaker. 'No celery stick,' Cloe adds.

He starts making the drink and Cloe watches him closely. His movements – pouring in the tomato juice, then vodka, Worcestershire sauce, hot pepper sauce, a pinch of salt and pepper, then a shake – the familiar rhythm of bartenders. She is searching for clues; Cloe has a visual memory.

The bottles of vodka we hid under mattresses, Francesc who ate tomatoes like apples, biting into the flesh with bright joy, followed by juice sailing down his forearms, the clinging sound of cocktail shakers last night. Cocktail shakers, most certainly. I use my intuitions to cross-examine my actions.

'Would you like some green olives to replace the celery for a garnish?'

She nods in agreement, and he serves her the cocktail: 'Yours – a combination of poison and remedy.'

What do you know about the remedy I need?

What do you know about poison?

Help, can you see me?

Cloe lifts the tall cocktail glass. She gives him a quick smile and takes a first sip.

On the other side of the bar, the bartender empties the dishwasher methodically and Cloe jumps each time two glasses clang loudly. First, he takes out a tray full of glasses, puts it on the counter, then he takes each glass in his hand, a tea towel in the other, a quick polish, and he returns the sparkling glass onto one of the shelves. Amid this repetitive work, he begins talking, not quite directly to Cloe, though she is sitting at the bar alone. Behind her, the room is loud with broken conversations.

'I always thought this cocktail was quintessentially British. Sunday lunches, the celery stick, Mary Tudor.' He glances at Cloe, who acknowledges him, so he continues. 'But it's all about marketing, I guess. A distillery came up with a centenary anniversary in 2021, a celebration of its creation at Harry's New York Bar in Paris back in 1921.' He stops, bringing one of the glasses closer to his face for inspection before discarding it inside a plastic bucket on the side. 'Something to do with a bartender nicknamed Pete who served drinks to the American expats who had fled to Paris during the Prohibition years. I wouldn't blame them, to be honest.'

He comes across as inoffensive, revelling in his gimmicky facts. Cloe eats the last olive and uses the cocktail stick to give her drink a faint stir, swirling the top of the glass. Surface, appearance. Lust, fear.

'My family always said the cocktail was named after Queen Mary Tudor, but that might be very English of us.' He takes another tray of glasses out. 'And we're Protestants as well.' He carries on polishing the glasses and goes on talking about Prohibition and alcohol, cocktails and the stories behind their recipes. Cloe pretends to pay attention, but her thoughts drift.

A woman slides out of the kitchen's fireproof doors. 'Don't let him bore you with his quiz facts!' she says in passing while carrying two large bin bags, one in each hand. Her cheeks are red and her forehead is crowded with freckles; Cloe notices the large, darker mole above the woman's left temple, a focal point when trying not to meet anyone in the eyes. The bartender doesn't have time to respond before the woman in the apron adds: 'Can you pour me half a Neck Oil, please? I'll have it at the bar with you. It's quiet in the kitchen.'

The bartender agrees and she walks out. When she returns, she climbs onto the stool next to Cloe and lifts her glass. 'I'm Gertrude. Cheers.' She delicately knocks Cloe's drink and takes a large sip of hers.

15

Mathilde and Sarah

In addition to the beer garden at the back, the Oldfield Tavern has a few picnic tables in front of the building. The division between visitors happens organically: families and those who come with a dog settle in the enclosed back garden while solitary drinkers, and those who don't want to mix, stay at the entrance. This organisation shows that beneath the apparent chaos of large cities, a set of unspoken rules, visible to the locals only, convey a silent agreement that makes life manageable on an individual level.

After lunch, Mathilde had popped to the bathroom, letting Sarah head out without her. She stayed inside the cubicle for long enough to read the handwritten notes some of the previous guests had scribbled, colourful and messy messages covering the walls. Names of lovers and politicians, football predictions, band names; Mathilde read some of the lines carefully, snapshots of lives and hopes, and pondered what could bring someone to write their thoughts on the walls of a pub toilet. Was her name ever written on one? Would she feel praised or sullied if she had known about it? A vortex of things people had either wished they could say or, the opposite, the ideas shame cancelled. Do the authors bring pens with them to the pub, planning to leave a trace, or are these urges? Mathilde has become scared of her own compulsions over the years, and she has learnt to control them, a skill she attributes to her success, working her way through a demanding career. She had started as a recruiting manager for a bank, then went on to apply her professional calm and strategic mind to a greater cause she cares for: Mathilde works as a legal advisor at a women's centre. But then there are the moments when, impulsive, a tide propelled by fear and anger hits her, occasions when she tinkers with control. When a child screams loudly and abruptly on the street, a fire or car alarm goes off; the vibrations of boiling water, they melt her armour against her will. If she had a pen, she would write on the wall – *I'm drowning. SOS*. But Agnes has never shown her daughters how to be humble and to reach out for help. Everyone asked Mathilde the same question – *What were you thinking when you decided to pour that pot of boiling water over yourself?* – but she doesn't have the answer. She was surprised when the therapist handed her a questionnaire and told her to answer with numbers on a scale from 0 to 10, an attempt to score her mental health. Her responses were fraudulent, commanded by the ingrained attitude of being a righteous student: Mathilde guessed what an appropriate score would be so she wouldn't be marked as depressed. There were periods when Mathilde would weigh everything in the house scrupulously, from herself to the bags of flour stored inside the kitchen cupboards. She didn't have an opinion about the numbers that showed on the scales' screen, but she gained a form of control each time she flirted with breaking apart. Data she could handle. Like a jigsaw puzzle of a painting by Renoir, Manet, or any of the impressionists she admires, Mathilde broke the world into smaller pieces so she could arrange them into a beautiful canvas. The mental health questionnaire required a different skill: a demand to quantify one's paranoia and social anxiety and paralysing thoughts and harmful intentions. She takes part in a similar system in the office, where her hours are dedicated to helping women who are victims of abuse to navigate the legal system. And there she learnt of its limitation: if impulses and emotions could be measured like marbles in a jar, our society could approach social and health issues with the logic of an equation. Except this isn't the case. The human heart beats unevenly between unfair and unflinching structures, and Mathilde can't recall what she was thinking when she poured the boiling water over herself. Acts of such desperation are not thought through before they are performed. *Be a good girl, will you?* Mathilde is afraid of what she could do, who she could hurt, apart from herself, when an impulse dictates her actions.

I have told you about the cravings, about roaming in my mind and from one room to another, craving and looking for the origin of my pains, insatiable. I can't explain why I chose to pour a pot of boiling water over me, but I know that I was empowered by it. It hurt like hell, but it had hurt before too. It stopped the pain for a moment though. The unanswered questions stopped when all I could focus on was how much my skin burnt. When I came back home from the hospital, I walked into the bathroom so I could check myself in the mirror. I spotted a grey hair, and since then I dye my hair.

At the end of her lunch with Sarah, Mathilde meant to leave the pub. She planned to walk along the high street, to stop in a shop or two, and to send voice messages to friends – mundane tasks. To go home and do the laundry, except that she sat on one of the benches next to the front door and she stopped *doing* in order to function. She played out scenarios about the people who were drinking and chatting around her. She halted her present with imaginary tales of others – love triangles playing out through meals, prosaic conversations about bathroom tiles and quiet couples caged inside a stare with one another. A loud table was reconciling the simple joy of good news, and she smiled briefly.

You might wonder how much time has passed since Sarah exited the Oldfield Tavern, but preoccupations limit the prospect of occupations. The past cripples and arrests the possibility of a future. Mathilde has told you she can't be trusted, and she wants you to know that numbing her thoughts with sitting still in a public space is progression from hurting herself. She asks you to be patient with her.

'What are you doing here?'

Sarah has returned to the Oldfield Tavern. She pulls her shirt down, self-conscious of her appearance, sketchy and tired.

With the outward confidence that characterises her, Mathilde replies: 'What are you doing here? You went ahead and left earlier.'

'I forgot my scarf.'

'Which scarf?'

'It's a new one, you wouldn't know it.'

'But what does it look like?'

Sarah shakes her head, peering past Mathilde into the pub.

Mathilde insists: 'Let me know what your scarf looks like and maybe I can help.'

'Yellow, silk, with a large tiger.' Matter-of-fact. Sarah hasn't looked back at her sister.

'This doesn't sound like something you'd wear.'

'This is helpful, thanks,' she says, still not looking at Mathilde.

'I haven't seen it,' Mathilde declares.

Then Sarah turns around. 'I told you, it's a new one.' She softens her voice, scanning her sister for hints on how to trade with her strange behaviours, and she adds: 'I must have hung it on the back of my chair when I sat down for lunch.'

Mathilde pulls her guard back up: 'Where is your scarf from? This one must be precious for you to come back all the way here. Aren't you on a deadline as well?' She spoke the three sentences fast.

'The library closes at five on Sundays. Anyway, Mathilde,

this is absurd. What's going on?' They lock eyes; no words. 'I left two hours ago.' Disorientated, Sarah adjusts to the present situation and finding her sister at the same location. She considers how much she has done and failed to do since she said goodbye to the woman she nicknames *Mathi the doer* after lunch – and the stillness she finds alarming. Sarah reckons with terror and Mathilde is embedded with it. They stare at each other, deeply and expectantly, the sour broken promise that they won't need to detail their sentiments, that ills will be identified inherently and fixed without the two siblings needing to say a word. That succession will play its role.

The silence persists; both are stubborn when it comes to hiding their passions. The daughters of Agnes.

'Do you ever think about that day?' Mathilde asks.

Sarah avoids eye contact. The recognition of a secret and the attached resentment for Mathilde to bring the topic up without warning; a chill weaves through her body.

'I can't move on from what I did to you,' Mathilde confesses. Sarah turns around to face her sister, sliding one of her legs on top of the bench and settling in, astride. The pair face each other, and Mathilde goes on: 'I'm grateful that you didn't die, but I know that my lies broke you.'

Sarah tries to interrupt her sister, puzzled by the revelation, a gust of wind switching her day from her present sins on to the secret that holds her and Mathilde close. Mathilde continues, her pupils wide and anchored onto Sarah. She wants to be heard: 'I can't unsee the links between your illness and you almost drowning. I'm in the shower or I'm washing the dishes, and there I picture you walking towards me: wet, your hair covered with lake weed. You're still six years old but I'm an adult.'

Sarah nods gently while Mathilde describes how her nose, eyes and ears look disproportionate during these visions, her face still the size of a child, her hair wet and dripping with water over the tiling of Mathilde's kitchen. In this imagined version of their sisterhood, Sarah peeps up to Mathilde because she has grown into an adult, while Sarah is trapped in a life of *what ifs*. She comes to show Mathilde that flirting with death tied her to a sickness for life, Mathilde adds. She explains that Sarah doesn't speak to her, her expression is resigned and the water drips down, soaking her t-shirt, then her stripy swimsuit bottoms and finally her jelly shoes. A puddle forms around her. She gasps and she struggles to breathe, but she doesn't die; she turns blue instead, bruising so hard she could never recover. In reality, Sarah was resuscitated and her brain was declared healthy. No apparent cognitive traumas, at least. Sarah's near-death experience is the ghost of an event they never talk about as a family. Mathilde's speech is calm, which worries Sarah, and she drops a hand on her sister's knee, joining her fingers with those of Mathilde. Consolation cannot be thought of; she must do something.

'Have you told someone about this? I mean a professional.'

Mathilde looks away, ashamed.

'When they checked you in at the hospital after your incident, did you mention these episodes to them?' Sarah reformulates.

'That night ... The boiling water was the only way to halt the visions.' And before Sarah can add something else, Mathilde insists: 'Remember what I told you about the American study and the blocked tears? (Sarah doesn't remember.) The water is the key to unlock our story and to release you from all these pains. You must know that with your research.'

Sarah looks at her sister, bewildered. Her lips are chapped and tight.

'Can't you see it? Our obsession with managing flows of water. There must be a significance to all of this ... There must be an end point.'

Sarah has never considered her academic subject from a subjective angle. Rarely does she allow herself to acknowledge that she almost drowned – she was so young, and she loves water and the idea of swimming. Memories come to her occasionally, when the tips of her toes meet chlorinated water and her arms push back to slow down the process of descending into the pool. Her head is immersed. The water blurs, dark green, a lake, the pale legs of her sister ahead; bright, a wish, the light of hope that didn't spark. Sarah had wanted to swim 'like a grown-up' and Mathilde wanted to complete her crosswords. She was so close to beating her grandfather; she stayed behind on the towel. Mathilde feared there would be repercussions for her choice when she had promised to look after her little sister who had just learnt to swim. She asked Sarah to keep her secret; she was alive. Time ratified this promise as their union, but Sarah never held Mathilde accountable for her accident, or any of its after-effects. Silent years also shifted both their interpretations of the event. When a fever runs high and clamps her forehead tight, Sarah questions if she would be so sick if it hadn't happened. She blames her fragility on having had her soul deprived of oxygen in a bout with death, but not on Mathilde. Sarah tells Mathilde as much and beyond: 'This is my story. Yours ended where our secret started.' She hates the sound of her voice as she does, an overly protective little sister who won't share her toys.

Sarah doesn't remember waking up – her memory fast-forwards to the end of the summer, September elevating moods and her walking through the gates at school. Both she and Mathilde were excused from swimming lessons.

As for the adults' accounts, the story goes: it was summertime, the pollen count was high, swollen hands and drowsy brains, a state one seeks only to regret soon after. The family had gone visiting the paternal grandparents in Wales, a house in the countryside where they enjoyed a taste of freedom. They foraged wildflowers and queried the names of the trees during long walks. A week was enough to recharge their tolerance for the city, the yearly visit falling during the month of June so the children could visit the Hay book festival, their parents keen to make them readers, and so it would be warm enough to swim in the lake. The rest of the story is a case of adults discharging their own responsibilities on to the other. One thought the other was watching the children. All were busy reading, checking emails, pulling up weeds or brushing mud off vegetables. It happened *so* fast.

'You're not listening to me. There is something with the water. Do you remember how cloudy the lake was? Slimy and dangerous.' Mathilde's voice has become lower, her alarm palpable. She speaks in whispers. 'Don't you remember how scared of the lake you were? You spoke about an enormous snake . . .'

Sarah hates being the younger sibling, a passive receiver of memory. And she has lost faith in Mathilde. Sarah thinks about her grandmother, a botanist with a long braid hanging down her back, who told tales of myths and stories of gods and witchcraft to the girls. Their nana always had her hands deep down in the land but didn't fear the grass snakes; instead she taught her granddaughters that knowledge was the key to keep phobias at bay. Nana told Sarah about the snakes that guard the underworld, living in crevices, serving as intermediaries to the upper world. She educated Sarah about nature and needing to respect its workings so that humans, flora and fauna can cohabit. Sarah looked for snakes everywhere she went after that. 'I wasn't scared of the snake at the bottom of the lake.' She speaks with gravity.

Mathilde, the sole witness of Sarah's accident, had been asked to summarise what had happened as soon as the ambulance arrived. They needed to know how long Sarah might have been immersed under the water, deprived of oxygen. The lie flowed from her tongue smoothly, like that of a serpent: the sisters were swimming together, with Mathilde leading the way. She was clearing a path as the water was obstructed and other bits made it harder for them to swim.

Sarah must have got herself entangled with a branch or something. *It happened so fast. It was so scary.* Mathilde doesn't know how long Sarah was underwater but it can't have been long. She was close to her. Mathilde didn't understand the concept of time as much as she does now, the notion trivial to a child whose days are framed by the decisions of adults. While Mathilde spoke to the paramedics, Sarah laid on the grass. A small, improvised curtain hung up so Mathilde couldn't see. She resents the adults for that decision because her imagination suppressed her perception, and she struggles to erase the false images she created. They carried out the resuscitation by the side of the lake and Mathilde remembers the terrifying silence. And then Sarah woke up, along with cries, questions, beeping machines, a cacophony for her second birth. She was wheeled away for examination. Their mother went with the emergency crew and the rest of the family drove in silence. Hours passed, which neither Sarah nor Mathilde recall; days spent walking up and down hospital corridors instead of a summertime playground, until a social worker invited them for 'regular catch-ups', as the family called the girls' talking therapy. The therapist asked questions about the accident, but also about their sleep and their appetite. Sarah repeated the same version of Mathilde's story. The sessions ended with the sisters returning to their known routines in London, then to school, and the episode was never mentioned again. A well-guarded family secret, but Sarah's body says otherwise. It clicks like a faulty chain inside the Jenkins–Bell machinery.

The grandparents planted an olive tree at the bottom of the garden, an offering of vegetation against the cursed element. Unpredictable water. The fruit doesn't grow well among the branches, but the leaves are coloured with a tender mid-point between green and grey.

Mathilde's fingers dwindle, bloodless; Sarah is pressing her hand as hard as she can.

'Do you hear yourself, Mathi?' Another squeeze. 'This is just a silly promise we made when we were children so we could cope with the shock of what had happened. This is irrelevant.' A pause. 'Let me go get you some water.'

As soon as she says the word, Sarah looks up at her sister with an apologetic expression. *Water* hangs between them.

A wave set in motion by an inherited line of trauma rolls over: Mathilde shakes her sister by the shoulders. Mathilde was the one in charge that day. The big sister who let her little sister down. She insists that the water is poisoned. Sarah has been so sick ever since. What if she hadn't lied and had told the paramedics that Sarah was underwater for a longer period because she wasn't looking? Would they have treated Sarah differently? The water that broke before both their births, the metaphorical water under which their mother immersed herself, the water pipes Sarah is studying, the subject that causes her all these worries, her loneliness – they are trapped inside a whirlpool. She has tried to free them by pouring boiling water over herself, by making herself accountable for her actions. She asked for forgiveness – tattooing pain over her skin with water for ink. Can Sarah not see what she did? She, the big sister, put herself forward to clear their name. Sarah must be familiar with whirlpools – plunging, circular, attracting forces – a one-way stream. But does she know that when a whirlpool is extremely powerful, the kinds that are found in oceans, then its name is derived from the Dutch language: maelstrom. 'A grinding-stream', from *malen*, to grind, and *stroom*, stream. A force, a black hole, that gulps any signs of life before burying them deep down, forever. That day at the lake launched a maelstrom at the centre of their lives and, Mathilde insists, they can't move on until they stop it at the source.

The deluge ends. Mathilde's eyes are dry, her hands tremble. She stands up, quiet and pale, in fight-or-flight mode. Sarah gets up too. Tears are running down her cheeks, a taste of salt.

Sarah looks at Mathilde in disbelief. It pains her that illness is all her sister can see in her, that Mathilde can't authorise her sister happiness. Sarah takes her hand away from Mathilde's, clenching her fists. She is the one who could throw a pot of boiling water over herself on this occasion, in a bid to reclaim her own life experience; her survival and the guilt she has inflicted over her sister, the antipathy her mother doesn't try to hide. This is her diagnosis, and it doesn't define who she is.

Mathilde acts self-conscious, and she considers apologising for her outburst.

'Let's go inside and grab a glass of something stronger.' Sarah steps ahead without looking back. The door doesn't close behind her. The pub is emptier than when they left after lunch – they can hear one another sigh.

Mathilde and Sarah head to the bar.

16

Cloe and Gertrude

'Are you not going to tell me what the number-one tune was on my birthday?' the bartender asks Gertrude.

'Ah, man, I can't believe this has become a part of my job spec.' Gertrude takes another sip of beer and gets her phone out of her pocket. 'Come on then, give me your date of birth.'

'18 September 2000.'

Cloe puts her cocktail glass back on the bar so she can look at him, and so does Gertrude before the two women turn to each other: 'Do you feel old too?'

'That's rude,' the guy moans.

'It shouldn't be legal for you to work in a pub if you weren't born before the millennium,' Gertrude says.

'Well, time flies. I'm above the minimum age. But, technically, I still need to show ID with the under-twenty-five laws.' He continues to clean glasses with the same meticulous method. A keen smile, his shoulders offbeat like a puppet, he adds: 'I laugh inside when I ask some big guy to show me proof of identity because they could be under twenty-five years old.' He puts the glass he was polishing away, then brings both his arms up, his fluffy hair blowing back: 'But what can I say? "C'est la vie!" And I'm the one who works behind the bar.' He walks towards the dishwasher, emboldened with confidence around two women who show him interest.

Cloe and Gertrude glare at him, then they eye each other with a complicit smile.

'Your song was "Music" by Madonna, by the way,' Gertrude shouts to his back. 'Don't get too excited. Stefano had "Vogue" so you're not that original.' He doesn't respond. 'Neither of you is,' Gertrude can't help but add, talking under her breath.

The young man doesn't engage; in the backroom, he ticks chores off.

'What was this game?' Cloe asks shyly.

Gertrude ponders for a second. 'Oh, what was the number-one song on your birthday? It's a silly thing I like to play with people when it's awkward. Or it's a good one for quizzes, or to create a fun birthday party playlist.'

A celebratory mood lightens Cloe's face. She wants to play and to discover which song was heading the chart when she was born too. She gives Gertrude her date of birth but she has this odd feeling, as if she was about to have her tarot cards read or as if the song could hold important clues about her identity and destiny. She brings her hand in front of her mouth, her fingers are covered with rings. She apologises for talking too much and asks about her birthday song again.

'"Hero" by Mariah Carey,' Gertrude tells her.

'Oh, that's nice. That's a nice one, right?'

Gertrude takes another sip of her beer in agreement. She is amused by this strange woman and the earnest tone of her questions.

'So, how does it work? Was "Hero" the number one in the UK or elsewhere?'

Gertrude looks doubtful as she starts scrolling down her phone screen impulsively.

'I don't know. I never thought about checking which number one I was looking at.' She frowns. 'Fuck, all these playlists I've made for people, and I never checked.'

'That was probably a dull question. It's the copywriter in me – "fact checking", "fact checking", "fact checking".' Cloe mimics a robot as she speaks; she sounds gauche but cheery. She laughs and takes another sip of her drink, not wanting to make eye contact.

Gertrude smiles.

'Okay, let's check. Because you might be right. It wasn't the number-one song in the UK since there is a specific feature for that on the website. Apparently, I can also give you the number-one tune in France, Germany, as well as the bestselling novel and so on.'

'Let's start with the number-one song in the UK on my birthday, please.' Cloe turns slightly so she faces Gertrude.

Gertrude mirrors her movement, then she responds, looking freakish, her face compressed: '"Mr Blobby" by Mr Blobby.' A sharp laugh escapes her as soon as she voices the last syllable.

'I swear, this is the story of my life!' Cloe snatches the phone from Gertrude's hands and looks at the photo of the bulbous figure. Bright pink with yellow spots, green and large eyes, and a disturbing toothy grin; she doesn't say a word.

'You okay, hun?' Gertrude asks dramatically, before they both erupt into loud laughter.

'No, seriously, this is so telling.' A short pause. 'Blobby, blobby,' Cloe says with that robotic voice again. 'No hero for sure,' she laughs.

'I wouldn't give it too much credence and I'm into all sorts of horoscope and star sign stuff.'

'Then you will know that I'm a stubborn Capricorn. Can you tell me what the number-one song on my birthday in France was, s'il vous plaît?'

Gertrude obeys. 'Okay, so don't over-analyse the lyrics – just hang on to the success story. It's "Living On My Own" by Freddie Mercury.'

'Right, I need another drink. Where is our underaged bartender?' Cloe downs her last drop of Bloody Mary.

'You're in luck, lonely hero, because I work here too.' Gertrude jumps off the stool and walks behind the bar. 'What can I serve you?' She shines with ease.

'I'll have the same as you,' Cloe responds for a dare.

'Two pints of Neck Oil then. (Gertrude avoids looking Cloe in the eyes as she speaks the next sentence.) I've peeled enough potatoes for each table inside this pub to order twice.' She places the two beers on coasters and walks around the bar, sitting back so she can face Cloe. 'Are you French?'

A hint of interrogation is cast over Cloe's expressions.

'My mum was.' Short answer.

Gertrude notes the past tense.

'That was unthoughtful of me, sorry. I only asked because you said "s'il vous plaît" earlier.' Pause, then comes her alibi: 'Everyone always asks me if I'm French because of my name, which is hilarious because have you ever seen anyone looking more English than this redhead Brummie before you?' Gertrude smiles, trying to put meaning behind the word *sorry*.

'I didn't know Gertrude was a French name.'

'It's not.'

They snort, a relief midway through an unexpected afternoon.

'Tell me, then, what's the story of your name?' Cloe asks.

'My mum lived in Paris for a while and fell in love with that bookshop you see around printed on tote bags, and the whole twentieth-century artists' circle thing that goes with it.' A sip of beer. 'Somehow she convinced herself that it would be empowering to call me Gertrude because she couldn't have gone for Alice.' She pauses. 'Sweet Alice B. Toklas, always so underrated.'

'I read that book for my A levels.' Gertrude doesn't reply,

178

allowing Cloe to pick up her train of thought. 'We read *The Autobiography of Alice B. Toklas* and I was confused for the first hundred pages or so because I had understood the title literally, like I always do. But it turned out it was the autobiography of Gertrude Stein.' Cloe drinks, her tongue slides between her lips. 'I think that's more about what happens in a partnership between two people. It's not that one sits back, at least not in a happy situation, but a case of both storylines merging into one, voluntarily or not, and then the one who shouts louder receives the credit for all of it.' She places the pint back on the bar, thoughtful. 'Like teamwork. It was never just the work of Gertrude Stein, but the efforts of both Gertrude and Alice, and I want to believe that they knew that. You know?' Cloe looks at Gertrude: 'It's another case of writing up history in shorthand because truth hides in the details and their ambiguities, and nobody really wants to hear the truth. The proof is, you're called Gertrude, not Alice, and the name is rather uncommon for a British woman of your age.' Cloe stops. She looks pale, as if she wanted to erase herself, seen for her ideas.

Gertrude gives Cloe a friendly smile before she adds: 'At least you haven't asked me if my brother is called Pablo, like a guy I met yesterday.'

Cloe smirks. 'Only because I didn't know you had a brother.'

Two clever women meet. What did you expect?

'Would you like to tell me more about that guy?' Cloe asks Gertrude as they click.

*

Enter two other women, one with long hair, her fringe longer in proportion, the other one with a short bowl haircut, which looks as if a continuous fringe draws a carousel around her head. The placement of their eyes, round and close to their nose, and the length of their necks, are similar. They share a shadow, a mark of sorrow; two sisters evident at first sight.

There are fewer plates left on the tables now, the playlist is friendly and easily identifiable, most of the crowd has moved outside in the back garden. Daylight hangs onto the clock until the early night, light jackets and seasonal smokers surface, spirits are elevated, and the outdoor bar is busier than inside for the first time of the year. Some spoon ice-cream, Aperol Spritz tops the cocktail orders, red bleeding into a summery orange, and lagers lead the overall chart. The magnolia trees have flowered with large and pink petals this year.

'Can I get you anything?' Gertrude asks Sarah and Mathilde after spotting them glancing between the menu and the other side of the bar longingly.

They stay silent, frowning.

'I work here. I'm not trying to chat you up, I promise!' Gertrude lifts her hands up in the air, palms flat and exposed.

'In that case, can we have a bottle of Sauvignon Blanc?' Sarah asks.

Mathilde puts her hands on her sister's arm in protest. Sarah ignores the gesture, and Gertrude opens the small fridge underneath the bar.

'And a few ice cubes on the side,' Sarah says. 'Thank you,' she adds quickly, her cheeks itching, caught under the sun.

Gertrude pulls her hair high in a quick bun, and Mathilde cannot take her eyes off her. Cloe makes way, putting one foot on the floor, half standing half sitting, pushing the stool on the left. The card machine glows on the bar, GBP 22.00, and Sarah taps.

Gertrude places the glasses on the bar, giving the two sisters a radiant smile that backs up her hospitality skills.

'I recognise you,' Mathilde says. 'You were at that bottom-less brunch place yesterday. Near Paddington.'

In a rush that surprises her the most, Cloe responds: 'We were just talking about that! How funny how small, small, small the world is.'

Gertrude notices that Cloe repeats the word that put her in the spotlight three times. She confirms: 'I was there having a truly terrible date.'

'Make it four glasses,' Sarah says firmly.

PART 4

Saturday Night

17

Cloe and Gertrude

To visit Colette forces Cloe to reassess how she conceives time. Its influence over people's behaviours and the coalition of seconds, days, months and years, looping in a race for evolution: Saturdays with her grandmother, the hours between each tin she gives to Massimo, the length of a movie listed on streaming websites versus the experience of watching it. Even the number of minutes required to read an article precedes its online publication – time informs decision-making.

In January, Héloïse bought a calendar from the Royal Mail in support of the RSPCA or Worldwide Cancer Research, or both, when the usual postman was sick but she didn't want to explain to the other man that she had one already. The paper calendar hung on the fridge door like a floating archive of how the family intended to spend another year, held by a magnet in the shape of the tower of Pisa.

Héloïse lost her temper and threw the calendar on the floor often, the ink of the pen they had used to mark dates fading, Cloe taping it back up afterwards, a museum for hobbies. The proof of an absence too, when mentions of movies and hair dyes were replaced with medical appointments so Cloe could track them (Héloïse would never pursue something or someone she couldn't hold sway over, 'like my death sentence, a waste of time,' she told Cloe). Until Héloïse didn't leave the hospital and Cloe had nothing left to record in writing; Héloïse was a realist who knew of her pleasures, not an optimist.

Without her mother to care for, Cloe gulps the hours before eight o'clock, slows down her pace with the afternoon and drags her existence into a capricious night-time. Insomnia gnaws at Cloe with a sense of loneliness inspired by not doing the right *things* – not being out, not reading but not sleeping, not enjoying being out and not sleeping enough. A life cut short haunts those who survive with the pressure of producing more, to be endurant to endure. Cloe would have insisted on filling the calendar with dates with her mother if she had known their time was up. Héloïse didn't need rest when they had never attended one of the planetarium shows at the Royal Observatory in Greenwich (they always said they should). They could have had a last goûter at the Maison Bertaux before heading to Seven Dials, dizzy and thirsty, pursuing the small joys that feed into happiness.

When eczema dried her skin and coughs and pains thinned her body, Héloïse spoke highly of Switzerland.

The Alps and the lakes with crystal-clear water that tastes of minerals, fields of tall grass, and health facilities where people are allowed to die with dignity. Colette and Héloïse argued about the ethics of euthanasia for weeks – Héloïse denounced her mother for denying her right to die on her terms; Colette responded that she was rescuing her daughter from a suicide attempt – generational disconnect and a deep love for the other interfered with their ability to be reasonable. The pair fought in French, a language they never taught Cloe so they could preserve this intimate grammar among themselves, the conductor for rules that excluded Cloe. Héloïse never travelled to Switzerland, but she died in winter with Colette and Cloe by her side. At the end, Héloïse spoke only French. Murmurs toned down her characteristic wit and demonstrated the ties between language and identity, so Colette stepped into the shoes of an interlocutor and Cloe cried silent tears for the words she wanted to say. *Tu vas me manquer, Maman.* She wanted to be called Chloë and wrote the letters in her notebook consumingly, adopting a cursive style she thought was taught in French schools. *Cloe*, a middle ground or the root that made her an ambidextrous person – *you're always so indecisive, Cloe.* If only she could tell this to Héloïse, but even a mother doesn't consent to be born, and nor does she consent to die.

Cloe has researched her mother's diagnosis and each one of the treatments she was offered, still does – compulsive anxieties, she can't stop herself. She bookmarked articles about trauma and the body and sickness. She discovered the links between illnesses, such as arthritis, dementia and cancers, and long-term stress and traumatic events, or about sexual assault and illnesses like Crohn's and fibromyalgia. Papers made connections with the functioning of the nervous system she didn't want to know. Cloe read and she was angry, defeated before the systematic favour of efficiency against prevention – *You speak English, no need to bother with French; shush, be good; medicines cure physical pains and paralyse mental illness; don't speak up, silly, hopeful girl!* Hope is a dangerous coping mechanism.

At the west end of the city, the signs of springtime lift moods. Londoners come together in parks, barefoot with portable stereos in hand, and bikes and scooters are abandoned on the grass. The bins inside Paddington station burst with cans of pre-mixed cocktails and lagers. Flappy shoes and swollen ankles, there is a sense of urgency – two teenagers run for a train, announcements about delays, a pug's head pops out of a backpack. Gertrude walks in, turns left, and heads down the stairs in the direction of the Bakerloo Line: a few stops to Oxford Circus, another promise of chaos, then a change for the Central Line, a long way inside a narrow carriage. She wants to go home, yet her gait is tentative, like a newborn. The gap she should mind, the hands of strangers she fears, the trap of being between stations. The swan in Stockwell, the rifle in Finsbury Park – the underground network of

London that reminds her she is an outsider in the city where she lives and works.

She walks back up the stairs and exits the station.

Gertrude grew up in a place where she knew the names of the shop owners and children were encouraged to play outside the house. On occasions, she travelled to London for day trips with her school. The class would walk up Whitehall and visit the Churchill War Rooms, followed by a stop at the Women of World War II statue in honour of their service. The monument is made of bronze with carved uniforms from the Women's Land Army, the Women's Royal Naval Service, a nursing cape, dungarees, a welding mask. The children stood for long enough to show respect and moved on to the next stop without a grasp of the historical context. They went to galleries, wandering around the rooms with questionnaires to complete, but their perimeter was limited between Westminster and Euston train station – a metropole in a classroom's nutshell.

The mood of her classmates was elevated, boys shouting at girls, girls shouting at boys, driven by a desire to break a rule while being in the big smoke. They stole bags of crisps from Boots when teachers bought tubes of sunscreen, ran secret errands to the corner shops for a bottle of sweet and fizzy drink, sometimes a can of the energising Red Bull. They told stories about a teenager who suffered a cardiac arrest inside a nightclub after mixing the drink with vodka. They shared more tales about who had lost their virginity and whose parents were getting a divorce and who didn't have their periods yet – frivolous rumours that scarred Gertrude. If you asked her, she would tell you that she felt crushed under a rolling pin. That her body was compressed by the expectations of what she should like doing – gymnastics when she was discouraged by the gender division in PE classes to join the basketball team; going to McDonald's with the boys, but not to speak like a boy – and what she should look like – cute and smiling and thin and graceful – demands she approached as homework. Still, teachers called Gertrude's parents to discuss anger management issues, and they reprimanded her with their anger; Gertrude wasn't academic.

When she was in London, Gertrude couldn't stop looking at the terraces outside of cafés and restaurants. Suits, large sunglasses, trainers and heels and hiking boots; chairs made of braided straw or plastic seats; umbrellas in case of a rainy interlude. Gertrude watched the performance of London with the attention of a miniaturist. There, in the European capital of musicals, despite the traffic, the high pollution rate alerts, the fog and the butter-like air, people still stop to eat and drink together. Coffee cups, Champagne glasses or pints of beer; bread and pickles, or cupcakes served on small plates; the terraces of London had always intrigued Gertrude. She started planning for a venue of her own: bacon and scrambled egg sandwiches, mimosa cocktails, scones, a selection of organic wines, finger food (but presented on elegant dishware). Chihuahuas on laps, sunglasses and newspapers that spread over long pages, the crackling noise of paper, but fabric napkins.

The embarrassing but pleasing croissant flakes, business meetings over breakfast – a ferociously childish and glossy vision of London that took her mind away from the schoolmates she didn't assimilate with. Gertrude saw herself as a director, never an actor: her escape was to facilitate the lives of others from backstage. This much she knew when she researched courses at the Cordon Bleu, the fees sky-high, and her parents adamant that training as a chef was not the type of graduate studies worth her time and their money. He has worked for an insurance company and she for a local solicitor, each for the same company for as long as Gertrude can remember. Gertrude still went to an open night during which canapés were served and a cohort of enrolled students, dressed in white aprons and chef hats, welcomed prospective students. Trainees referenced success stories, smiled and dropped names, but shed not one sliver of light on the financial transactions required to run this show. If you pestered Gertrude, she would admit that she had hoped to find the grass greener elsewhere that night, but reality thundered the same aftershock as the lifestyle her parents were imposing on her and Liam – one in which compromises flatten individuality. Prayers and sacraments, narrow but sharp comments about gender and its illusions, what pronouns Gertrude should identify with, the corruption of ideas and money. Gertrude looked at the uniforms the chefs in training wore, plain white and impersonal, and she felt cold. Cold in her bones. She remembered the white, plain and impersonal clothes she had worn for her baptism – a full immersion in stagnant water at the age of eight – or the plunge into an era of disbelief. This was also the day when her parents smiled with the most teeth. The day when she lost trust in their preaching, although they used the word teaching.

One can never really say no.

Gertrude left the event before the end. She finished school and moved to London with one backpack, and the untested but motivating conviction that being on her own would enable her to find herself. She met Stefano at the second hostel she checked herself into. He recommended her for a job at the Oldfield Tavern, and she worked her way into the kitchen via the front bar. She still dreams of opening a venue of her own and doesn't want to mend her relationship with her parents. It baffles Gertrude how fast people around her fall in and out of love and yet none of them believe that she could cease to love a family member. Every month her credit card bill takes a deeper dive; interest rates are 21.9% APR (variable), but she refuses to be corrupted.

Gertrude exits Paddington station, walks through the taxi corridor, and stands in the area dedicated to the *other* cabs. She queues. The woman next to her could be cast in a luxurious perfume ad; three men behind her devour kebabs loudly; Gertrude breathes in the mayo-yoghurt, pickled cucumber and meat shavings. The traffic on the road is at a standstill, cyclists zigzag around cars. Gertrude looks at them – they who are heading somewhere; she who nests on the side of hospitality – and she exhales, unseen and calm. Her phone vibrates, a notification pops up; the driver is approaching.

Saturday night in London, Cloe is heading out. She stands before the long mirror in her bedroom and finds blemished skin with purple vessels that draw spiderwebs over her eyelids – clues of the secrets she keeps close. Dark hair, the colour of an uneventful night, a prominent square chin she inherited from Francesc while Héloïse had an upturned nose. Narrow forehead, like her mother, who repeated she was too small to swim fast. Her eyes cast over the clock on her bedside table – Cloe is running late.

In the kitchen, a quick spaghetti, pesto (basil) and shaved Parmesan cheese on top, works like an emotional sponge after an afternoon spent with Colette. She must adjust her moods, a birthday party for a childhood friend and the celebration of youth. Cloe eats standing up and in rapid mouthfuls that hurt her thorax.

I owe it to her, a good story to bring home with me.

She plugs in her hair straightener and mixes gin and tonic together. She adds a drop of inexpensive, sour whiskey for Héloïse because her mother knew how to speed up a party, swirling around with allure and delivering quirky anecdotes to friends and acquaintances. She embarrassed Cloe when she joined the parents' evenings at school, only so she could militate for the science curriculum to include, in her words, 'proper' sex education. She initiated public arguments with the council gardeners about their trimming methods after one too many tablespoons of whiskey in her G&T. *It'll be tomorrow's good story, Cloe.* It took a relentless approach for Cloe to convince Colette to let her choose what to write as a dedication on her mother's tomb – *Héloïse, forever tomorrow's good story.* Cloe's chest tightens with the guilt of not having visited her – what if moss covers the writing? Will Héloïse notice that her daughter has not come? – she shakes her head rapidly and downs her drink. Héloïse had a way of knowing everything, the instinct of a woman who had been cheated repeatedly, acute but unreliable. Cloe pours herself a second drink; the straightener has heated up.

With the help of pins, she separates her hair into sections, then grabs a first piece of hair and lifts it up with the straightener, before returning it down, warm and soft. She sips her gin and tonic between patches, the perk of being ambidextrous. Once she is pleased with her hairstyle, she applies a simple combination of foundation and mascara. A denim skirt with a gold sequinned top tucked inside, a quick fix for her nail polish (read: extra layer), electric blue; she clips hoops into her ears and finishes her drink; then a final touch of lipstick, rosy lips before the night.

18

Mathilde

Mathilde goes up two sets of stairs and stands still before the front door of her flat. Her handbag drags her shoulder down as she scrolls through social media, sprinkling half-hearted likes under posts. She soaks in passive updates: Sarah has left the library, the sun sets over Regent's Canal and groups of people sit on the fake grass by the water. The sky is overcast in north London; the city never stops surprising her – its radius, and how varied the forecast can be across neighbourhoods.

A slight dread prevents Mathilde from jiggling her keys inside the lock. Chris, a tall man with no chin, a self-proclaimed pub-quiz champion, her husband-to-be, is waiting so they can cook dinner together.

Mathilde and Chris met at a wedding. They bonded at 1 am, a pivotal time when a hungry stomach cries for carbs and the mind claims another drink. He was sitting by himself on a garden chair, one of his long legs crossed on top of the other, looking at the dance floor. Mathilde had emerged with the same sparkle in her eyes Chris mentions often, grabbed a chair next to him and said, matter-of-fact: 'I'm not sure about the playlist, but lunch was good.'

The ceremony was held at the college where the newly-weds had studied. Chris and Mathilde sat with a leftover bottle of Prosecco, two plastic cups and a few slices of pizza, and they talked at length – about money. In the course of three years of studies, Mathilde had never met someone with whom she felt safe to share her opinions about wealth. At home, her father spoke about finance. In the classroom, the subject was either a topic for arguments with the students who lacked funds or one of fury for the majority who burnt money. Mathilde wanted to understand the workings of finance. Her interest intensified after reading an article about women's wealth: research had found that women were less likely to invest their money, saving it in safer but less profitable bank accounts instead. The journalist concluded that this 'risk-averse' behaviour kept women poorer than men overall and therefore financially dependent. Mathilde was angry. But she had identified the source of her limitations, and Mathilde draws confidence from knowledge.

The communal experience of university – living in student accommodation and meeting classmates at the coffee machine outside the library to plot rebellions that didn't materialise; dating Chris, her great first love – to be away from home, granted Mathilde the aplomb that she can do what she puts her mind to. She was a passionate and dedicated student. Mathilde thinks that she can control who and how she loves, too.

Mathilde slides her engagement ring up and down her right finger, a corner smile lightens her face. She had worried about optics when she decided to switch hand for the ring after her accident, so she wouldn't draw attention to her scarred skin. Chris responded, candidly, that they make the rules under their own roof – and Mathilde had raised her eyebrows with scepticism. So Chris found a grounding fact that Mathilde could use to justify her personal action: his great-grandmother was Norwegian, and in Norway the custom is to wear engagement rings on the right hand. Mathilde never checked his source – although Chris's mother had told her about their family history – and decided not to know more. She has a truth of her own to hold onto, and that matters. She opens the door.

'Do you remember the promise we made to each other the first night we met?'

'You smell of wine.' Chris drops a kiss on Mathilde's dimple.

'But, honestly, do you remember what we said?'

Chris looks at her attentively and reaches for his phone inside his jeans pocket, his eyes locked on Mathilde's. 'The wild card,' he says.

Mathilde nods.

Chris hands his phone over to her. 'Here. I look at it often.

It's not much, but it's there waiting for us whenever we're ready to jump.' Then he approaches her, their shoulders brush against one another, and he starts showing Mathilde where she can access the rates fluctuation history and see the total amount they have saved.

A specific tone distinguishes Chris's voice when he explains something. The words flow slowly but sharply, an ownership that arouses Mathilde as much as it did when they first started dating.

'If we ever wanted to use it, then we would need to request the money by clicking here.' He taps on the screen; a new tab appears. 'See? This is how much we would receive and below there are two lines: one for the bank fees and one that shows by how much our initial investment has grown.' Mathilde pays attention, quiet with the determination that is characteristic of her intentions. The dimple Chris loves delves further into her cheek and her eyes narrow – her facial expressions are more pronounced on the left side than on the right. Chris details the process: 'We're lucky that for now we've made money, otherwise the last line would show a minus instead of the addition sign of course. I'd have to check the terms again, but the money should be with us within seven business days from the moment our withdrawal request is approved.'

'With the rate written here, regardless of what happens across the financial markets during the transaction period, correct?'

'Indeed. The figure you see here is the money you're

guaranteed to receive as of today.' He looks at her again, but with an added layer of accountability. 'But do you remember the first thing I told you when we wired the opening sum?'

'It's a long game,' Mathilde grins, not looking at him, 'like us.'

'Exactly. If we go on to the next page, we'll find some prognostics about what to expect over the next one-, three-, five-, even ten-year periods. None of this is certain, especially now when it's all so unstable, but it gives you an idea of how much of a risk you're taking.'

He zooms in on a graph, and Mathilde grabs his phone.

'We have been together for eight years,' she murmurs.

'And we have proof.'

Mathilde takes Chris's hand in hers and kisses the back of it rapidly.

The story of the night Chris and Mathilde met goes on with the pizza. Chewy cheese and chilled tomato sauce, or with a bite the way Mathilde likes hers. The Prosecco was flat and sour, the night wound down as guests started to leave and the playlist ended. Mathilde and Chris kept talking about what consumes and scares them, breaking into the secrecy of the latter as soon as the crowd faded away: astronomy, cancer, wasps, *The Office* (UK edition), road tunnels. The waiting staff was moving around with oversized bin bags, cleaning and folding trestle tables and chairs. Chris suggested they take a walk, an invitation Mathilde welcomed with enthusiasm, but specifying that she wanted to head to the river Cherwell, a tributary feeding the river Thames. Along the water, she told Chris about missing London, the city where she was born and raised. She described the riverside footpath in Hammersmith, taking sneak peeks at the terrace outside of the River Cafe and stopping to greet the old man who sells jewellery from a small stand further down the way; Mathilde detailed the plurality of London. She was finding life in Oxford asphyxiating, as if she had been set up to fail by an institution protected by a rigid hierarchy that made debating a one-way road to concurring. Chris had agreed with Mathilde on the topic of academia, a system built around quoting and referencing sources that discouraged new knowledge, but he added that nothing ever changes in London either. The functioning of the city was modern, but a whirlwind. Chris confessed to Mathilde that he found the pace too fast and that the constant flow of people, information and happenings made him feel insignificant – a never-ending rush hour that prevented anything new from maturing. Mathilde acknowledged his concerns, but she reframed his views with the notion of scope: things could be different because there is enough unknown to accommodate dreams. This is what is so peculiar to London for Mathilde, who had defied Chris to walk along the Strand without picturing a sudden, vivid fantasy of himself pursuing a career as an actor in a musical; it was *impossible*, she spoke highly. London contaminates its inhabitants with eventualities – *it is toxic*, Mathilde clarified, *like any addiction that needs to be chased until the next fix, on repeat* — a stimulant. The conversation switched gear with the use of the first person next. Mathilde spoke the most: she told Chris that she wanted to make things happen for herself, tiptoeing with shorter sentences. She needed to break up with her parents and their agency over her. She was scared because she had only lived above a safety net. She didn't know if she was fit for anything else. But she had ideas and opinions. She had passions. Chris squeezed Mathilde's hand — a new beginning. Mathilde circled back to the research about women's wealth: she needed to start investing in herself. Chris nodded and told her that he was an impatient child and when he set to learn something new, his mother always told him that even if a mountaineer had already climbed Everest once, they still needed suitable boots the second time around. Mathilde asked Chris about his mother's name and added that she was a wise woman.

The night escalated: he opened a banking app on his phone, swiftly accessed the 'investment' section and talked faster. Chris selected the 'medium risk' option, Mathilde sent him half of the £50 minimum fee required to open that investment account and she set up a direct debit into his account. £20 on the first of each month for what had become their 'shared investment for hopeful break-ups'.

'You can't possibly ghost me now,' Mathilde had said after confirming his sort code.

'Neither can you,' Chris responded.

They walked back to the city centre, where they stopped for a croissant at the bakery near Mathilde's place. They met again for lunch, a few hours later, then dinner, and a series of meals through summertime while they applied for jobs. They found work and then moved in together to a basement flat on the north corner of Putney Bridge. Everyone warned them about it being premature, but they were in love, and the cost of renting a room in London justified their choice. They commuted to the office and fell down a cascade of deadlines, networking events, kilometres on a treadmill, nights out and overtime at work. Chris met Mathilde's friends and he introduced her to his colleagues; each crowd might have had different occupations, but they shared similar roots – approbation was easy to obtain. Mathilde's parents adore Chris, and his mother tolerates Mathilde when she is there, while she grows fond of her when Mathilde steps aside so her fiancé can invite his mum for dinner.

They bought a flat in north London a few years later (the dates aligning with the passing of Chris's grandfather). They still haven't dipped into the investment trust. It has become theirs officially, instead of Chris's in which Mathilde chips in, when they signed the paperwork for the mortgage on their flat. Their credit history merged. During the appointment at the bank, Mathilde pointed at the small typeset paragraphs at the bottom of the pages and asked questions.

'You grilled that guy,' Chris said when they walked out.

'You wouldn't buy a pair of hiking boots without trying them on first, would you?' Mathilde responded.

*

Today, Saturday night: Chris and Mathilde are standing between the living room and the narrow kitchen in their flat, half hugging, half contemplating the phone screen before them.

'Do you ever think about what we could do with this money?' Mathilde breaks their silence.

'I thought about using it for our honeymoon.'

Mathilde considers his suggestion for a few seconds. 'That's not right. This one is for "hopeful break-ups", money for the things we wouldn't use our savings for.'

'And what would that be?'

'Risks!' she says in a breath, before she pauses. 'But that's unfair. I asked you.'

A laugh escapes Chris.

Mathilde picks up the conversation. The thinking wrinkles on her forehead come forward. 'We should also start investing some of our money properly. Check if the fund is green and put in a heftier sum so we can plan for the more traditional things too.'

She has caught Chris's interest. He rubs his nose against her neck as he whispers: 'Tell me more about these traditional plans so I can advise.'

She brightens. 'Like a mini you and me, their education, a house with an actual garden.'

'Interesting. Tell me more about our minis.'

'Plural, I see. Well, between you and me, no blond heads. Hazelnut eyes, verging towards the green, maybe. Clumsy but cute.'

'Cute but clumsy.' He straightens his back so he faces her again. 'Then we're lucky that I've already opened other saving accounts.' He brings her back closer to him, a squeeze, and he adds: 'I take my role as father-to-be very seriously, Mathilde Jenkins-Bell.'

Mathilde's reaction differs from what Chris had pictured. She steps sideways, her eyebrows thick with interrogations, so he starts mumbling with a defensive tone – something about making money work efficiently with interest rates. 'The markets are so unpredictable at the moment,' she hears him cry before explaining that his boss hooked him up with an accountant after handing him his last bonus. His words build patronising sentences that remind Mathilde of Friday night dinners with her family when she was growing up. Her father butted in most conversations with comments about incomes and safety and growth; a discourse meant to assert that only he knew the cost of their comfortable life. Until today, Mathilde entertained the portrait of a relationship of equals with Chris – they both work full-time; they are planning a *modern wedding*. She has always known Chris likes to be in control, but so does she, and she wanted to believe that the equation would balance in their favour.

Mathilde shivers and lets go of a soft cry. 'I hate this.'

Chris stands still. Like a good politician, he dislikes wasting time with counterarguments.

She speaks. 'When were you planning to tell me about this? It's my money too.' She adds something unintelligible, then she says: 'What happened to your great morals about trying on new boots together? You blindsided me.'

He stays quiet, but he gapes. *But I'm telling you now,* she can hear him say.

'If this money is for our future, why wouldn't you want to involve me? You know how important it is for me to pay my share,' Mathilde says.

'I can explain.'

'It's a bit late.'

Mathilde is resentful; Chris knows as much.

He turns his neck away, scanning the kitchen where vegetables are scattered over the counter. He had gone food shopping on his way home after the gym, for an evening he had intended to be predictable. He thought they could divide the chopping duties between them and open a bottle of wine. He anticipated that Mathilde would gobble the olives while talking about her appointment at the hospital earlier this morning, then she would apologise and serve another round of snacks, moving the small serving bowl away from her. He bought a large jar. They would have detailed the rest of their Saturdays to each other, Mathilde sharing the latest gossip from her group of friends and describing the food, including what people at the tables around theirs had eaten, and he would have listened while cooking the curry. Then they would have settled on the sofa, with their backs bent over the small coffee table, and they would have watched a few episodes of *Friends* because when the reunion episode had come out, Mathilde realised that Chris had never watched the iconic series. It was her goal to have him caught up before their wedding day. They have reached the eighth season: a *good thing* that came out of their decision to postpone the wedding after Mathilde's incident. *More time for* Friends, they share an inside joke, an example of Mathilde's conviction that one has agency over love.

Instead, they spoil their appetite with a fight that is explosive at first – reflections on trust and family fly fast without consideration for the point the other is making – then they settle into an apparent truce, built on small talk, which Chris honours but Mathilde attacks.

'How was your lunch with the girls?'

'Women.'

Mathilde has always called her friends *the girls* until this evening. Chris is swirling the vegetables around the pan, refusing to apologise. He avoids conflict, but he hates unsolicited stings the most.

'It was nice. A lot of talking about weddings and babies. They all seem in good form.'

'Good. How was the food?'

'Good.'

He pours in the coconut milk then turns around to look at Mathilde. She responds to sweet scents and his lips unlock tenderly as her nose twitches. 'Well, I'm confident dinner is about to be good too.'

Mathilde blinks, and says: 'Any news about the case in the office?' She regrets asking that question as soon as she does. She means to show Chris his own faults and why he can't bypass her when making decisions – she wants it to hurt, but she nips herself with the broken mirror of a future marriage.

'Not that I'd know of. It's Saturday.'

'It's not like you never work on Saturdays.'

He inhales slowly.

'Is there something you'd like to ask me?'

She is biting her lips and he has noticed. Mathilde must speak her mind.

'I want to hear your version of the story. I've only had the official party line about them having a "playful relationship" and her suddenly calling it "sexual harassment". And, I suppose, while I understand he is your boss and that she was an intern, she deserves to be treated with respect.' She breaks to appraise. 'In my experience, it's never a *sudden* (she spits the word) thing, sexual harassment.' Mathilde grimaces but he isn't looking at her, so she adds with a grave tone: 'She is not making small accusations, and the idea of your name being attached to this story worries me.'

He taps the wooden spoon against the casserole edge brutishly and turns around to face Mathilde. 'I'm confused. Are you worried about the intern's wellbeing, my reputation, or your reputation?' Chris strikes back.

Mathilde refills their wine glasses. She mulls over the problem Chris has just raised.

'All three.' Mathilde is honest. 'Mum was asking me about it the other day and I didn't know what to say,' she adds by way of example.

He thanks her for the wine and takes a sip. Mathilde's

pupils are dilated; Chris cannot move away from their jurisdiction.

He explains. 'I don't like it either. But we've put a plan in place for her to get better. She has received medical help and she is being seen by a therapist who handles sexual harassment cases in the workplace. According to her state-ment, he never touched her. There were just some emails and photos I wish I'd never had to picture.' Mathilde gasps to interrupt him, her blood boiling at the use of the word *just* and disappointed with herself for not having asked about the girl's name, but Chris's talking pace doesn't allow her to jump in. 'As for me, I want to do the right thing. I've had meetings with our communications department, and I'll publish an official statement to condemn his actions as well as to denounce how unresponsive the trustees were at making the necessary structural changes.' He drinks more wine. 'As for you, this was never about you, so you'll have to explain your concerns before I can answer.' His bottom lip hangs open.

Mathilde steps in front of the hob and stirs the curry absently. A long minute passes.

'People are always more intransigent towards women. They'll praise you for speaking up, but I'll be blamed for not stopping the story before it broke.'

'But you don't even work there.'

Both have forgotten about the intern at this point in the conversation.

'Whether you want it or not, we're teamed up.' Mathilde

switches the cooker off, then covers the casserole so the curry can settle.

'Do you even want to be teamed up with me?' he asks rapidly.

'I do,' she slips. 'But I also care about my work at the women's centre. Have you thought about that? This could hurt my professional reputation. Things are real over there and we can't afford to exploit people's life stories like politicians do.' Credentials matter to Mathilde.

'Are you implying that I knew what was going on with the girl?' The girl creeps back in his mind, a messenger coming to serve him. This loud voice doesn't suit Chris.

'Woman.' Mathilde hears him become defensive, like someone who has been found guilty.

Chris tucks his chin inside his neck, his eyes shallow, immobile. He covets Mathilde's verbal fluency.

Mathilde restarts, with a softer cadence: 'I don't think that you knew.' She touches his hand briefly before stepping away. 'But I wish you had involved me from the moment you heard.'

'I can see that.'

She looks him in the eye.

'I'm sorry,' he adds.

She grabs two bowls inside the cupboard. 'Marriage is hard work. I need to be able to trust you.'

Mathilde is serving portions of rice and curry. Chris stands at the other end of the kitchen counter.

'Is this about the savings account again?'

'This is about us building something together. Can you grab forks?' He does. 'Next week, I want us to find a moment to go through the paperwork and for you to bring me up to speed with our finances.'

Mathilde is holding the two fuming bowls, facing him. Chris nods again before asking: 'Could I also show you the press release we drafted in the office? I'd like to publish it on Monday.'

'Let me guess, not a single woman was in the room when it was drafted?'

He smiles briefly. 'And I'd love your opinion.'

'The food is getting cold,' she says as she steps forward. 'Bring both the release and the wine with you. We have a long night ahead of us.' She walks into the living room, and he hears her reaching for the place mats inside the chest of drawers. Mathilde is settling at the dining table.

Chris sits next to her. She slides the place mat sideways, so it lays before him, her eyes inquisitive as she pivots her body to face him.

'It's easier to look at the release in front of us if we sit next to one another,' he explains.

19

Gertrude and Cloe

Gertrude touches both her shoulders, signing a cross at the door of her flat. The gesture surprises her; a sneeze, she dusts her superstitions away with rapid head movements. Gertrude is not religious, but the child of pious parents, and tonight she prays for Liam not to be home.

On the way, Gertrude built an unapologetic appetite. She wanted to chew dinner loudly without the fear of a consuming silence and not to split the bill, to date herself – *yes, yes, this is pleasure* – so Gertrude executed the fine, urban art of timing both her cab and takeaway order.

Lights off, she steps out of her shoes, then she drops her bag and the pizza box in the living room. Her choice is endorsed by the smell of Gorgonzola, rich and cloudy.

guilty pleasure, flaws, a steal

She heads to the bedroom, braids her hair roughly, takes

off her bra, and trades Liam's shirt and jeans for loose-fit clothes. Saturday night patching over an afternoon hangover: Gertrude cheats with her routine.

Upon arrival at the club, a robust and smiley bouncer greets Cloe: 'Can I see your ID, love?' He scans her from head to toe, toe to head.

She slides a hand inside the pocket of her blazer without taking her eyes away from him, and she shows the bouncer her driving licence. Cloe steps inside the club and the music blares out – disorientating, the spotlights on the ceiling flash blue and pink. Self-conscious, Cloe hides her confusion by heading to the bar. She must find her friends.

'A shot of tequila and a bottle of San Miguel,' she orders. Her voice sounds louder than necessary, unpleasant and impolite, yet the bartender asks her to repeat her order. Cloe does, he acknowledges her, she pays. She downs the shot and walks away with the beer in one hand. People in motion blur her vision; in the spotlight, she pulls her skirt down like a good pupil before a supervisor who measures the length of skin between girls' knees and skirts. A ten-centimetre rule to define how appropriate a person should be, a prejudice. Cloe mutters, but nobody can hear a word of what anyone is saying – nods, thumbs up, fast movements, the loneliness of a crowd. There are party balloons with Happy Birthday written on them tied to the back of chairs, though not the birthday she has come to celebrate, and coats are piled up on velvet sofas and feathers are sown over the dance floor; solo dancers and those who draw circles among themselves; signs show the direction of the smoking area, a meeting point for anyone who loses their peers. The night elevates outside: music bloats out and chatters break into conversations, blinding garden lights under the deep night sky. Cloe heads out.

'Do you have a lighter?'

'What's your name?' the man asks in response. He is ruffling his hair with one hand and holding a cigarette in the other.

'Sorry, I'm just looking for my friends.'

He hands Cloe a lighter and adds: 'It's busy tonight. You can stay with my lot, if you'd like.' He points his finger at a group of men behind him.

Cloe examines her cigarette, pivoting it sideways with one hand, and she draws in two fast inhales. She can't smoke quick enough when he is looking at her.

'I should really find my friend. It's her birthday.' Cloe walks towards the ashtray but he stops her, his hand holding the top of her elbow.

'I really want to know your name.' His breath strokes her face, standing too close for her taste.

'Cloe.' She steps back, and he lets go of her arm.

'See you in there, Cloe.'

Inside the enclosed nightclub, Cloe follows the logic of moving in the opposite direction of the enthusiastic tide of partygoers, a self-preserving strategy to avoid mingling. She walks up the stairs first, fast, before making her way back downstairs. She swipes through each room, stopping at the bar on the second floor for another bottle of beer, the fresh liquid; strange bodies step aside so she can walk past them. She should be dancing too. She should be smiling. She should be waving at the DJ when they interrupt the music to shout vague political statements – strikes, Tories and utility bills – but Cloe feels twitchy instead. She hears cheap arguments; everyone watches but nobody listens. She has no phone signal between the thick, fire-proofed walls – one, solitary tick next to her text messages to her friend. Cloe steps into the bathroom, a final stop before heading home.

Women talk to each other from one cubicle to the other, paper rolls unrolled across the floor, water leaks, make-up retouches and sprays of deodorant. Those who fix their hair-style under the hand dryer. Static electricity, camaraderie, an ask to be seen instead of looked at, the energy echoes with her memory of the changing rooms at the swimming pool. A place where friendship seeds, matures and rots swiftly because reflections inside the mirrors of public spaces tear apart the image one entertains of their self. *I love this top! You look great!* The welcome reassurance from a stranger; generous in part, an upbeat gesture to hear *so do you* in return, an inclusive but demanding exchange. Cloe stands, immobile, slowly washing her hands once, twice, staring at the dichotomy between her perceived and actual selves. Flashy sequins design her top, the hair she had styled with care now appears dry and heavy, her pale complexion marks the promise of showing bags under her eyes tomorrow. The ugly side of going out, the forced effort to mix and match; she walks back outside.

'Cloe. You again.' She has fallen face to face with him. 'Do you want to dance?'

'Okay,' she surprises herself.

This is when the rhythm of Cloe's night quickens. Another shot of tequila, climbing up to the third floor of the club where electronic music hammers through large stereos, a break on the ground floor where a playlist of classics initiates new friendships, a gin and tonic, maybe two, dancing and befriending strangers. Fun, until. Flashes.

Thin pizza crust, the safety of grease and carbs after a social afternoon; a dairy cuddle and the purple rain of onions. Eyes itch, redden, tears.

> *i slice*
> *thinner, thinner, thinner*
> *i bite,*
> *i slice, i eat*
> *pat on the back, i slice, i bite*

Gertrude grabs a small plate, a knife and a fork, so she can drag dinnertime on into a lasting affair. She sits on the floor and cuts each slice into smaller bits of dough. A TV show streams on her laptop while she consumes more media on her phone. She lists the meals she would like to cook, the documentaries she should watch and the books she must read in her notebook, juggling fork, knife and pen – a show of Gertrude's distracted effort to have something to say to someone who isn't her. She swallows, pumping noise inside her ears as the screen before her renews images – a so-called 'reality' TV show portrays lives far from her truth.

'A group of men and women participate in a series of tasks with a partner who they swap until they meet the love of their life,' the show description reads. *The love of their life*, Gertrude repeats to herself with a soft tone, her voice almost inaudible. She takes another mouthful of pizza – the modern need to frame the illogical emotion of loving – and reads the description again. *They swap until they meet the love of their life.* She considers the sentence – *isn't it what we all do?*

> *i swipe,*
> *i date, i swap*
> *a bargain to love,*
> *i trade to be loved*

Gertrude trades fork for hands. Another mouthful of pizza in pursuit of her appetite to bypass, to live, to be insatiable. She begins doodling something – Gertrude who can never focus fully, she who starts with putting on a pair of socks when she dresses and who catches herself brushing her teeth with half her clothes on. Her parents had instructed her child-self to take pills under a strict schedule – *to calm your nerves*, they had justified – and she visited a speech therapist weekly – *to help you make sense of your thoughts and to organise them*, they explained – she who always needs correcting. Liam, in comparison, had good grades despite a poor school attendance, scoring high with the rugby team; Liam who makes everyone laugh. Gertrude who can't spell.

> *i audition*
> *for a role in my life;*
> *will you pick me?*
> *even if i tell you the truth about me,*
> *if i say no to who you wanted me to be?*
> *i audition,*
> *a sunflower in winter*

By the time Gertrude has finished the pizza, her doodles have consolidated into a familiar drawing. You would see plays on forms, colours and perspective and you would call the result abstract, but Gertrude sees a swarm of bees. Not any bees, the ones that chase her – they are remorse, solitude, abandonment. Gertrude stands up, pins and needles tickle her ankles, she grabs her laptop and moves into the kitchen. *Let's take care of you*, she whispers as she reaches for the jar where she stores her sourdough starter. The TV show still plays in the background, a row of men and women talk to the camera while they sit on a large, burgundy sofa. As if they were kneeling at the confessional, they lie about their emotions and achievements. *Sad girl sourdough, it's between you and me tonight* – Gertrude pours a spoon of the mother starter into a baking bowl with some luke-warm water. She uses her fingers to break the mixture, pleased with the self-assignment of following a recipe. She sets the bowl aside and begins measuring two different types of flour: two hundred and fifty grams of wholemeal and one hundred and fifty grams of spelt. She combines the diluted starter and the mixed flours, and she begins kneading with confidence. The dough dries out, so she adds another gulp of lukewarm water, slowly. More water, then she continues to work her fingers. Chemistry and feelings combine, the familiar fragrance of homemade bread, the minimum knowledge required to make the final product rise inside the oven and taste good. She works with a 75 per cent hydration dough, roughly; she bends the measurements rule the most, the season weighing in, shifting temperatures, humidity, air pressure. Gertrude recognises her intuition when she bakes with her sad girl's sourdough starter – a row of small happenings that heal her fidgety brain. Focus and purpose, one task at a time. Once the dough has come together into a homogeneous ball, she leaves it to rest under a tea towel for ten minutes. She watches the TV pro-gramme with more attention during the waiting period: two couples are on a date. Candles fire things up, chimichurri sauce dresses steaks. He is wearing a gold silk shirt and she is dis-playing beautiful, colourful jewellery around her neck and on her fingers. *Obviously*, Gertrude breathes out, and she kneads for another ten minutes. The ten-minute break repeats: he is asking her about her parents, if they are married, what they do for a living, and she laughs softly between each response.

Typical, Gertrude sighs. Inheritance and identity. She kneads for another ten minutes. The woman on the TV has taken over the questioning, asking him about his work and where he sees himself in five years. He stutters – Gertrude stops kneading so she can watch him battling with language. She has lost count of the number of kneading rounds she has completed, but she persists until she finds a balance between holding an elastic and a strong dough in her hands. Gertrude returns the dough inside the bowl, covers it with a tea towel, and leaves it to rise in a corner of the kitchen counter overnight.

The primitive relationship between ownership and touch – *mine.*

She fetches a chocolate bar from inside the cupboard – milk, extra creamy – and sits on the sofa with the laptop on her knees. The date ends with a romantic dream of a part- nership and a soft kiss. Gertrude tidies the chocolate away, her mouth furry and her teeth thick with a sugar coating. She sits there, in silence, immobilised by an afternoon gone with the waves. Her defensiveness, the German boy she went on a date with, the location and why she had agreed to meet him in person. Him, a random man, someone she had only texted before. The social work of being herself while show- ing that she tries hard enough to be compelling to others. It was easy to believe that he could be a good one; it will be harder to mend the side of herself he uncovered – embit- tered, watchful. Yet it was fun, thrilling to tell Liam and to ask him to dress her, to borrow his shirt. She felt close to her brother – to her family.

Gertrude thinks of loving and fucking as a troublesome pair. Her sexuality and her relationship with sex, her choice to reject what is imposed yet doesn't work on her; the possibilities of love and pleasure, the simplicity of feeling for someone and this beckoning sexual attraction, a miss; the secret she keeps from others.

> *love me, love me not*
> *a choreography with my identity*
> *don't touch but*
> *love me not, love me*
>
> *would you still love me*
> *if I said no,*
> *no to sex, would you still love me?*
>
> *i never want to die for love*
> *no,*
> *i never want to say no*
> *to reason, not for love*
>
> *love me not, love me*
> *a choreography with my identity*
> *don't touch but*
> *love me, love me not*

'It can all happen again. Petals fall off flowers, you'll remember. Deep down, you've always known.' Gertrude checks her horoscope on her phone and goes to bed.

20

Sarah

Since when do you change your passwords?

Online. Typing . . . Nothing. *Typing* . . .

What do you mean, dear?

Never mind.

Ok. Good night my dear.

Sarah huffs. She enters another password – error message – so she waves at Agnes for help.

I wanted to listen to an audiobook while I take a bath.
I have one downloaded in your library already.

Without delay, the response arrives.

Why didn't you ask me?

It's been a stressful day.

Can you give me some context?

It is as if her skin was about to explode into a rash, only it never does, and therefore there is no treatment for this state of being. She reckons that her body will attack itself until it stops operating. She considers saying exactly that to Agnes – plainly – but she refrains herself. If only her mother could understand her daughter's pains without needing her to explain.

Sarah's chronic pains have made her someone who anticipates the unplanned constantly. She expects a flare-up will make her cancel on someone or change tickets for an exhibition; don't mention booking holidays to her; Sarah has stopped pencilling dates in her diary. When she feels hopeless, she bookmarks sensational articles listed at the bottom of websites: 'This miracle gloss whitens teeth without the intervention of a dentist!', 'This is how this woman bought five sports cars!', 'The secret behind these revolutionary hearing aids!' Fake or real news, it doesn't matter to Sarah because they convey life to her, something irrational and hyperbolical. Just today she read about a mother who was watching *EastEnders* lying on her sofa at home until a car crash on the TV triggered an 'out-of-body' experience. The woman told the journalist that she had jumped out of the house in her pyjamas and had driven to her daughter's house without thinking about which direction she was going. 'Her instinct had taken her to her daughter,' the article detailed, and this is how mother had found daughter sitting in her car, the engine still off but the keys inserted, unconscious after having suffered a seizure. The last sentence confirmed the daughter was fully recovered and had been diagnosed with epilepsy when she was twelve years old. The interviewed mother reported having been subject to many of these 'out of-body' experiences, *her choice of name,* the article detailed, since her daughter's diagnosis – and this made Sarah envious.

It still pains Sarah that Agnes had refused to look at her daughter's symptoms truthfully when they started – 'Have you taken an Ibuprofen, dear?' Agnes yelled from the kitchen on the ground floor – bouts of fevers and regular visits to the doctor's after Sarah's swollen joint in her left foot made her limp. She didn't suppose it was a cause for great concern – 'She'll be fine. She is growing too fast for her body to cope,' she justified, stubborn with her use of the third person even though Sarah was sitting next to her. Her refusal to see her daughter's body fail. Agnes didn't object to Sarah's loss of appetite; her dry eyes were caused by all the hours she spent in front of a screen, headaches because she didn't eat, and the subsequent fatigue; anecdotes that excluded something bigger. Still, when a flush derailed into a high fever, Agnes stitched Sarah's mind back together with dignity, patting wet flannels one after the other over her daughter's forehead, pearls of sweat and feverish confessions past midnight. While Sarah's mother doesn't subscribe to small attentions, she is pragmatic. She kept a specific diary for medical appointments and tidied the referral letters inside a folder, whose colour she had asked Sarah to choose. Agnes stirred the fizz away from a glass of Coke after each stomach upset, she held Sarah's legs slightly up to release some of her back pains, tireless through nights of nursing. Between waiting rooms, blood tests and scan results, Agnes had lost her temper only once: when the family doctor prescribed steroids to Sarah at the early stage of her treatment. A short period so Sarah could recover from some of the inflammation and grow stronger, but Agnes cawed. *I can still hear her bones cracking open.* The doctor reassured her that the prescription wouldn't be long enough to cause osteoporosis. She cried again. They would monitor her. *Her bones broke like glass.* Agnes stamped her foot and Sarah understood that *Her* referred to her grandmother and that no questions should be asked. Ibuprofen works, but her stomach has softened. Sarah never held her father accountable for any of the above – but she couldn't articulate why if you asked her.

Mum, please. Can I use your account?

A second, rapid message: It's included in your subscription.

Ok.

A short break, palpitations and glassy eyes.

It's the day of Mathilde's birth, 05 and your
year of birth.

05. Agnes doesn't specify that the number stands for the
month of May, when she was born, streamlining the data that
spells her password. *05*, or an example of the pride that steals
her mother's joys. Agnes can eat profiteroles with a gargan-
tuan appetite, but always leaves the last one for Sarah because
she knows the cloud of cream and melted chocolate will
make her daughter beam. The details she knows instinctively
so Mathilde can have the best of hen dos. The shadows of
Agnes, or the domestic life of their family, daughters before
mother before public appearances.

The phone vibrates again: Keep your inhaler next to
you. You're prone to attacks when you're in water.

Sarah considers telling her mother that she is learning to
swim again. She goes to the Brockwell Lido on Tuesday
evenings where she has a personal instructor, a man in his late
thirties who wears the same burgundy swim trunks every
week and who looks at the water the way someone who hates
being wet does. She wonders if he knows how to swim. She
loves to pet her pruney fingers at the end of a lesson – swimming frees her sheltered body and removes her tag as the girl
who almost drowned and who has been ill ever since. She

started with lengths of breaststroke to gain confidence, then she learnt how to crawl. She can do the crawl! Sarah fell for the practice of swimming: the mechanics of her movements and the logic of her fingers and spine flow-through, so she can brace more water with less physical impulsion. Her senses lift when she performs strokes, then dives and swims back, shorter sight and compression, a funnel that forbids her from thinking. Sarah doesn't tell her mother about the swimming lessons – she is protective about her source of pleasure, a selfish joy.

Love you mum she sends instead.

Sarah opens the tap, the distant sound of a waterfall, a squeeze of shampoo instead of bubble bath, an old candle she struggles to light. The wax has melted and the wick is cut short, but she succeeds and re-loads the audiobook platform on her phone while the bathtub fills up. Foam forms, she logs into her mother's account, tries to pair her phone with the Bluetooth stereo once, twice, she swears, and she repeats. She places her inhaler (the *little worm*, as Mathilde called it when they were children) within easy reach, then she turns off the tap. Sylvia Plath; the audiobook launches, a favourite at the end of a day when she feels unheard.

The narration begins. A suffocating summer in New York City, the year when the Rosenberg couple was electrocuted. Sarah puts one foot inside the bath and sees her ankle colour into the shade of an immature cherry. She waits so she can acclimate while the voice narrates something about nerves and being burnt alive. Electrocution. Sarah hums a song by the famous French singer who died in his bathtub briefly. She vaguely remembers lyrics about Alexandria, the rumours about a hair dryer and the dangers of a bathroom. She is standing still with one foot inside the bathtub only; the water is too hot for her taste; she always makes the same mistake. She loses balance and takes a plunge. She settles, closes her eyes and tries to find calm against Esther Greenwood's angst.

How long has it been?

Probably half an hour.

'Chapter Two,' the narrator reads.

Only page 13. Sarah knows the book well. She has a bias towards the modern classics she has either read or listened to compulsively over the years – penned societies of manners constructed around identifiable and therefore recognisable patterns that tame her fears – and so *The Bell Jar* appeals today. She could use her library card to access more audio-books, but this wouldn't give her the same thrill. Sarah wants her mother to help her – she wants it to sound needy but for the execution to feel cosy, like a privileged demand to be loved.

Sarah turns around, sliding onto her stomach, her back bending with her legs up and her feet curving around the bath taps. Her big toe burns against the hot pipe, she bends her back further, her toes are touching the backs of her thighs, making a knot in her spine. She flips around again.

The water is putting pressure on her chest, warmth invades her thorax like a high tide working its way along her throat. *I cannot breathe.* What if this Saturday is the day when she cannot breathe *for real*? *Don't cry wolf, Sarah bird!* she hears.

She closes her eyes and focuses on the audiobook. *Focus on Esther Greenwood, Sarah. Focus.*

A yellow striped swimsuit, her hair the colour of smoked walnuts as a witness of summertime. The visage of a child, round and puffy. Sarah hid her face inside the stomach of her stuffed toy while the adults talked about her during the blissful periods they spent in Wales as a family. The days gravitated around walks and long meals, the house was made of white stones. Sarah misses her grandfather who smells of Jakemans' liquorice sweets, her grandmother and the bouquets of apple, cherry and plum tarts drawing her silhouette along with the seasons. The family never returned to Wales for a week-long holiday after Sarah's accident, however exhausted their mother was, despite the grey tone of their father. He talks behind his hand when he calls his parents on the phone. They send cards for Christmas, New Year, Easter and birthdays. Mathilde, Sarah and their father took short weekend trips when Agnes had social engagements elsewhere (the kinds that made good excuses: fundraisers, an opening at the gallery where she works part-time), and the grandparents visit occasionally. The last time was for Sarah's master's graduation ceremony. The mood was fine: the adults had tuned their memory harmoniously, yet they couldn't escape their respective culpability. Sarah knows the truth too: her mother refuses to be anywhere near that body of water, but nobody wants to name her trauma. *Agnes was the mother*, if this silence could speak. Accountability, a deceitful postpartum, whether the family wants to address the topic or not.

Sarah pushes her hair back so she can wash it, but not deep enough to submerge her face fully. The water murky, she yearns for the aquamarine of the treated pool. A quick shampoo, and she is out. The water empties, gurgling down the drain, and Sarah sits on the edge of the bath, wrapped up inside her bathrobe. The timer on her phone screen reads seventeen minutes, the black and gold audiobook cover, an alluring helix and the oneiric name of *Sylvia Plath*. Thirst. Sarah pushes her palm flat underneath her collarbone, the weight of her thinking, the raft that rescues her, or the mind she can put to work when her body won't follow her ideas.

Sarah stays there, still with her hair dripping, her stare facing forward but cut short by the wall of her narrow bathroom. She stays like this for longer than she was in the bath – a moment of her own and the result of having tried and loathed dozens of meditation apps over the years. Breathing exercises or small meditative workouts that fit around a modern lifestyle (they suit an office job!). She even found one that had introduced her to morning pages. Sarah bought a yoga block, a wristband made of silicone that promises better balance and something about how energies flow between bones, muscles and nerves. She routinely spends more money on stationery than she is willing to pay for her weekly food shopping. She has become a skilled planner when it comes to completing her thesis (deadlines, word-count targets, keywords for each chapter), and she masters Trello boards and Google Calendar features. She has bought calming sprays and other natural remedies. Then she renewed her relationship with water; two ways. At the lido, Sarah found the possibility of active meditation with the help of goggles and the guiding lane lines at the bottom of the pool. With swimming, Sarah has discovered that a different fight with life takes place in water, and she feels rewarded when she walks out of the leisure centre. There, on the edge of her bathtub, with her skin steaming and the stinging odour of trapped humidity, Sarah can inhale and retain a thought.

Past conversations resonate differently inside the white noise of water too. Sarah lives in student accommodation for which she receives a preferential rent rate as part of her studentship. The building isn't located on campus but in south London, and homes both postgraduate students and university staff. The hall is wide and the floor is covered with a carpet made of synthetic fabric that is cut short and sharp, the colour of thick petrol with the addition of indiscernible geometric shapes. It reminds Sarah of space maps for children, a hint of astronomy to give dimensions to the narrowness of the lives of those who reside in the building. She had shared her observation with Mathilde, who questioned her views.

'How do you know their lives are sad?'

'I didn't use the word "sad".'

'Narrow is pretty sad.'

'No, not necessarily.'

'I think so, Sarah. What's the point of a narrow life?'

'What's the point of happiness?'

'Don't attack me.'

'I meant narrow as everyone seems to have a definitive routine. I cross paths with the exact same people in front of the lift every day.'

'They must think the same about you.' She paused, looking expectantly past Sarah's shoulders, and added: 'Or they probably have office hours.'

'I never said I was better.'

A silence settled.

Sarah continued: 'It gives me some David Lynch movie vibes in there.'

'What, like you're expecting to see some replica of Elephant Man walking out of the lift?' Mathilde replied and Sarah sat back.

'No, more like *Blue Velvet*.'

They both whispered of night skies darker than velvet – the iconic soundtrack of nightmares catching dreams.

'All these locks and fobs, they make me suspicious. What do they all have to hide so carefully?' Sarah asked.

'People want to feel safe,' Mathilde responded. 'Which is understandable.'

'But it's quite the opposite. I feel there must be something really ugly hiding under the surface if we all must take cover behind locked doors and habits.'

Their eyes met, but Mathilde didn't engage with Sarah's point. She offered material solutions instead: they could go shopping for some organisers for Sarah's jewellery and stationery, then to another shop for some curtains and perhaps a bedside table. Candles and bedsheets too, and Sarah learnt that since her sister moved in with Chris, she has become a linen sheets type of person. She woke up, suddenly, when Mathilde said her name – *Sarah bird, are you listening? We need to build you a nest* – insisting upon her sister's assent. They could end the trip with a lunch.

Sarah resented Mathilde for suggesting she should own more stuff to compartmentalise her existence, and the Jenkins-Bell sisters never went homeware shopping together. Mathilde and Sarah are sisters indeed: they know the other genealogically, but not presently. They are bound to disappoint one another.

Sarah's studio flat has plain walls (the lease agreement forbids hanging frames), a two-person table made of white plastic, but the chairs are turquoise. The kitchen is composed of a small fridge, one work surface and an induction hob. The kettle was provided, white, and the knives are safe for children to use. The bed fits perfectly between the bookshelves and the wall, there is no room to walk on either side so Sarah must jump in from the end of the bed – a detail she often uses to describe her home: narrow.

The usual Saturday night disruptions unravel outside of Sarah's window. Smoke plumes from portable barbecues and weed; the smell of grass, picnic blankets and circles of people scatter across Peckham Rye. That is Sarah's definition of solace. The crowds outside, their howling, a distraction while she cooks a meal for one.

She uncaps a bottle of lager, and she cooks. She follows one, simple rule in her kitchen: the setting only accommodates recipes with three ingredients. Tonight is spaghetti with courgettes, eggs and Parmesan. Four ingredients, but three if she omits the implied carbs, Sarah corrects. Sarah talks with herself when she is alone; her anxiety runs loose in the absence of a spectator. She starts with cutting the courgettes into long, thin strips. Sarah approaches the task slowly, the blade of the cooking knife she gifted herself sharp and the few sips of beer she has drunk already making her feel fuzzy, the warmth of living on the eighth floor of a building. She groups the chopped vegetable on one side and begins organising the work surface with the method that suits her brain: the packet of spaghetti is placed near the hob, the induction cooker beeps, and the water is set to boil; she grates Parmesan cheese and leaves it in a bowl next to the courgettes. The box of eggs is also open and within reach; she has plotted a chain of ingredients. It feels good, after a day of looking at a blank page, of reading over what she has already written – *The opening chapter is a wonderful exercise of style*, her first assessment had concluded. It was a relief, considering the amount of time she had spent working on these same pages, her commitment not to produce anything new, her refusal to write more, hence her relentless editing of the past. The blank page, a gulp of olive

oil and the sizzling noise of frying food ahead of summer –
she throws the courgettes into the pan and stirs until they are
tender. One hand swirls, then the other brings the refreshing
beer to her lips, cool and bubbly. Heat off, Sarah sets the courgettes aside and adds a pinch of salt to the boiling water, then a
handful of pasta and a couple of extra spaghetti strands to ease
her worrisome appetite. She looks at the long sticks loosening
as they dive into water. Some are entangled and others stick to
the side of the pot: Sarah attempts to rescue them but forfeits.
She smiles, still, a thrill settling in her lower stomach. She
beats one egg together with an extra yolk and the Parmesan
cheese. She beats with more energy than she thought she had
in her, Sarah *the hyper*, Sarah who can be in charge. She knows
the pace will quicken next (this is her signature dish), and so
she moves the bottle of beer out of the way to the dining table.
She returns the courgettes to a low heat, making sure they
don't overcook but are warm enough that they will lure the
egg to form a glossy coat without scrambling. She adds the
pasta and mixes everything: the noise satisfies her, a mush,
a child jumping inside a puddle, with yellow rainy boots;
Sarah turns the heat off and incorporates the final touch of
egg, together with a spoonful of the cooking water. She stirs,
stirs, stirs. This is what hunger can make her do, her desires
that subject her to doing. Dinner time. She eats with her hair
still wet, sirens populating the streets in the background, a
buzzing city, she lives.

When Sarah walks back to the sink, she checks her phone
on the way out of habit, and instantly regrets doing so.

Breaststrokes

Kristina: What are you up to?

She drops the plate into the sink and she takes a deep breath.
Turns the tap on, off.

Sarah: Come over.

21

Cloe

The intensity of a workout, a vivid heartbeat pulses inside my neck, the stretch of my muscles and the feeling of breaking free from the limitations the shell of a body imposes over a woman's life, but the lightness of being carried away with the tempo and then the pleasure of falling out of it. This is how I dance: a bond between the day that has gone and the night ahead, a show and tell, an expression of myself and the opportunity to rewrite who I am. My eyes are closed when I dance, my head empties and my feet tap. Tap, tap, tap. My knees bend and my arms extend – stretch, stretch, stretch – my forearms waving as an invitation to the rest of my body to follow the gesture, to lengthen and to inhabit a space. Just like I swam to become a woman, I exist when I dance; I do and I feel. I dance, I sweat, I close my eyes.

I thought about going home. I went to the bathroom, a final stop before the bus journey, the infamous red blotches of London's roads.

There I saw them – the unapologetic women – and I wanted to be one of them. What I felt was envy. There is no other word for this seizing burst of jealousy that could have made me do anything. I craved luscious lips to turn my lipstick into an accessory other than a costume, I wanted a piercing on my belly button and the confidence to show it; I wish I could walk and dance perched on heels. They made my tattoos look childish. I was convinced that I was alone, and I am. I miss my swimming team. I could have done anything to join their movement, screaming fiercely from each side of the thin panels between the toilet cubicles, them rowing and a silent version of myself. My silence.

I find talking difficult. To speak up is harder, but even the chatting part I find difficult. There is a certain kind of pressure when looking for the correct word – to grant meaning to a felt experience that would be accurate from my perspective and the one of others. That is the challenge: I want the description to be truthful to my experience and for it to translate so my interlocutors can portray me with realism. My reality. But the problem is that I never had a creative flair – I have endurance and I could hold a plank for the longest in my team, but that is it. I'm raw. If I tried to describe the situation with words, then I would acknowledge an event has taken place; then, if I shared these words with others, I would ask them to acknowledge that specific event has happened to me. I would redefine myself before the eyes of those who surround me, making me vulnerable. A submissive woman, but I can manipulate and be vain and spit over truth. I'm raw and rotten. You would be too. I have tried to lay down some of my thoughts on paper, in part for myself, but also so I could share them with others: a mea culpa against my passive lies. I don't say no, therefore I say yes. I don't speak up, therefore I agree. But I cannot write the words. I have managed hasty notes on my phone because typing accommodates my thoughts best, a brisk expression that won't be regarded as serious, a hiding place where I can be honest with myself. A room in the cloud of my phone storage where I have no jury apart from my own self. The speed of writing on a keyboard allows intimacy, and so does dancing more than talking does. So, last night, I stepped out of the bathroom, and I took a hopeful plunge.

I danced to say that I am sorry.

Sorry that I don't talk. Sorry that I don't take part in the political discourse more actively. Sorry that I buy fast fashion. Sorry that I don't have a firm opinion about the Depp v Heard case. Sorry that I buy leeks and courgettes in plastic packaging. Sorry that I didn't post on my social media about the Roe v Wade case, that I haven't quite understood the meaning of it – a Supreme Court ruling that made abortion illegal in thirteen states – that I defer the judgement to something far away from home. Sorry that I keep rewatching Annie Hall. *Sorry that my choices are not political. Sorry that with my silence, I consent.*

I remember meeting him again. There he was, standing on the other side of the bathroom door with his shiny hair, looking odd and inoffensive. I found him attractive. I didn't want to feel this way, but there I felt noticed, therefore there I existed. He asked if I wanted to dance, and I said yes. To that, I said yes. I had consumed my cocktail for confidence: a shot of tequila with a side of San Miguel lager, the kick of white alcohol and the cooling follow-up. I know that I would have lowered my guard after that pairing. Still, I drank it. I can trace three rounds from my credit card statement, with a more expensive transaction on top. Later in the night, maybe drinks for the two of us? I must have agreed to pay because my credit card doesn't allow contactless payments.

I can see lights, flashes of them, I can see hands, brushing the air along with the booming sound of the music, a mass on the brain, a lift underneath the feet. Flashes from phone screens and selfies, an invitation to record our transgressions into the night. The regrets that arise early in the morning – pink sky and purple clouds, dreamy and intoxicating London – the meticulous choreography between those who are heading home and the ones who jog before work. The drought inside my body and the layer of grease over my hair, a perfume I don't recognise, an itch, itchy itchy skin. I was touched, this much I know. I'm scared and I pass my fingers through my panties, swollen and warm, my cheeks burn but my tears are ice-cold.

I'm sorry that I cannot remember the details about what happened. I'm sorry for myself that I cannot tell my story. But I do have an instinct; would you listen to that narrative? Would you trust my instinct the way I can feel it plucking my cells? The shame that is burning my skin from the inside. I didn't want to sleep with him, you've heard me say it now. I have lost a piece of myself in the process – a few hours of memory and my integrity – and I hurt. I'm sorry about the women in the bathroom, that I couldn't be their ally. I'm sorry that I let this happen to me, like I always do ... What if? I should have known better. I should have gone home. I should have worn something different. I shouldn't have been drinking that much. Or maybe he shouldn't have benefited from the situation? Did he ask? Did I say yes? Three letters that are easy to guess when someone is failing to articulate properly, an easy word to put into someone's mouth. I know as much, but I don't know how to convince you with my suspicions.

I should have said no.

Could I have consented to something I don't remember? Who establishes the rules about what consent is? Who owns the language around its narrative? How can a system accommodate the subjective experience of individuals? How can policies bend to the lexicon of the traumatised selves? Does last night stamp my body as political? Do scars speak for themselves? I wish, I hope.

I find talking difficult and I'm sorry about that. Even when I'm silent, please consider that I might be saying no. Please do not take my consent for granted – I am my own person. All I wanted to do was dance because I don't know how to speak up on behalf of my feelings.

PART 5

Sunday Evening

22

Cloe, Gertrude, Mathilde and Sarah

Gertrude grabs an extra couple of glasses and pours a few drops into one for Sarah to taste first. She nods with approval, and Gertrude goes around anti-clockwise to serve wine to the three women, the colour of crystal under the sun. Mathilde is served last, and she thanks Gertrude, only to ask the question on the tip of her tongue: 'Can we know more about your date?'

Sarah squeezes her sister's wrist, a rushed reaction initiated by a mixture of envy and embarrassment for the entitlement behind Mathilde's effective voice. For her inherent long-ing to know.

Gertrude defies Mathilde. 'What would you like me to tell you?'

Sarah begrudges Gertrude's confidence not to ask Mathilde why she wants to know, but what information she would like to have. A trade, or a conversation between two socially trained adults.

'How did you end up at a bottomless brunch for a first date?' Mathilde mimics Gertrude's gestures.

'How do you know we were having a first date?'

Sarah interrupts: 'Well, the way you said hello, apparently.' Bitterness takes control of her trademark self-censorship.

Gertrude rolls her eyes towards Sarah, gently, acknowledging her before facing Mathilde again. 'Are you two sisters?' she asks.

'I'm the big sister,' Mathilde says quickly. She allows a short break and adds, her voice softer: 'There is something about you and that man yesterday that troubles me. I was excited for you at the beginning. You looked handsome together, but it felt so intense. So many things that could go wrong.'

Gertrude chuckles: 'This is a fair assessment. I'm enviable from the outset, off-putting once you know the details.'

Nobody responds.

This interplay between assumptions and ideas, revelations and secrets, tests their typical behaviours. Gertrude can't stop looking at Mathilde either, a woman she only met this afternoon, but with whom she has crossed paths before. The recognition that they will have had common experiences – the quest for happiness, needing to answer yes or no, finding a purpose for themselves – but they don't hold any intimacy or context about one another. As their meeting unfolds, you will wonder what facts about yourself you would have shared with these women if you were in that situation – what specifics about your story you would choose to disclose to them so they could re-construct your persona through their own perception. Keep in mind that some signs will be out of your control too. As they talk among themselves and as you read, your biases will overcast the interpretation of the data they will share, either consciously or subconsciously. You may measure their achievements (intellectual, financial, familial, other), but your reference point will be different to theirs, so it will be for happiness and stress and trauma. As much as they will try to extract themselves from the aura of meeting someone new, the familiarity of their daily lives will resonate – the dutiful habits that led them to cluster at the Oldfield Tavern; the customs that enable transport companies to plan bus and train timetables, the needs that motivate councils when they grant business licences and misinform estate developers when they map new building sites; forces that keep citizens in lanes. The poison of wanting to fit in also prevented them from declining the drink in the first instance and will contaminate their sentences and gestures. Beware, listen and observe, but don't internalise their signals and words; give Cloe, Gertrude, Mathilde and Sarah a chance – they mean to be relatable rather than truthful.

Gertrude lets go of a small sigh, *fuck it*, before speaking fast: 'We met on a dating app. We spoke for a while, which was nice frankly. He was funny and he was relaxed about my hours here at the pub, so when I finally had a Saturday off, we agreed to meet. He chose the place, and I wasn't brave enough to tell him that going for a bottomless brunch in Paddington is an awful idea.' Gertrude briskly looks at the three women in front of her, then she starts talking again. 'He is German and works in wealth management, so I thought this might be the type of things he does. I was curious to know his London.' She pauses. 'I also didn't want to give him reasons to ghost me,' she adds, picking at her nails.

'What do you mean by "his" London?' Mathilde asks.

'I never go to Paddington. Do you?' Gertrude responds.

Sarah jumps in: 'She was having brunch there just yesterday.'

An attack; her spilling uncovers her insecurity.

'It's a convenient place to meet with someone who doesn't live in London or lives on the other side of the city.' Mathilde tells Sarah defensively, as if she doubts this logic too. She turns around to face Gertrude; the four women are sitting in a row at the bar, with Cloe at the upper end. 'I'm more curious about the "activity choice" (she marks the air quotes). It's risky to go for a bottomless brunch on a first date.'

'I can see your point. The core, bottomless principle of it removes the option of having an obvious end point,' Sarah agrees.

Gertrude snaps in response: 'It didn't go well.'

Regardless, Mathilde doesn't soften her line of questioning. 'That's what I mean. This date was sabotaged from the outset. Why did you even say yes?'

'How could she have said no?' Cloe joins the conversation.

Cloe's grammar indicates that she was asking Mathilde to

explain her thinking, but Gertrude pinches the skin on the back of her hand nervously and responds instead. 'It's true that I wanted to meet him because I was curious. His reality is so far removed from mine: he lives in a second language, works for a large corporation ... He is the prototype of the *single professional* you find on the Rightmove ads.' Gertrude lists attributes but it is unclear if she is describing abstract listings or his specific flat: 'Leather sofa, floor-to-ceiling windows and the docklands. I guess I was curious to know how the other half lives.' Louder, she adds: 'I wanted to be served food.' Gertrude's cheeks are red, making the complexion of her hair pop darker, her features luminous. Mathilde hasn't stopped looking at Gertrude, her pupils closing to a restrictive yet tireless focus, a sustained stare to decode a new encounter. She hums, a gentle sound effect before the following question: 'Shall we get some snacks to mop up the wine?' Gertrude exhales.

'Is your shift over?' Sarah can't hide her disappointment about socialising with strangers when Mathilde has just taken a step forward in her direction. She looks over at Mathilde's hands, spotting the first lines of the scarred patches on her sister's skin, clues about their contrasting memory of the lake in Wales. The accident that taught them that the length of one's life stretches and bounces back no matter what social status or genders one subscribes to – the duality of hope.

Gertrude glances at the room behind her, where people have sprawled over reading chairs and a dog lies on the wooden floor. The light levels tone down, exposing the oak tree texture of the tables. Sunday comes to an end. It rained early this morning, a necessary introduction to a brilliant day, the sunshine breaking through later in the afternoon. Londoners were compelled to plot a day: they headed to parks and beer gardens, red like lobster shells, and they wished they could have travelled to the seaside. The pond in Hampstead Heath is fully booked and swimmers reconvened at the *Hackney Riviera*, or the river Lea, despite the rumours of raw sewage and health hazards. 'It's quiet and we don't serve food on Sunday evenings, other than the leftovers from the lunch menu.' Gertrude justifies herself for having deserted the kitchen. The other truth is that she can't remember the last time she had an interaction of this level with strangers, let alone with women around her age. The social overload and thus consequent loneliness of London, combined with her hunger, calls for rapid decisions. She jumps off the stool, refills all four glasses, and walks towards the kitchen. A few steps in, she loops back and looks from one to the other – Cloe, Mathilde, Sarah – 'I assume everyone is fine with chips?'

'Yes,' they all reply.

Gertrude responds with pride: 'Great, because that's all there is.' She disappears through the back door.

Back in the kitchen, the steel of the counters sparkles clean. Two of Gertrude's colleagues are sitting on the small stairs just outside the back door, listening to music and smoking, until they startle – the door slammed, Gertrude stands behind the duo. She smiles at them.

'How are we doing with the stocks?'

One of the two men drops his cigarette on the side of his shoe, then replies to Gertrude: 'We're doing fine. We don't need an extra kitchen aid tonight.'

'Yeah, it's quiet. You can go home if you'd like,' says the other.

'That's fine. I'm just by the bar with some,' she breaks, 'some friends.' She finishes the sentence with ease. A slip of the tongue that favours room for interpretation, rather than a lie.

Something you should know about Gertrude: she is more intransigent with herself than with anyone else. The men react as you would expect them to at the prospect of spending the evening at the pub with *some friends*. They return to their chattering, one of them holds a phone between their shoulders and switches songs hastily, one after the other, mumbling about their merit.

'Just grabbing a few plates of chips,' Gertrude says as she stands before the fryer.

When Gertrude joins the three women at the bar again, she is craving something real.

'Did I miss anything?' she asks as she drops the two serving baskets on the bar, both with paper cups of mayonnaise and ketchup sauces enclosed.

Don't you also want to know what they have been talking about since she left?

'My boss finds it entertaining to guess the colours of mine

and my female colleagues' underwear when we walk into the office in the morning,' Cloe says as she chucks a chip inside her mouth.

'That's gross,' Gertrude says. 'Your boss, I mean. He is gross,' she clarifies, licking salt from her fingertips.

Mathilde agrees; she nods.

'It's fine. I usually work from home. But we were asked to wear red panties to the last Christmas party,' Cloe details. The three women look uncomfortable with both recognition and resentment for that recognition. It is Cloe's turn to tell a story, to speak under the spotlight. She continues, her pace fast and her tone working hard to entertain a light mood, a pretension that she has agency over her body and sexuality and that she is unaffected by this episode. 'He calls the office his "harem", standing at the end of the open plan, speaking loudly like a boy who was educated at some private school, but who splutters when he gets excited.' She smirks with herself. 'He obviously has no sense of the cultural history of the harem. He simply thought of the word as a short cut to affirm that he is "the man" among us.' She pauses, then rephrases: 'The boss.'

Mathilde outbids Cloe's story: 'When I was in my first job after university, my boss used to find it hilarious to introduce me as "his mistress" (Mathilde winks comically) every single time I brought him and his guests hot drinks. I had just graduated from Oxford with distinction, I can speak three languages but, still, I was there doing that job because I was the boss's mistress.' She drinks, and Cloe stammers – *gross gross gross*.

Sarah is dipping a chip into the mayonnaise then into the ketchup, rotating it between her two fingers slowly until she bites into it. Her arm extends, reaching for another portion of food, the corner of her lips flavoursome with condiments, and she speaks without looking back up at any of the women. 'Once someone sent me a text message to apologise for ghosting me. It had been over a year since I had sent the last text, and we had only gone on three or four dates.'

'Why would they do that?' Gertrude questions.

Sarah shrugs, then she sets forth: 'The text had a photo of me attached.' She eats another chip, dipping the top of it into the sauces, mixing them both despite her sister's obvious irritation. Sarah is confidently greedy with her food. One of her hands covers half of her mouth as she chews and talks at the same time: 'The photo was odd as well. It was taken when we went to one of the Friday night Lates at the Tate ("With Uniqlo! Love, love, love these," Cloe interrupts). The light is off, and my head bends in a way that makes my nose look bumpy. I hate to know this photo exists and that I don't own it.'

'I'd hate that too,' Cloe confirms with an apologetic tone after barging into Sarah's story.

'He is a creep,' Mathilde says with authority.

'*She*,' Sarah looks at her sister. 'She is a creep.'

'She is a creep, and you're better off without her,' Mathilde corrects herself with a vigilant gaze.

Sarah laughs and Mathilde is struck by how much she loves her sister's giggle, the expression of her empathy and

251

the execution of the life Sarah conducts, a burst of emotions that are often contradictory but felt nevertheless; deeply felt, under the thin skin of a perfectionist. She considers adding something else to acknowledge her sister and the pronouns she has decided to disclose. She must be contemplating an apology for having been blindsided by her own worries, but Mathilde who normally speaks her mind says nothing, and her sister shows grace for this decision. It would have broken Sarah to be othered in front of strangers after telling Mathilde who she desires.

The conversation carries on with each woman being oblivious to the extent of the others' revelations. Today's encounter between these four women matches the setting of a market square, a melting pot of stories, lies, accuracy and rumours, when each person follows their own agenda but is still eyeing the items that colour the baskets of others. A dash of jealousy, too.

Gertrude elaborates about the danger of photos with a story of a friend of a friend who once found herself featured on a strange dating app profile. It seemed that someone was using some photos she had posted on Facebook years ago to create a fake profile, and Mathilde became more invested than necessary. She asked what the woman in question had done about the situation. Had she reported the fraudulent user to the dating app's management? Yes. Had she followed up about what they had done about it? No, but she had checked, and she couldn't find the said profile anymore. This wasn't enough, Mathilde insisted. This is a case of identity

theft, therefore the story needs to be escalated and reported –
if this had happened to that one woman, surely a bigger issue
of impersonation exists and the people who manage the
app need to address this security breach. Had she contacted
the app through their FAQ or via social media? Gertrude
doesn't have more insights; she doesn't know if this is factual
or gossip; she shortens her answers after each new question.
A tension around whose responsibility it was to report the
issue builds, so Cloe widens the topic by asking Gertrude,
Sarah and Mathilde if they are on social media. A set of wary
eyes welcome the dreaded topic and the assumptions of what
a person should do with their public-facing persona. They
all are on Instagram – Mathilde and Gertrude have their
profiles set to private – only Mathilde is on Facebook – for
Messenger, she stipulates – and Cloe and Mathilde are on
Twitter, but only Cloe tweets. She has an engaged following
as well, she 'thinks thinks thinks'. Sarah admits that she is
glued to Instagram.

'Same. Not that I post anything ground-breaking on any
of my socials, but I like to share what I'm reading. And my
outfits,' Cloe explains.

Gertrude speaks with an absent voice, as if grappling
with the meaning of her observation as she goes: 'It's insane
that our generation and future ones have all these personal
branding resources available. Think about it: in the nineties
you'd read about a celebrity's blood type diet or other bullshit
on the pages of a glossy magazine, but these days everyone
can share their "secret to a flat tummy in thirty days" and

sound like they know what they're doing.' She is peeling the label off the wine bottle, and then concludes: 'I guess it felt unreachable before, like "only celebrities can be that thin", whereas now the beauty myth is totally democratised.'

'Exactly that,' underlines Cloe.

'Social media can be a good place to challenge your opinions with others,' Mathilde says.

Gertrude responds: 'I'm not sure this is true ... No dialogue takes place on social media. It's another platform where people are expected to become social regulators.'

Cloe keeps which hashtags she follows to herself.

'Isn't it a good thing? It's democratic,' Sarah says.

'This is an illusion. It makes you believe in the possibility of opacity, but it's black or white really.'

Cloe joins: 'There is this woman I follow on Instagram. She shares mindfulness advice. She posts reels of herself getting dressed and I love them. But the other day she made a video where she gets into a skirt and when she does, you can see her underwear for a brief moment. Like a second, not even. You wouldn't believe the comments.'

'I think I can,' Gertrude lets go.

Cloe quivers. 'It made me really self-conscious about my own selfies, you know?' She posted a photo before going out last night, a lengthwise shot taken standing in front of the mirror inside her bedroom. She liked how she looked, so she posted it.

Sarah raises her glass. 'Yep, you women should be shielding yourself from all the violence. I think they call it prevention?'

'Depressing,' one of them whispers.

'While I can't offer a solution to that issue, can I suggest that we open another bottle of Sauvignon Blanc?' The question is characteristic of Gertrude, avoidant after revealing a fragment of her opinions. The gap between who a person can be and the presupposition of who they are determines Gertrude's relationship with the world and others. When social media frames selves into high-resolution squares, Gertrude melts into a puddle on the other side; caramelised sugar, sticky and lumpy because the substance doesn't hold together in its new form.

'I'm game,' says Cloe. And so is Mathilde, who slides her arm on top of Sarah's shoulders as she responds — a squeeze to end the gesture.

'No . . . I can't.' She turns around to look at Gertrude first, then at Cloe, and back to lowering her gaze above the empty wine glass, ice cubes liquefying into tasty water. 'I'm on a deadline for my PhD,' she explains.

'She's always on a deadline,' Mathilde seconds. Her voice sounds annoyed despite their public setting — Sarah's hair stands on end. She doesn't look at Mathilde, refusing to acknowledge what she has made official.

A pause to reassess the dynamic: only the two sisters Jenkins–Bell knew each other before tonight's encounter with Cloe and Gertrude; a playful mood of learning and guessing, to reveal and hold information, is staged between the four women. Intentions, gestures and words are withheld, overshared, projected or misinterpreted; don't judge them swiftly.

Gertrude stands with her two arms open on each side of her waist, her blue denim shirt crisped, her expressions interrogative. Mathilde nods decisively, and Gertrude bends down to open the fridge door. When she stands back up, she uses the guise of a genuine question to distract the women away from her hands: 'What are you studying, Sarah?' She is opening the bottle of wine.

'I'm researching access to water, and water systems.'

Gertrude doesn't shy away from the shortness of her response: 'This sounds like a valuable topic. Like private water access or . . .?' Neither does she finish the sentence since she doesn't have a clue about the said topic. Gertrude doesn't act pretentiously. Mathilde remains quiet and Sarah wishes her sister spoke on her behalf.

'I'm focusing on the social housing site of Thamesmead. It's part of a funded studentship so there are clear limitations about the research area and the methodology. And there are deadlines to meet to continue to fulfil the criteria. It's not only about my research; there is a bigger picture to this project.' Sarah opts for specificity, a strategy to derail any further lines of questioning; the last sentence was directed to Mathilde, and so she catches her eye as she says it.

'There is always a bigger picture, isn't there?' Cloe wonders, but she is ignored after such an allusive query. The four women haven't reached a sense of reciprocity yet.

'It all sounds brilliant and important,' Gertrude says, validating Sarah's work as she refills her glass of wine. 'You deserve a bit of moral support,' she concludes with a playful smile.

'Thanks. Can I have a squeeze of soda with it, please?' Sarah asks shyly. 'I'll be grateful tomorrow morning.'

Gertrude reaches for the bar gun, a splash, and Cloe reveals that she loves the fact that, after today, she will be able to say she befriended one of the Oldfield Tavern bartenders with great enthusiasm. The three women have pinkish cheeks, they seal their lips. They are at a pivotal moment in their coming together: they are getting comfortable with each other – and there is no urgency to speak, topics will flow in naturally with the appropriate setting. A friendship is born, however strong the bond will be, however long it will last; the moment is as such. This is when Cloe steps in, vulnerable and honest: 'I wish I had known the bartender last night.' She lowers her voice and apologises for being weird. 'It's just that I've had a tough day and I don't know what to do.' Another break. 'Ignore me, I'm probably just hung-over and it's messing with my brain. Hair of the dog.' Cloe sighs loudly, lifting her glass up to her mouth. She is working her hardest to pretend that she means not to bother with this conversation. Mathilde excuses herself and walks to the bathroom; Sarah mentally steps away from the group, her back bends over her phone, chin resting over her hand.

*

When Mathilde returns, Cloe and Gertrude have broken into a separate conversation. Their foreheads touch close and, from where Mathilde stands, their exchange follows a palpable, compassionate pace. Angular eyebrow shapes give away who is confessing and who is hearing a secret; Gertrude nodding with serious expressions, Cloe avoidant before her. Sarah is shrivelling over her mobile, still, the line of her spine drawing a bump at the top of her back, on which Mathilde drops the palm of her hand delicately. A light caress as she sits back by her sister's side: 'Was the yellow scarf hers?'

Sarah remembers the missing scarf; apprehensive, she scans the room. Then she turns back towards Mathilde: 'Wait, do you mean the woman who ghosted me for over a year before sending me a strange photo of myself?' Mathilde doesn't respond, her hand lands on her sister's upper leg. The kind gesture sets her apart from Kristina's grip when she wants reassurance that they will meet again. Familiarity, not vulnerability, speaks. 'That one has long gone. It's the scarf of a colleague. I should really find that scarf, actually.' Sarah slides away from Mathilde.

'Wait,' Mathilde says. 'Why do you never talk to me about these things?'

Sarah looks at Mathilde apprehensively. She is flooded with all the *things* she would like to tell her sister – *the horrid mole I spotted at the back of my knee; the sex toy I bought once but then never felt brave enough to try (Have you ever shopped for one? I should tell you that they come in anonymous parcels, brandless like an elegant treat); my swimming lessons of breaststroke, crawl but no butterfly or backstrokes, the numbing fragrance of chlorine I find enticing. I'm sorry that I have to tell you that I don't have enough money to go somewhere sunny and salty for your hen do.* The things she wants to ask Mathilde – *Do you think Dad prefers me and Mum prefers you? And did they negotiate such a division with the view to be fair parents? Could you help me rearrange my flat so it looks brighter and more spacious? Do you think I should stop seeing Kristina? Do you even want to know about Kristina? Do you think that I'm fragile? Too fragile to make good decisions for myself?* Sarah moves her lips slowly; words come out with a short delay: 'I do, I just did.' She walks past the bar and on to the dining room, where she had lunch with Mathilde earlier. She must find the scarf, a task to fulfil.

Mathilde tops up her glass of wine and whirls back to face Cloe and Gertrude. Cloe talks slowly, with the rhythm of someone who is disorientated inside the hall of a train station, unsure about the meaning of the full sentence she speaks as she places sense in the words she picks. Cloe tells Gertrude about the shot of tequila and the side of San Miguel, about the sequins covering her top, how they break her nails, and the brilliance of the women she met in the bathroom. The stairs were made of metal, with bumpy arrows on them to avoid slipping; 'Durbar stairs,' clarifies Gertrude, before specifying that she only knows their name because she ordered some for the pub recently. A material acquisition to prevent customers from falling. Cloe acquiesces and recalls the open wounds across her knees because her school was built across a high building and they would have to go up and down the stairs more than once a day; *they*, a bunch of overly excited pupils roaming between classes. Digressions spark a light over the women's identities, their heritage lurking behind the assumptions that frame their present portraits. Gertrude catches herself drifting and moors her focus with Cloe's words. She is also aware of Mathilde, who is waiting for an occasion to rejoin the conversation. The interactions between the four women are scattered after an immediate bond on the back foot of an impulsive decision, and the regrets that hit afterwards – Sarah asked Gertrude to add two extra glasses on top of her initial order, but excused herself for the second round; Cloe, who was quiet initially, overshares; Gertrude was liberated from her shift duties and is itching with guilt for cheating on the timesheet; Mathilde has become quieter, slipping down a stream of consciousness. Raised by Agnes, Mathilde has learnt how to extract more information from others than she is willing to give away. Cloe continues her account with the revelation that she smokes when she goes out – the first puff disassembles her brain, foggy, and the next ones slow down the temptation of alcohol, her favourite cigarette – and the smoking area is a good place to hang out. Fresh air under the night sky accommodates fantasies. She relishes the smoking areas of nightclubs because they scream the name of Héloïse, her energy and her eagerness to meet people for who they are and not what they do. Cloe elaborates without revealing that Héloïse is her mother and that she has died. Gertrude interrupts Cloe by saying that she also enjoys a cooling cigarette, like the one she shares with Stefano mid-shift, when they can grab a few minutes of calm. She explains that each shift is different, the affections from her colleagues' moods and the various hiccups across the pub, a late delivery or the sink that needs replacing, recurring blockages and overflows. But there is that one moment when all the tables seem to agree to pause, always. She can't explain how such a symbiosis happens quotidianly and randomly at the same time – forks are put down next to empty plates, there is a break before another round of drinks, the wait for the bill to arrive, the kitchen slows down and the staff are allowed a short break. Gertrude briefly contextualises her story by saying that Stefano is her closest colleague in the kitchen, a friend, and then offers to get more food for them. Cloe ignores the invitation for nutrients and asks Mathilde what she does for a living.

'I'm a legal advisor for a women's centre,' she responds with apparent pride.

Raw, perceptible jealousy: Mathilde has a *valuable* job.

Mathilde continues, her voice composed: 'We provide consultancy and advocacy for women in dangerous and difficult situations, but we also offer advice about women's health, mental health support, and we run various workshops to build a better future for women who are isolated.' She sips her drink, and Gertrude stands up to go get a carafe of water on the other side of the bar. 'The problem is that we're short on funding, so at the moment we can only help women who are resident in our borough. It's tragic to turn down a request for help based on a postcode.' Another sip, then she adds, softly but seriously: 'The thing is, we don't. We amend

261

addresses and we make it work. Well, we try to do that as much as possible.'

Gertrude serves four glasses of water. 'It must be mentally exhausting to hear so many horrific stories.'

'I already struggle to read the news,' says Cloe.

'It does put things into perspective,' Mathilde replies. 'But it's also my job. I approach it pragmatically, and this allows me to set boundaries.'

Mathilde is impressive when she speaks about her work; she knows. 'I focus on finding solutions, if that makes sense,' she adds.

'Can I ask you something?' Cloe mutters.

Mathilde squints her eyes, her left one almost closed, as she tells Cloe that she can ask her anything. *Anything*, or the privilege of being confident.

'I was just telling Gertrude that I'm feeling uneasy today.' Cloe is holding her left wrist with her right hand, her shoulders are tightly closed over her chest, words escape her mouth slowly and her lips spasm. Shame, overcome by a self-afflicted need to share. She quickly looks up at Gertrude and Mathilde, then she launches herself: 'I woke up at this guy's house this morning and I can't quite remember how I got there. I met him inside the club where I went out last night. I know that I met him at the smoking area and then again outside of the bathroom, when he suggested we dance, and I said yes. We danced, and I don't remember what happened after that. And—' Her voice breaks. ' . . . I'm scared of what it is that I can't remember.'

Sarah has joined Cloe, Gertrude and Mathilde again, sitting at the upper end of the bar in silence, but showing concern. Gertrude stands close to Cloe. The three women are quiet so Cloe babbles: 'Because I know I did something. I can feel it.' She joins both her hands, tighter between her legs, avoidant and tense. 'I feel funny, you know? Something isn't quite right.'

'Of course, darling, this is distressing. If you were out with friends, then you could call them and ask if they know something that might help you remember?' Mathilde suggests.

'I went out to meet a friend for her birthday, but I never found her.'

Gertrude puts her hand over Cloe's wrist, her fingers moving gently, working to untie Cloe's extremities.

'I tried to text her, but I had no signal,' she adds, resigned.

'It might be worth giving her a ring anyway. Maybe you found her later during the night, but you can't remember,' Gertrude says.

Cloe's body blanches under the pressure of being torn between her felt and experienced truths. 'This, I would remember,' she says, sharply enough to dissolve the contradiction of her statement. 'He rang me on my mobile this morning to ask if I got home safely. He said he had offered me his sofa last night because I was too drunk to go home on my own.' She pauses.

'What did your instinct tell you when he told you that?' Mathilde asks calmly.

'I've had blackouts before, so I've reason not to trust myself.'

'But what is your instinct telling you?'

'Something isn't right.' She shivers. 'I think that he had sex with me. I asked him if he was a friend of Lucy to test his story and he said yes. But I don't know of a Lucy.'

'Before anything else, you must know that it wasn't your fault so you must not justify yourself,' Mathilde says with assurance.

'I don't even know his name!'

Gertrude chips in: 'I agree with Mathilde. But what I find confusing is that he called you.'

'I thought the same,' Sarah says, 'but then he probably wouldn't think he's done something bad.'

'Like what? That Cloe just needed a little push to fancy him?' Gertrude speaks cynically.

'Mm-hmm,' a faint gust escapes Sarah's tight lip. 'And he probably thinks that he's done right by her with this call. That he put things to bed.' *To bed*, palpitations infuse Sarah with anguish as she copes with her clumsy language.

'I've learnt that people make illogical decisions when they realise that they could be incriminated for their actions, guilty or not,' Mathilde announces. Sarah thinks that murderers often return to a crime scene, but she holds back this banal information before Mathilde's professional knowledge. She bought their mother a book about the 'untold lives of the women killed by Jack the Ripper' last Christmas, penned by Hallie Rubenhold and highly reviewed. Sarah had thought Agnes would enjoy the read, she who prefers a backstory over a plot, her family who was from Whitechapel originally, except that her mother avoids any information that reveals clues about the origins of her name. Mathilde laughed as soon as Agnes unwrapped the book – 'mauvais goût', she snorted – and Sarah understood that, like all performing ego-centrics, her mother cannot enjoy learning about anything that might affect the public narrative she has instituted. *Did I ever tell you that I was named Agnes because* Agnes Grey *by Anne Brontë was my father's mother's favourite novel?* Agnes told her daughters at bedtime. Mathilde and Sarah never had an opportunity to check the veracity of this information. Still, they have used it to thread the story of their family.

Cloe looks pale. Gertrude tightens her bun back up and addresses her next question to Mathilde: 'What do you think Cloe should do?'

'It's a personal choice, but a suspicion of sexual assault should always be investigated in my opinion.'

Cloe freezes. The policing body steps in.

'I meant to ask for your advice on how to do that,' Gertrude clarifies firmly.

'She could go to the police,' Mathilde says, and immedi-ately realises that she is talking about Cloe in the third person in front of her. She turns to face Cloe, then she continues: 'I'm sorry, Cloe, you could go to the police with someone you trust. They will ask you to make and sign a statement about what happened, and they might carry out a forensic medical examination. Or, if you aren't comfortable with that, there are organisations that can help you. You could start with calling the women's centre in your borough, but whatever you decide about reporting the assault, you should seek medical help.' Cloe shivers again and Mathilde gently smiles at her. 'The NHS has a dedicated, twenty-four-hour service called Sexual Assault Referral Centres where they can provide physical and mental health support. We can find the nearest centre if you'd like?'

'I don't want to waste their time. I'm not sure if this *was* assault,' Cloe admits, dragging her voice out. 'Because I'm not sure about what happened.'

'If you're unsure then there was a form of abuse,' Mathilde says factually.

'Really?' Sarah questions. 'Surely it's more complex than that.'

Mathilde is taken aback by her sister's intervention. She passes her fingers through her fringe, her remedy when she is on the edge of talking *too* truthfully and her words could hurt. It has been a uniting day for the Jenkins-Bell sisters, so she pauses. Then she explains, with paralysing authority: 'Generalising doesn't stand a chance if one starts digging into such a complex issue. There will always be exceptions and conflicting cases in which different factors come into consideration. However, in relation to the topic of consenting to have sex, there is one reference word, and that's "yes".' Mathilde could stop here, but she fears the sentence will make her a conservative before the three women. 'The things I have seen, the stories I have heard, have shown there is no other word than "yes" to determine if consent was given or if it was abused.'

'And what if I can't remember saying "yes" to him?' Cloe is picking at her fingernails, red with inflammation and cuticles flaking.

'Then one can question if you were in the position to say it, and even if you meant to say "yes" in the first instance. There is a context to consenting too. The mind is good at forgetting what the body went through, until it doesn't any-more,' Mathilde says back to Cloe, without allowing a break for relief nor thoughts. 'Until it breaks under the weight of intuitions,' she ends.

'Are you saying that it's the responsibility of your sexual partner to check if you mean it when you send the signals that "yes" you want to have sex with them?' Sarah is look-ing at Mathilde with an expression only they can spot and understand wholly (absent, her hand digs to find the inhaler inside her pocket, the 'little worm' Mathilde will also search for with her eyes in a few minutes). She wants to engage, but she fears an exposing disagreement.

Mathilde opens her mouth softly, making sure to compose her words with clarity as she responds to her sister. 'This rhetoric has been used a lot to close cases in the past, as in arguing that the assaulter didn't know the assaulted didn't consent. Sex is complex and there is a blurry line between testing a limit and passing it, but it is part of the partnership that all people involved should make sure everyone in the room consents. If there is a doubt, then that agreement wasn't sealed properly, therefore consent was breached.'

'This sounds good in principle, but I'm not sure how it

267

translates to everyday life,' Sarah summarises. 'And I hate that it always comes down to women having to police their consent. What if I don't know what I want yet?' she challenges Mathilde.

Mathilde responds: 'I said I was generalising to discuss the issue of reporting sexual assault. I'm not talking about sexual desire.'

A pause. They contemplate talking about desire bluntly; tender, violent, regretful, a quickie or a slow burner, the dissident pleasure.

'A third bottle would be pushing it, right?' asks Gertrude.

'I'm up for another portion of chips,' Cloe says.

'The chips are gone sadly, but there is a large amount of vanilla ice-cream. Would that do the trick?'

'Totally!' says Cloe with enthusiasm, and the three women cannot help but smile before her. She comes across younger than them.

'What about chocolate?' asks Sarah.

'Only vanilla, I'm afraid. The chef here is a total cheapskate. Don't quote me.' Gertrude winks and walks towards the kitchen. She types a quick text to her brother as she goes – Gonna be a late shift, don't wait for me to have dinner – to which Liam responds instantly: Are you pissed off about this morning? I didn't think you'd be into her!! Of course Liam would think this is about him, and Gertrude puts her phone back inside her pocket without sending a response. She doesn't hold a grudge against her brother, but she likes to let him sweat over it because it hurts that he doesn't know her well. She found the neighbour attractive, but she doesn't care for one-night stands, or about having sex. She recognises hints of physical attractions in some people, she enjoys the warmth of pleasing someone, their style and intelligence, the details that define their character and the signs of a reciprocal feeling – but the physical contact, she doesn't understand or crave. These are emotions she processes internally, through her brain and her experiences, not with touch. It suffocates Gertrude, it undermines her expressions of love to be touched – but how can she explain this to someone, without scaring them, when they are on a first date? And wouldn't it be unfair not to tell them from the beginning? That she would love to see the person again, to date, to be romantically involved, but not to have sex, ever. The simple thought of that one sentence makes her heart swing, beats that bite her guts, so she undermines each one of the dates she goes on before they end. Books, movies, people's accounts, she has consumed and listened and watched to be defeated – our social organisations approve and differentiate familial, amicable and romantic loves through the spectrum of sexual attraction. Its forbiddance, restriction or execution. Gertrude doesn't know how to explain to her brother that she felt threatened by his ease to be intimate with someone else – and that by sleeping with the neighbour he took away the illusion that Gertrude could entertain a relationship with her. *She is into sex, like I should be to be desirable.* She exhales and walks back to the bar with a container full of ice-cream and four spoons. 'If my boss sees me, I'd probably get fired,' she says as she hands one spoon to each woman.

'I'm happy with a bowl as well if that's more suitable,' Sarah says.

'This is fun,' Cloe squeals, bringing her hand in front of her face after a mouthful of ice-cream. 'Brain freeze!'

'Fuck it,' Gertrude concludes. 'Where were we at?'

'The broad subject of consent,' confirms Mathilde. 'But to return to your question, Sarah, I would say that there are two spaces to consider: the private sphere, and the world outside of it. In private, we can approach a situation through the question of language and communication with the assumption that there should be a history of understanding between the two participants. One was either ignored or made to believe they wanted to do something that they didn't want to do. Again, keep in mind that I'm generalising for the sake of arguing here (Sarah flinches at the word "arguing"). When it comes to people who have never met before, and when alcohol or other substances are involved, there is an added layer of complexity about what signals one sends, the meaning they had in mind and the perception of these signs, on the basis that all substances were consumed willingly obviously.' She inhales and exhales: 'But I'll bet that each one of us has had enough of this culture that interrogates and blames victims for their doings – *What were you wearing? Were you drinking? Did you take drugs? Why did you go out on your own?*' Mathilde swallows. 'As if any of the answers would alleviate the consequences of having been sexually assaulted. It's not a question of not having said "no" clearly enough, but it's down to an assaulter infringing someone's right to oppose. And nothing can excuse the crime.' Mathilde stops to enjoy a spoonful of ice-cream. Her eyebrows release, and her face lightens peacefully as she turns towards Cloe. 'If you decide to report him, make sure that you go with someone you trust and who is going to stand up for you.' Then she adds, emptied: 'When it comes to sexual assault cases, the system follows the rule of presumption of innocence with rare efficiency.'

The women rub their fingers, sticky with dairy, the air thick like cream when the ice has chilled their minds, a downside for the overworking of wine. Gertrude pours water into four tumbler glasses while talking: 'If you ask me, I don't see how one can police sexuality. Love, sex – they are two irrational forces. Humans spend a lot of time thinking about the two, together and separately, and sometimes we love and we fuck, or we do one or the other, and often it's the restriction that turns us into beasts.' *We*, an enduring place to hide.

'No one here is saying we should police sexuality or love orientations, only that consent is the foremost requirement for both to thrive.' Mathilde tends to speak for all. *She knows*, she thinks subconsciously, and therefore she talks as if she does. Her interlocutors trust that she does.

'You're better at arguing than I am. Let me rephrase.' Gertrude takes a sip of water, and so do Cloe and Sarah. 'What I wanted to say is that I don't think a fair penal system to evaluate how love and sex are anticipated and performed can exist . . . so we can't judge consent through a traditional juridical route. The idea of such a judgement being "systematic" goes against the issue.' Another sip. 'I guess I'm creating a problem rather than suggesting a solution, but it's not like the current system works well for women and minorities.'

'I think about this often too,' says Sarah bashfully, a spoon still in one hand. 'But also at an individual level, how can someone be asked to communicate what they are consenting clearly if they don't know themselves yet?'

'True, and I wonder how we account for the fact that it takes time for a person to admit that they were in a vulnerable position,' Cloe says. 'I think power plays a big role too. You can't emancipate yourself from someone who has agency over you.' She sounds mature and wise as she speaks with the wealth of experience and with each word chosen and enunciated carefully. 'It's a lot to ask for a victim to list what they consented to and what they didn't. The two influence the other.' She looks up at the ceiling, rolling her eyes: 'There is only abuse under an administration.'

And with any forms of power, consent is most likely to be wronged before it has been considered, Cloe could add, but goosebumps hold her still. *Pick your battles, Cloe*, Héloïse had taught her. Her mother had vocal socialist ideas but found a sustainable happiness in an individual execution of pleasures – disarmed by the laborious process of revolting inside a policed state. Héloïse grew up into a generation of disappointments, post-May '68, when communes and civil resistance movements were defeated by a societal disinterest – the rise of individualism. Despite Nathaniel Baldwin's breakthrough invention at his kitchen table years prior, the commercial and portable headphones were introduced on the market in 1979 with the Walkman. Baldwin died financially ruined, but the Sony Corporation introduced an era of walking down the streets with blocked ears and a sealed mind, an inward experience. Héloïse loved people and a party, but she was afraid of crowds and obsessed with the smell of sweat she snuffled everywhere she went. Cloe could tell you plenty about the loads of laundry her mother washed and that Héloïse didn't bother to vote in elections anymore.

Gertrude, Mathilde and Sarah are confronted with the realisation that while they are debating academically, Cloe is talking with immediacy and is preserving her safety by agenting her own storyline.

As you read, consider pausing to ponder if the topic of consent can be theorised meaningfully. If you hear the word *consent*, do you picture freedom or submission? Consent to do, consent to decide, consent to speak – the issue widens beyond the topic of sex. The storm of common decisions that need taking so we can file a folder and wire money and put bread on the table, one stroke after the other, our consent to keep business as usual. More, our hard work to *make sure* business is done as usual and that we perform, from bringing good grades home to securing a job that will pay the bills, and the social interactions we pencil in our diaries in between. Living triggers side effects, so consider the individual perspectives as you read on.

'I relate to the power-play comment,' says Sarah cautiously. 'It's so difficult to make your desires understood when the person who triggers them is a figure of authority in your life.'

'What do you mean you can relate to Cloe's comment?' Mathilde questions with a noticeable tone switch as her focus sets on her sister. 'Also, just to be clear, I'm not advocating that victims should be accused of not being responsible enough. Quite the opposite,' she insists, worried.

'I mean that the recognition of who owns power is primordial to the establishment of a fair consent between individuals,' Sarah speaks confidently. They have finished the second bottle of wine and the ice-cream; pearls of condensation run down the tub's edges. Furry mouths, boiling ideas.

'Have you guys heard of the iConsent app that was launched in Denmark?' Sarah asks.

Mathilde gets her phone out. She hates not knowing the ins and outs of the debated topic. Cloe withdraws and the three women don't see her for her specific concerns anymore, but as an example to debate a general issue. Power plays out despite their warning – none of them would want to know what this behaviour reveals about their privilege.

'This is a basic capitalist answer to the question of consent. Data policing,' Gertrude says.

Mathilde is scrolling down her phone as she speaks: 'It's a pragmatic way to address the issue. Clear rules and an official recording system for them: consent prequels intercourse, one consent is valid for one intercourse over a period of twenty-four hours. Any sex without consent is rape: the rule must be simple enough to be incriminating at a judicial level.'

'I guess lawyers are smart enough to get anyone out of a sticky situation?' Gertrude asks with playful eyes; she doesn't expect Mathilde to answer.

'I just think this app is totally disconnected from the reality of women,' Sarah adds.

'Any non-binary people and women,' corrects Gertrude. Again, she tightens her hair bun.

'Right,' Sarah says with a dry voice. 'What I meant is that we're being told yet again that there isn't a safe way to have genuine, rules-bending sex. This app is a quick fix, not a solution.'

'Maybe if I had had access to the app yesterday, my situation would be clearer today.' Cloe returns to the pool, watchful as she ponders what would have possibly happened if he had asked her to click on a green 'I consent' button before unclipping her bra. *I can feel the warmth of his breath close, the coldness it brings inside my body. My collarbone is sore, I hurt. My pee was a yellow mustard colour this morning. He had sex with me last night. This much I know, but I don't want to know, and you don't want to know either. Otherwise, we would need to do something about the shouting girl who shows you that sex can be so pleasurable and consuming and destructive all at the same time. Pleasure burns, abuse drowns. My back is facing up, mountains of*

*pillows cover my mouth and cut my breath short. I'm silent when he
asks how much I like it like that. I am scarred, violated.*

'Do you really think so?' asks Gertrude.

'It'd ease my doubts.'

Gertrude ignores Cloe's hypothesis and responds to her
own question. 'Let's say he drugged you last night, then he
could have made you click on any buttons without a fight.
If you were drunk to the point of suffering from blackouts
today, even if you drank this amount of alcohol voluntarily,
one can easily argue that you didn't tick the "I consent" box
with your full mind, that in practice you didn't consent to
consent. Do you see the snake biting its own tail here?'

She pauses, nobody speaks. Cloe has glossy eyes, the scare
of having been drugged kicks in with a recollection of a past
headline about an increase in spiked drinks with GHB and
other drugs in nightclubs across the country. The article went
on detailing a new practice with women waking up with
bruises and scars on their arms and shoulders after nights
out in France and Spain. It appears they had been needled
with a mysterious substance that is untraceable in their fluids.
The journalist wrote a hopeful closing paragraph about the
security response at venues and that medical testing had
concluded the needles were most likely empty – 'a condemn-
able act, but not a real danger for the victims' health' – and
Cloe had laughed out loud. *Naïve.* Empty needles stitch up
the consequences of not knowing, disparate patches cover
realities we don't want to see, sewing in a loop to protect
the establishment. *Did I read this?* Cloe scratches her eyes.

Colette and Héloïse had warned her not to ever leave her drink unattended when they dropped her off at parties. *Look after yourself, Cloe*; they had told her to be responsible. Tears overflow and she begins crying silently on account of Gertrude's judgement, her past, present and future selves, and the fact that even an app wouldn't have saved her. *Because I would have consented to please. They advised me to avoid a situation, but they never taught me how to say no. Not in the changing room at the swimming pool, nor when I started going on dates with these boys with blackheads covering their foreheads, nor when my boss suggested that I'm charming with the older, white-collar men. I fit the bill better when I smile, not when I write good copy. The origins of my problem weren't born last night. I miss my mum. Héloïse would have answered my call, and she would have walked me to the health centre Mathilde mentioned. What was the name? The acronynm echoes one of a sexually transmitted infection. Héloïse would have waited for the results with me, eating bowls of instant noodles in bed and watching* Amélie. *She would have commented on each scene loudly and admitted how envious she is of Audrey Tautou's lips. Did he give me an STI yesterday? Something incurable, other than the poison of distrust. Other than stealing my body away from me, a ghost. What if he has left me with a child? A witness. Héloïse always wanted to be a grandmother, but Colette dislikes repetitive patterns, 'great-grandmother'.*

Gertrude squeezes Cloe's hand gently. 'What I mean is that such an app works on the assumption that two well-intentioned adults who understand each other are using it. It works with people who don't need them the same way a

Guardian article demonises Brexit to Remainers.' Her lips pinch in the corner of her mouth. 'If you burst that bubble, then it's likely to fail to be representative. My bet is that the app won't be used in premeditated cases, and when it will have been used, the victim will be accused of having wronged the aggressor because they consented.'

Mathilde quickly casts her eyes over Cloe, a kind roll before she starts talking back to Gertrude. 'I see your point about the app not solving the philosophical question of what consent is and how to determine it in our society, but it does give a metric tool for criminal assessments. Unsexy as it may be, we need a framework as a society, so it'll be possible to love and have sex freely and safely.' Pause for breathing. 'In this instance, no click equals legal ground to investigate a case of rape. This, on its own, would make Cloe's declaration to the police easier, and more likely to trigger actual actions than her current case does.'

'I'm not going to the police,' Cloe says loud enough so Gertrude, Sarah and Mathilde must notice her distress.

'Nobody is forcing you to go,' says Gertrude. 'But I do think Mathilde was right to mention the health centre so you can get checked.'

Sarah seems distracted. She doesn't intend to be insensitive to Cloe's situation, but all these opinions about consenting and sex put a weight on her chest. She wants sex to be fearful and risky and good. She would click on the 'I consent' button if such an app existed between Kristina and she, but isn't this exactly the problem? She would because Kristina sits on the throne in the hierarchy in their relationship – she is the supervisor of her PhD research, and Sarah is the one who is into her the most. Does Kristina even like her as a person? She desires her, this much she has figured from the movements of her hands, the bites she leaves inside her thighs, the taste of Kristina in her mouth after they spend the night together. Sarah doesn't want to dig into the complexity of what should be involved for sex to be right – sex with Kristina is a result of an impulse Sarah cannot police – because it would mean undressing herself before the rest of the world. It would be impossible for Sarah to have sex with Kristina again if the materiality of their being together translated into a quantifiable concept. She wants to have sex so she can learn about her sexuality and desires. Alcohol makes her ears buzz; is Kristina thinking of her when she is not there? She wants her.

'I'm scared of hospitals,' Cloe admits.

Mathilde would like to chaperone Cloe. She feels close to her with her thin hair and almond-shaped eyes, an elegant line so taut she wonders if she can see properly, but she is afraid of hospitals too. The windowless corridors she strolled yesterday already, the arrows drawn across the floors, colour codes to guide patients from one service on to the other. Most of the gowns lack one or two ties, the concept of privacy is erased as soon as one steps into the building. The phlebotomist nurses are the most fun, the radio plays loudly in their room, while the authoritative radiographers and the witty neurologists are the heart of the building in

Mathilde's experience. The kind of nods people exchange inside hospital lifts only. The list goes on. Mathilde cannot accompany Cloe tonight.

'I'll come with you,' says Gertrude with a simple and assured voice.

'But you don't know me.'

'What do you make of this evening?'

Cloe smiles, bright and hopeful.

'Let me look for the nearest centre,' Mathilde offers.

'It's good that you're seeking help,' Sarah says to Cloe to sign off their encounter.

'What's the postcode?' Mathilde asks, typing on her phone. 'Never mind, I found it!' She scrolls through her phone for another few seconds, before she puts it back on the bar, screen facing up, and gives directions to Cloe and Gertrude.

'I know where that is. We can walk to sober up,' Gertrude suggests while making a point to smile at Cloe.

'I'll get us a cab, Sarah.' Mathilde puts on her jacket as she instructs her sister and Sarah doesn't mention the lost scarf again.

They split the bill four ways and they leave the pub. Sarah and Mathilde jump into a taxi (grey Toyota Yaris) while Cloe and Gertrude walk along the pavement. The sky wears the colour of linen, a few timid clouds, and a seagull flies as a flag for the sea a whirlpool away from London. If only they took a plunge; if they could swim through their desires assuredly, so they wouldn't drown for wanting.

23

Mathilde and Sarah

They fasten their seat belts, a clip, the noise of safety. Sarah and Mathilde settle at the back of the taxi and the driver confirms both booking name and destinations, which they approve. He checks the itinerary on his phone, propped in a holder suckered onto the windshield, and asks if they intended to schedule the stops in that order. He clarifies that they will be making a loop across the city, from the Oldfield Tavern to south of the river Thames to drop Sarah off and then back to north London, round the corner from the pub, where Mathilde lives. Mathilde approves the route.

'Wait, why are you dropping me off?'

'I like being in a car. It helps me think.'

'Lucky you. I always feel nauseated.'

'It's always been like that,' Mathilde adds with a corner smile. Another detail Sarah doesn't remember, and she waits for her older sister to gift her a family story. 'I would ask Mum and Dad to drive, while you insisted that we should walk. Sometimes Dad would go places by foot with you, and I went in the car with Mum. I guess it hasn't changed much; you still walk a lot.'

'This is called living in London on a budget.'

'Fair. Anyway, why don't you talk to me more?'

Sarah takes an apparent deep breath. 'How can you say that after today?' She checks on the driver and lowers her voice: 'You're the most honest person I know, Mathi. Don't play hypocrite with me.'

'I'm your big sister.' The light is red, and they both pause to watch the pedestrians cross – age, outfits, attitude, a quick review distracts them from the self-involved complexity of being the Jenkins-Bell sisters. Mathilde speaks again, but softly: 'I mean it, Sarah. I'm here for you and you should come to me when you need to talk about things. When you want to celebrate too.'

'It's you that our parents want to celebrate. I'm the broken one.'

'Who is acting like the little sister now?' Mathilde brushes Sarah's shoulder, their smiles match with complicity. 'Come on, tell me. Who is she?' Sarah peeks out the window, quiet. 'Who is this woman who has *agency* over you?'

Mathilde always speaks her mind, regrets Sarah. She considers the engine whirring and the driver speaking through Bluetooth headphones, his voice muttering in a foreign language and the satellite navigation occasionally breaking in with the cheery innocence of turning left at the next junction. She bends over to share a secret.

'I'm seeing my supervisor. Kristina.' She names it; her. The words are easier to say than when she had rehearsed. The car speeds up and Sarah is lighter of one secret, discharged.

Her epiphany is interrupted by a quick reaction from Mathilde: 'Your supervisor? I can't believe it,' Mathilde titters, then she picks up the pace with an excited voice: 'Sarah, this is so cliché! Mum would love the gossip.' She passes her fingers under her eyes and Sarah looks at her, bemused. Mathilde's face gives her amusement away, the freckles that speak for her when summer sparks. 'Well, until she realises that we're talking about her bloodline,' she adds, then she laughs loudly. Sarah joins her with the welcoming continuity of being validated for her desires. The end of the story, the beginning of the affair. Sarah explains that the yellow scarf was a gift from Kristina and she describes her to Mathilde with a noticeable, agitated voice: the length of Kristina's eyelashes and her confidence and stinky collection of stamps, how proud she is that she can draw every single country flag from memory, she swears by it, and she swears a lot too. Mathilde appreciates her sister's empathy for Kristina. Sarah is reborn talkative; she tells Mathilde about their first dance, the karaoke that introduced her to *Tina* and the sex they have (but she keeps the encounters at the library secret); Mathilde teases Sarah about her constant 'deadlines'. Kristina has formed into a leading character in Sarah's play of life, a step outside the cage of her mind. The two sisters are grateful for the long stretch between one end of London and the other as they talk and listen and converse – it tastes sweet and it smells of alcohol – the discussion of pleasures between two women who used to share toys when they were girls.

'Because sex with Kristina is fun and scary and . . .'

'You're learning things about yourself,' Mathilde adds.

'Yep. Like what it is that I really want, stuff I wouldn't have dared say out loud before.'

'Like?' Mathilde dares Sarah.

Sarah talks. She eyes the driver in the rear-view mirror, and she lowers the timbre of her voice again. 'But there is also the stuff I'm learning I like doing to others . . .'

'Right, got it, no more details needed,' Mathilde smiles as she speaks.

They each nod in silence.

'How are things with Chris?'

'Good. You know Chris, he's busy with work and taking care of things.'

'You're busy with work and taking care of things too.' This, too, hasn't changed. Sarah has always tended to repeat what her sister says, but with the years came a pattern of removing herself by switching the subject back to Mathilde.

'You're always so harsh on him. He's clumsy but he means well.' Sarah doesn't respond to Mathilde, who adds: 'What I meant is that we're boring, not like you and your sexy fling.'

'But being sexy hasn't secured me anything yet. I'm still living in student accommodation, still not writing my thesis and earning no money. I even need my sister to drive me home.'

Sarah speaks with the unfiltered sincerity of a family member. Mathilde hears false modesty.

'You're being unfair to yourself.' The driver changes gears with a second's delay after each red light, bumps and doubts as Sarah and Mathilde navigate the consequences of an afternoon spent sharing new information. Susceptibility stalks the words they speak. 'And to me,' Mathilde adds. 'I worked hard to get where I'm at in my career and with Chris. I still do.' She doesn't tell Sarah about the fight they had last night because this would stain the public appearance of their relationship – an example of when Mathilde allows her reason to skip a beat in favour of the demands of her heart. 'Relationships are hard work.'

Sarah pushes her chin inside her neck like a timid child. Quiet, they notice the environment changing outside of the window as the car cruises: the magnolias and the ash trees, the Victorian houses and then a square surrounded by Georgian buildings, the familiarity of Peckham finally. With a few minutes left on this ride, a rush takes hold of them before they must say goodbye. 'You should tell Kristina how you feel about her. She needs to know what it is that you want so she can give it to you,' Mathilde says with her renowned approach to problem-solving: to enable with a set of ground rules.

'How is it that I feel about her?' Mathilde raises her left eyebrow, so Sarah answers her own question: 'I don't know,

Mathi. I like her, but she is my supervisor and my academic career is important. And, to be honest, I don't know if I'd like to have something more serious with her.' Sarah furrows. 'We don't do much else apart from have sex.'

'Sounds like a good enough reason to try.'

'Says the woman who opened an investment fund with her husband-to-be on the day they met,' Sarah attacks in the name of insecurity.

Mathilde flushes with the nostalgia of a happy recollection. 'Because that's my type of fun with Chris. Yours is different, and so is your relationship with Kristina.' Mathilde solves two equations at once while the car parks in front of Sarah's building. Then she reaches out for her sister's hand, hastily, before Sarah unclenches her seat belt. 'She needs to know that you want to be loved.'

This is how the sisters Jenkins–Bell communicate, mulling over in their head before gasping confessions at inconvenient times.

'Are you sure you're okay? You got me worried at the pub.'

'I'm fine now. You keep researching those water systems and having good sex with your supervisor, okay?'

Sarah presses one hand over the door handle as she shares a last revelation, an organic step forward: 'I've started taking swimming lessons at the Brockwell Lido. I go on Tuesday evenings. Come.' Mathilde raises her eyebrows higher, lifting her fringe comically, and Sarah exhales sharply. 'I've fallen in love with swimming again and I'm sure that you would too. It's like meditation but proactive. I don't know how to explain, but when I put my swimming cap on, my ears are tucked underneath it, and I break free.' She speaks effusively. 'It's silent and loud at once, as if I am doing breast-strokes through a scream. There is nothing that I can hang onto anymore, and there I can let myself go.' The driver clears his throat and the two sisters give him side-eye. 'Will you come with me?'

'Are they private lessons?'

'Yes.'

'I'll text you.' Mathilde points at the door and Sarah drops a kiss on her sister's left cheek.

'Tuesday, six-thirty in the water. Be good.' Sarah steps over onto the pavement. She turns around and adds, her voice blurred behind the window glass: 'I'm sending you the address of the Brockwell Lido,' she points at her phone with one finger.

The car drives off, and Mathilde lowers the window. A fresh breeze unties her chest, her lungs open and she breathes out. She stays still before straightening her back up, her phone in one hand. It vibrates: **SE24 0PA. I don't owe you my fears, love you.**

Mathilde clears the message notification and opens a browser page. She types 'swimming caps' into the search bar and is dazed by the diversity of the offering as she scrolls through size guides, material descriptions and considers colours; she is delicately rubbing her fingers over the scar on the side of her belly. Mathilde closes the browser tab and writes to Chris:

Margaux Vialleron

On my way, but slightly drunk. Can we have pasta
for dinner?

I'll pop down to the shop. Long or short?

Long. I'm in the mood for love.

24

Cloe and Gertrude

'Do you think I'll get home in time to feed my cat?' Cloe asks with the premature assumption that Gertrude will be able to answer.

'I didn't know you have a cat.'

'Yes, Massimo. Technically he isn't my cat, but he was part of the sublet agreement I have with this guy.' Cloe slows down as the two women are getting accustomed to their respective walking paces. 'He calls himself a "digital nomad", which means that he works remotely while travelling around Portugal, and says that his lifestyle isn't compatible with having a cat. So, Massimo stays with me, which is absurd because I'm not a cat person.'

Gertrude sighs with disbelief. 'I understand each one of the words you've just said. But I can't make sense of the full sentence.'

'The digital nomad bit is confusing. Basically, I've got a cheap gig to sublet this flat while the guy who officially rents it travels because he doesn't want to let go of his lease. But, as part of the deal, I need to look after a ginger cat called Massimo.'

Gertrude smiles to herself. Cloe, who reads and interprets sentences literally, as well as her tendency to add more details when she attempts to simplify something, is charming.

'Massimo is pretty low-maintenance to be honest,' Cloe specifies.

'Better than my sourdough pet then,' Gertrude adds.

'What's that?'

'I confess, I have one of these sourdough starters. Which is like having a pet. It needs feeding, and it's sensitive to temperature and the change of seasons, so I'm like an attentive mother. I call mine "sad girl sourdough", which is rather sad in itself.'

'Do you bake bread with it?'

'I do. Pizza doughs as well. I feel responsible for this thing now that I've given it life. I know I sound silly, but I can't throw this odd organism in the bin. (Gertrude's voice peaks higher for the next sentence.) I spend a fortune in bags of flour, but it grounds me that I'm responsible for keeping it healthy.'

Cloe and Gertrude are walking in the direction of the Sexual Assault Referral Centre. At the SARC they will find doctors who specialise in crisis care, medical and forensic examinations, emergency contraception and testing for sexually transmitted infections. They will be greeted by someone at the front desk – and taped paper sheets around the reception area will feature portraits of the nurses and doctors who work there, introducing them and specifying their favourite snack or the name of their pet. The course of actions will be normalised and polite. Cloe and Gertrude will sit in a waiting room where leaflets will be spread out on a shelf next to battered paperback books, donated by either members of staff or patients. There is always a copy of *Bridget Jones's Diary*. One will ask if they have read the book and the other will respond that they have watched the movies – a short relief in a 24-hour hospitalised facility. They will cast their eyes over the documentation that lists things they don't want to know: it is common for the person being sexually assaulted not to carry identifiable signs or physical injuries from the outside. *How many are we? Me too; us too. How many do I know?* they will ask but to themselves. They will find diagrams that summarise commissions and report that assaulters are often known to the victim, and the information will be perplexing – known but unwanted; reassuring with reckoning but frightening to acknowledge publicly. On the walls of the waiting room, a poster will be hanging with definitions that mean to ease newcomers to the centre, but Cloe will note the authoritative language and thus she will question her eligibility. *Consent means saying "yes" to what happened.* Details and phone numbers to join support groups will also be offered, with a range that span from online to in-person meetings, to dog walking and religious gatherings.

The infographics will be colourful, with speech bubbles that tell readers that *Being intoxicated, not being asked, saying nothing, or saying yes to something else, is not consent. Being in a relationship or married to someone is not consent.* They will also learn that the first SARC opened in 1986 at the St Mary's Hospital in Manchester and they will think about the women before them.

In the present, the sheltering setting of the pub has hazed and a tentative cadence forms around Cloe and Gertrude's movements and chatters. Walking soothes their state, blood running through their legs and ideas circulating, a slower thinking that allows for peculiarities to cohabit between their bodies. Gertrude continues: 'Sourdough starters are a living, fermented culture. Maybe they aren't made of fur and cells, they don't meow or cuddle, but they're alive and they feed because they're the enabling agent for many bread-based recipes.' A light wind picks up, the branches of trees whisper. 'I really sound dull, don't I?'

'Not at all. I wish I knew something about cooking.' Cloe's disinterest comes across, regardless of her striving for it not to.

'But it's not about cooking. It's more that I know there is something else that needs me to be consistent to survive. A sourdough starter should be fed with water and flour at regular intervals, and that keeps me focused.'

'Accountability.'

'Absolutely.' A large smile escapes Gertrude, the consequence of recognition.

'I wish I wasn't so accountable.' They are walking through the park behind the pub, where a church has been rehabilitated into a community centre with a café on the ground floor and public toilets at the upper end. Tennis and basketball courts, an empty swimming pool, llamas and goats caged behind a fence, children run after balls and adults break into groups. Those who sit on a bench on their own with their headphones plugged into their ears. There is a path that cuts through the park, with young trees on each side, a pond where swans and ducks reign is located at the south end – Gertrude knows the area well and Cloe follows her. The absence of buildings, thus the blue of the sky, enlarges their perspective; the theatre of a closed public space has ended, Cloe unveils. 'My grandmother lives in a care home, which she hates because she is the most independent person I know. The nurses are lovely, but the place is sad. The kettle is the most talkative habitant and I can feel her personality withering through my veins. She is there with me constantly (Cloe pats her heart, unconsciously): her faff to keep anywhere she goes tidied, her firm opinions about everyone's whereabouts, the magazines she reads with her breakfast. Colette dedicated her life to enabling others to live, and she can't do that anymore.' A pause before Cloe's assured voice: 'Because humans move there to die, and my grandmother isn't someone you can lie to.'

Gertrude flinches. Cloe is being heard, so she continues: 'She has given up on life and I feel responsible for keeping her going when, maybe, I should let her go. You know? She is relatively healthy for her age, but she has lost her purpose now that Héloïse is dead.' Cloe stops talking for a few seconds, conflicting heartbeats echo through her ribs. 'Héloïse is my mother. She died of breast cancer last year.' Cloe requires another break, the shortness of her sentences challenging the pace of her breathing pattern. Still, she is unstoppable, unloading. 'My mother was the link between all of us in the family. She was the type of person who stayed in control until the end: she knew which treatments she wanted to try, she investigated alternative options, and she decided when it was time to check herself into the hospice. She organised her funeral.' Pause. 'And ... and I like to think that she knew when to take her last breath, except that this is when life took back control.' The two women stop without a hint. Gertrude looks Cloe in the eyes, who asks: 'Have you ever seen someone dying?' Gertrude shakes her head; a lucky *no*. 'The thing nobody tells you is that there isn't one, final breath. The body fights because the human instinct is to survive until the end, just like animals. Dying isn't in our nature.' Cloe starts moving again and Gertrude follows, falling a few steps behind but close enough to hear Cloe say: 'The dying body gasps and spasms: it takes time to die for real and it'll take me a lifetime to forget the scene of my mother dying.'

'I'm so sorry, Cloe.' This is one of the two sentences Cloe hates the most: *How are you?* and *I'm (so) sorry.* She has heard them often since the death of her mother, yet they never capture the emotion. The opposite of empowering, the words coerce her into impuissance, pushing her under the spotlight as if she was the sole composer of her sorrows. What about the ascendency of social and structural systems on someone's identity? The death of her mother caused Cloe's body to wound – her forearms, literally, were spotted with small, purple pinches – and her brain divided in two, a driving and efficient mode (but senseless) and a monotonous, thinking state. Grief, a tidal disturbance, tears flooding her sight before future droughts, draining desires away from her; the dream of a colossal wave hitting her instead, a punch she could address.

Gertrude fantasises about knowing what to say to Cloe, she who has estranged her own parents. They live but she decided to remove them from her life, a passive murder for her sanity. She thinks, she digs, she bites her lower lip, but she chooses honesty: 'I'm terrified of death, hence my obsession with keeping that "sad girl sourdough" alive, or the smartwatch I'm wearing and all the data I monitor with it. I'm one of those people who are so scared of dying, that they prevent themselves from living.' Cloe notes Gertrude's self-awareness. 'I don't even know how to swim,' Gertrude admits as they walk past the empty children's pool in the park. A hint of chagrin drags the last sentence.

'What do you mean you don't know how to swim?' Cloe's focus is on the particular, always and despite the alarming bigger picture.

'That I'd drown if I were pushed into a body of water and I wasn't able to touch the bottom,' Gertrude explains, calmly. She feels the pressure of his hands over her shoulders, her body immersed in water, drowned to be reborn baptised, the beginning of a lifelong lie. She picks fire over water.

'This is counter-intuitive. You must learn to swim so you don't drown,' Cloe says with a seriousness that alerts Gertrude.

'It's too late for me, and I'm not one for taking risks.'

'But you went to a bottomless brunch on a first date!' Cloe isn't good at lightening a mood. Her language tends to be repetitive, loading instead of distracting. 'Seriously,' she adds self-conscious: 'I can teach you how to swim. I miss swimming so much and maybe this is the reason we met today. We're each other's invitation to visit the pool.' Cloe turns to face Gertrude: 'Swimming has played a huge role in women's liberation movements. And I've always wanted to try one of the famous London lidos,' she gusts.

'Fair. I remember Rebecca Adlington swimming on telly. (Cloe smiles.) How come you're into swimming so much?'

'I used to swim competitively when I was younger. Breaststroke.'

'In that case you could legitimately teach me,' Gertrude agrees. 'But why did you stop?' she adds suspiciously.

'You do worry.' Cloe lets out a soft laugh, giving herself some extra time to consider what to say next. The ethical pressure around consent and the burden of a lie she started years ago weigh on her shoulders. 'It became too much between the training and the competitions. I guess I wasn't up to it.'

'I hate the smell of chlorine.'

It worked; Cloe concludes after Gertrude's trivial comment: 'Fair enough. It makes you wrinkle; it's awful.'

'One more argument in favour of not learning to swim: check!' declares Gertrude with generous self-derision.

'Can we stop for a minute?' Cloe sits down on a bench on which a small golden plaque is fitted at the top, *In memory of.* She casts her eyes over it and Gertrude joins her, settling at the other end so she doesn't get in the way of Cloe's gaze. 'I chose the words for my mother's memorial sign. *Héloïse, forever tomorrow's good story,*' Cloe whispers. 'This is what she'd have told me if I had called her this morning – "Don't worry, Cloe, this one will be a good story tomorrow" – and I'd have believed her.' Cloe puts her hand on Gertrude's leg, her grip soft and harsh, a gesture born of fear, unexpected but shy. 'My mum was the most committed person to being alive that I knew. A friend of any outcasts and a doer that nothing could stop. I admired her strength, especially at the end of her life, but I resented her for it too. Not all stories can have a happy ending because their narrator decides so like she told me.' This conversation follows a random rhythm between a tendency to overshare, encouraged by the aftermath of sharing drinks and snacks and pains, a craving to be acknowledged and a bout of confidence because they may never meet again. 'I think "sad girl sourdough" is a great name by the way.'

Gertrude has joined her fingers with those of Cloe. Her religious upbringing has taught her how to facilitate a confession, an interlude that merges guilt and pride into a moral lesson, ugly and human, a conversation in verses.

Cloe speaks again: 'My mum was obsessed with the Grimms' fairy tales. It was the only book we had in the house, but we owned an unnecessary number of editions in French, Catalan, Spanish, German and English. She couldn't read German and only my father knew Catalan. Not that he read books but, anyway, my point is that she thought fear was a weapon any individual could master.' She squeezes Gertrude's hands, who pulls back before the memory of the illustrations inside the *Little Red Riding Hood* picture book she owned when she was a child. 'We sat and we read the tales together. We built an auditorium in our living room with pillows and duvets, and she taught me how to be scared. I guess I'm thinking about this now because we read *Hansel and Gretel* often. She wanted me to learn about hunger and self-sufficiency because I don't have any siblings.'

Both need to pause to process the flow of information.

'If my mother hadn't suffered from complications after having my little brother, I'm sure that I would have more than one sibling. In my house, what mattered was that we did well as a family.' Gertrude sighs deeply. 'The "we" had priority over "I".'

The light is shifting, the London sky has a low anchor. Children kick footballs, agitated, and cyclists affirm red leather courier bags as fashionable items. Smoky breaths dance before the lips of pedestrians.

'If you're ever hungry, you can have a piece of sad girl sourdough starter,' Gertrude adds with a bright voice.

'I would be clueless about how to keep it alive.'

'That's the thing. You need to start feeding it so you can understand its composition. It grows by being shared.'

'I guess I could give it a try, then,' Cloe says, and Gertrude nods. So Cloe makes a stroke forward. 'The reason I stopped going to swimming practice is because our coach wasn't appropriate with me and my teammates. He made comments about our appearances, spanked my bum when I'd walk past him. He entered the changing room without knocking on the door. Nothing too awful either, you know, but we were small girls.' Cloe stops, her mouth dry and small. She swallows a few times in a row, preparing to talk again. Gertrude is also gearing to speak, but the anticipation of the words she will say revolts Cloe, who doesn't want pity. She jumps in: 'Don't be sorry for me. I'm fine, but I'll never forgive myself for not having said anything against him. I'm ashamed of myself.' And she can't hold the next sentence any longer: 'Ashamed that I'm complicit, and that I let other girls be groomed. But . . . I couldn't betray the team.'

A disclaimer about what comes next: Gertrude will be responding to Cloe after receiving an unreliable set of information, a mixture between what Cloe told her, what Gertrude has guessed and what she has soaked in from her experiences, and the specifics Cloe assumes others have understood, however subconscious any of these moral and social treaties are.

*

'I'm so angry on your behalf.' Gertrude spits the words, quickly and matter-of-fact. Cloe's head bounces back with shock – a shared anger is something new to her, whose initial instinct is to keep her head down, fighting with doing. Gertrude repeats the word and elaborates: 'I'm so angry that you – we – are made to believe that because we have violable organs we must make ourselves inviolable at all costs. And that we must make sure others don't get violated either.' Gertrude meets Cloe's eyes. 'Just because people can't think of a worse crime than grooming doesn't mean that it doesn't happen.' Cloe opens her mouth in protest, but Gertrude doesn't give her a chance. 'You don't have to feel guilty for what's happened to you.'

Past cases and research have shown that there is a tendency to think about child abuse as something happening to children far away from us or from another period. Categorising it as an unpredictable crime that can't be prevented, the product of an identifiable type of person other than a friend, a family member or a colleague, serves the purpose of easing adults' consciousness but doesn't protect children. As with most cases of abuse, the abuser is a person close to the victim, an apparent safe figure, an authority a child wouldn't want to question publicly. We must listen, and we must trust that we didn't see the signs until we are told about them. We might never see the signs, but we must consider them fairly and allow ourselves to acknowledge that they have happened. Witnessing a crime doesn't take away moral credits from a person, but it tests the said person's integrity – to review the crime of another human being, especially if the person comes from a similar social sphere, means one must face one's own prejudices.

A silence settles, fists clenched, and Gertrude rues her outburst. She shakes her head rapidly. 'Sorry, I didn't mean to sound angry at you.'

'It's fine. *I'm* angry,' Cloe says in one breath.

'Me too,' Gertrude smiles. 'One of the first things I remember learning as a child was to keep my emotions to myself. My parents hated any type of public demonstration, either happy or sad.'

'My parents were the opposite. My mum had the ability to pick a fight with anyone.'

They stay silent again because anger speeds up ideas but bars movement, other than the impulsive kind. And impulse wouldn't be appropriate in this situation.

Cloe speaks: 'The last time we went to a restaurant with my mum, we sat next to four loud guys. We had some wine and Héloïse was becoming infuriated by their accounts of ghosting women after one-night stands. Until she stood up and barked at them. The staff asked us to leave, and we never went back to that restaurant. I can't believe it's changed anything about how these men will treat women in the future though.'

Gertrude checks in with Cloe for approval; she moves her chin forward and Gertrude picks up the thread: 'I can relate to that. If anything, it has given these guys something else to say about female hysteria.'

'But, on the other hand, if you don't say anything, you have to live with your complicit silence.' Cloe releases her fingers from Gertrude's leg, her knuckles white under the grip, but Gertrude intercepts them. She tightens her hand across Cloe's, who resumes talking: 'For years, I've been feeling like I'm being punished for not having said "no" and then for not reporting our coach. I was afraid about what the story would say about me.' She drifts away and looks back at Gertrude: 'I also don't want this episode to become something emotional through the interpretation of others. Because I have always treated it like a bruise. Something physical that happened to me and that can heal.'

Vulnerability is a complex emotion. It consumes a person from within – an act between being defensive and a need to seek reassurance. The conflicted feeling feeds a structural system, a spiderweb through which authority equals agency and subordinates are entangled with guilt. Guilt settles into shame and prevents victims from speaking up and reaching out to an administrative office (either legal or private) for help – trauma is passed on from that generation to the next one.

Cloe inhales. 'Still, it has become who I am. I'm a liar trapped inside a lie.'

'We all lie about who we are to survive.' Gertrude untangles her hand away from Cloe. She grabs a tissue inside her pocket, the polluted air stings.

Cloe speaks: 'I'm tired of lying. It's like I'm stuck in a time loop until I do the right thing.'

Listen to Cloe as she sits on a public bench with a woman she has met today. They are discussing the circumstances of being morally and physically abused as a child and an adult, yet Cloe assigns her future to her *good* conduct. You have heard the sentence 'she was asking for it' before, and so has Cloe, often enough for the words to be assimilated. The product of an ingrained approach to assault, rotating around the victim's behaviours, feeds into a punitive culture in which victims – and those who fit in a similar class and/ or social categories to the victims – should learn a lesson so the event doesn't repeat itself. Popular science differentiates the human condition from that of animals with the ability to solve complex problems and the capacity for introspection, however such a comparison fails to address the fact that civilisation has upturned the natural organisation of species with the implementation of a hierarchy. The latter divides and silences its own injustice, leading to the prosperity of the few who exercise power.

'Why did you tell me all of this?' Gertrude asks.

'I guess I wanted to see if it'd make sense out loud.'

'How could abuse ever make sense?' Gertrude raises her eyebrows and faces Cloe.

'It has to make sense so I can fight it.'

'That's fucked up.'

The two women sigh before smiling at one another. This much they agree upon. They sit quietly for a few minutes because it doesn't end here – consent to buy clothes that have been manufactured through unpaid, underaged labour, consent to buy food that was grown with pesticides that will increase their chance of developing a type of cancer, and consent to buy medicines from profit-led pharmaceutical companies. They consent every day and consistently because there are no alternatives.

'Shall we start walking again?' Cloe stands up as she speaks.

'No,' Gertrude responds firmly.

Cloe trembles with surprise, her knees bending to sit back down, until Gertrude laughs sharply and shortly. 'I'm kidding – just rehearsing! Let's go,' she adds.

A drizzle breaks through, the smell of rust and wishful thinking for greener days, Sunday night.

'It's a difficult word to say, "no", however short,' one of them says as they walk away.

25

Cloe

I sit on the edge of the swimming pool with my knees up and my toes clenched. Inhale, focus. The grout lines dent my skin, scarring and sucking my blood. Focus, exhale. I fit my goggles, tighten them at the back of my head – tighter – and I plunge.

Head-first, breaststrokes.

Out-sweep, in-sweep, breathe; lunge, extend, breathe; repeat.

I'm not Cloe anymore; I'm no woman; I'm no human. I'm no one but I.

I swim and I hunt and I swim swim swim. Until I catch him. His body purple, cold, deprived of oxygen and poisoned by lies. I scratch; I disembowel him. Them. All these years I spent sitting back to watch Colette while she gutted fish and plucked pigeons in our bathtub. She performed clean cuts across the animals' chests, backs, bellies. She pulled out their organs and rinsed their cavities under cold water, the water running and she never drawing back from the meat. I swim.

Margaux Vialleron

She dropped leftover cuts into a steel bucket – dinner for the neigh-bour's dog. I don't smell chlorine but blood – pennies – and rot – an old rain jacket trapped inside a drawer between seasons. I swim.

Out-sweep, in-sweep, breathe; lunge, extend, breathe; repeat.

I scratch scratch scratch until his corpse dissolves, and they become nothing. I think of the shadows that roam above a body of water at the end of a boiling hot summer. His presence evaporates. They leave and I swim.

I. I'm reborn. I'm Cloe.

Out-sweep, in-sweep, breathe; lunge, extend, breathe; breaststrokes.

I swim. Breaststrokes until my hands reach for the edge at the upper end of the pool. I pull my body out of the water. I swam, I walk, I will dance.

Look at me

Listen to me

Trust me

Epilogue

Anyone, Any Day

If you or someone you know needs help, please consider reaching out to one of these organisations:

Galop
galop.org.uk

A charity that provides helplines and support for LGBT+ victims and survivors of abuse and violence.

0800 999 5428 (10 a.m. – 8:30 p.m. Monday to Thursday; 10 a.m. – 4:30 p.m. Friday)

help@galop.org.uk / Live chatbot available at their website

Mind
www.mind.org.uk

A mental health charity offering information and support for people who are experiencing, or have experienced, any sort of mental health problem.

0300 123 3393

info@mind.org.uk

The Survivors Trust
www.thesurvivorstrust.org

An umbrella agency, of which member agencies provide a range of specialist services to survivors including counselling, support, helplines and advocacy services for women, men, non-binary people and children. These agencies are mostly charities and are independent of the police.

08088 010 818 (10 a.m. – 12:30 p.m., 1:30 p.m. – 5:30 p.m., 6 p.m. – 8 p.m. Monday to Thursday; 10 a.m. – 12:30 p.m., 1:30 p.m. – 5:30 p.m. Friday; 10 a.m. – 1 p.m. Saturday; 5 p.m. – 8 p.m. Sunday)

helpline@thesurvivorstrust.org

Rape Crisis England & Wales

rapecrisis.org.uk

A charity that provides specialist information and support to all those affected by sexual violence. Help can be found online, via the phone and at one of the centres across England and Wales.

0808 500 2222 (freephone 24/7)

Samaritans

www.samaritans.org

A charity aimed at providing emotional support to anyone in emotional distress, struggling to cope or at risk of suicide.

116 123 (freephone 24/7)

Write to SAMARITANS LETTERS (freepost)

jo@samaritans.org (it may take several days to get a response by email)

Acknowledgements

I owe the title of this book to the Marshall Pool.

I dedicate the fictionalised life of Sarah Jenkins-Bell to the memory of Sarah, who lives long with us.

I'm grateful to my best friend and business partner, Irene Olivo, the eternal summer of my years. I owe a great debt of gratitude to my early readers, Johanna Clarke and Valentina Paulmichl, for their generosity with their time and advice. Irene, Jo and Vale: thank you for reading and hearing me.

Thanks to my friends for our conversations and our silences, which challenge, rejoice and inspire me daily: Giulia Bernabè, Ludovica Bevilacqua, Nicoletta Bucciarelli, Camille Dougé, Annalisa Eichholzer, Jemima Forrester, Céline Giraud, Alice Howe, Marine Ollivier-Lestre, Alexia Tassin and Laure Tavernier.

I'm thankful to my editor, Clare Hey, whose honesty and trust guided me through the process of writing and editing this novel. It takes a team to produce a book and I'd like to thank everyone at S&S for making this possible. Thank you, Louise Davies, for your patience and care with my queries. Thanks also to Kirsty McLachlan and Rebecca Wearmouth, my supportive agents.

To Charline: allez viens, je t'emmène au vent. Always.

And, Ludo: thank you for dancing with me like you do.